P9-CFN-788

THE BORROWERS

THE
BORROWERS

Mary Norton

ILLUSTRATED BY BETH AND JOE KRUSH

SCHOLASTIC INC.

New York   Toronto   London   Auckland   Sydney
Mexico City   New Delhi   Hong Kong   Buenos Aires

ISBN 0-439-32510-2

24 23 22 21 20   16/0

Printed in the U.S.A.   40

First Scholastic printing, September 2001

For Orlena

Chapter One

IT WAS Mrs. May who first told me about them. No, not me. How could it have been me—a wild, untidy, self-willed little girl who stared with angry eyes and was said to crunch her teeth? Kate, she should have been called. Yes, that was it—Kate. Not that the name matters much either way: she barely comes into the story.

Mrs. May lived in two rooms in Kate's parents' house in London; she was, I think, some kind of relation. Her bedroom was on the first floor, and her sitting room was a room which, as part of the house, was called "the breakfast-room." Now breakfast-rooms are all right in the morning when the sun streams in on the toast and marmalade, but by afternoon they seem to vanish a little and to fill with a strange silvery light, their own twilight; there is a kind of sadness in them then, but as a child it was a sadness Kate liked. She would creep in to Mrs. May just before tea-time and Mrs. May would teach her to crochet.

Mrs. May was old, her joints were stiff, and she was—not strict exactly, but she had that inner certainty which does

3

instead. Kate was never "wild" with Mrs. May, nor untidy, nor self-willed; and Mrs. May taught her many things besides crochet: how to wind wool into an egg-shaped ball; how to run-and-fell and plan a darn; how to tidy a drawer and to lay, like a blessing, above the contents, a sheet of rustling tissue against the dust.

"Where's your work, child?" asked Mrs. May one day, when Kate sat hunched and silent upon the hassock. "You mustn't sit there dreaming. Have you lost your tongue?"

"No," said Kate, pulling at her shoe button, "I've lost the crochet hook." They were making a bed-quilt—in woolen squares: there were thirty still to do. "I know where I put it," she went on hastily; "I put it on the bottom shelf of the bookcase just beside my bed."

"On the bottom shelf?" repeated Mrs. May, her own needle flicking steadily in the firelight. "Near the floor?"

"Yes," said Kate, "but I looked on the floor. Under the rug. Everywhere. The wool was still there though. Just where I'd left it."

"Oh dear," exclaimed Mrs. May lightly, "don't say they're in this house too!"

"That what are?" asked Kate.

"The Borrowers," said Mrs. May, and in the half light she seemed to smile.

Kate stared a little fearfully. "Are there such things?" she asked after a moment.

"As what?"

"As people, other people, living in a house who . . . borrow things?"

Mrs. May laid down her work. "What do you think?" she asked.

"I don't know," Kate said, pulling hard at her shoe button. "There can't be. And yet"—she raised her head—"and yet sometimes I think there must be."

"Why do you think there must be?" asked Mrs. May.

"Because of all the things that disappear. Safety pins, for instance. Factories go on making safety pins, and every day people go on buying safety pins and yet, somehow, there never is a safety pin just when you want one. Where are they all? Now, at this minute? Where do they go to? Take needles," she went on, "All the needles my mother ever bought—there must be hundreds—can't just be lying about this house."

"Not lying about the house, no," agreed Mrs. May.

"And all the other things we keep on buying. Again and again and again. Like pencils and match boxes and sealing-wax and hairpins and drawing pins and thimbles—"

"And hat pins," put in Mrs. May, "and blotting paper."

"Yes, blotting paper," agreed Kate, "but not hat pins."

"That's where you're wrong," said Mrs. May, and she picked up her work again. "There was a reason for hat pins."

Kate stared. "A reason?" she repeated. "I mean—what kind of a reason?"

"Well, there were two reasons really. A hat pin is a very useful weapon and"–Mrs. May laughed suddenly–"but it all sounds such nonsense and"–she hesitated–"it was so very long ago!"

"But tell me," said Kate, "tell me how you *know* about the hat pin. Did you ever see one?"

Mrs. May threw her a startled glance. "Well, yes–" she began.

"Not a hat pin," exclaimed Kate impatiently, "a–whatever-you-called-them–a Borrower?"

Mrs. May drew a sharp breath. "No," she said quickly, "I never saw one."

"But someone else saw one," cried Kate, "and you know about it. I can see you do!"

"Hush," said Mrs. May, "no need to shout!" She gazed downwards at the upturned face and then she smiled and her eyes slid away into distance. "I had a brother–" she began uncertainly.

Kate knelt upon the hassock. "And he saw them!"

"I don't know," said Mrs. May, shaking her head, "I just don't know!" She smoothed out her work upon her knee. "He was such a tease. He told us so many things–my sister and me–impossible things. He was killed," she added gently, "many years ago now, on the North-West Frontier. He became colonel of his regiment. He died what they call 'a hero's death' . . ."

"Was he your only brother?"

"Yes, and he was our little brother. I think that was

why"—she thought for a moment, still smiling to herself—
"yes, why he told us such impossible stories, such strange
imaginings. He was jealous, I think, because we were older
—and because we could read better. He wanted to impress
us; he wanted, perhaps, to shock us. And yet"—she looked
into the fire—"there was something about him—perhaps
because we were brought up in India among mystery and
magic and legend—something that made us think that he
saw things that other people could not see; sometimes we'd
know he was teasing, but at other times—well, we were
not so sure. . . ." She leaned forward and, in her tidy
way, brushed a fan of loose ashes under the grate, then,
brush in hand, she stared again at the fire. "He wasn't a
very strong little boy: the first time he came home from
India he got rheumatic fever. He missed a whole term at
school and was sent away to the country to get over it.
To the house of a great-aunt. Later I went there myself.
It was a strange old house. . . ." She hung up the brush
on its brass hook and, dusting her hands on her handkerchief, she picked up her work. "Better light the lamp,"
she said.

"Not yet," begged Kate, leaning forward. "Please go on.
Please tell me—"

"But I've told you."

"No, you haven't. This old house—wasn't that where
he saw—he saw . . . ?"

Mrs. May laughed. "Where he saw the Borrowers?
Yes, that's what he told us . . . what he'd have us believe.

7

And, what's more, it seems that he didn't just see them but that he got to know them very well; that he became part of their lives, as it were; in fact, you might almost say that he became a borrower himself. . . ."

"Oh, *do* tell me. Please. Try to remember. Right from the very beginning!"

"But I do remember," said Mrs. May. "Oddly enough I remember it better than many real things which have happened. Perhaps it was a real thing. I just don't know. You see, on the way back to India my brother and I had to share a cabin—my sister used to sleep with our governess —and, on those very hot nights, often we couldn't sleep; and my brother would talk for hours and hours, going over old ground, repeating conversations, telling me details again and again—wondering how they were and what they were doing and—"

"They? Who were they—exactly?"

"Homily, Pod, and little Arrietty."

"Pod?"

"Yes, even their names were never quite right. They imagined they had their own names—quite different from human names—but with half an ear you could tell they were borrowed. Even Uncle Hendreary's and Eggletina's. Everything they had was borrowed; they had nothing of their own at all. Nothing. In spite of this, my brother said, they were touchy and conceited, and thought they owned the world."

"How do you mean?"

"They thought human beings were just invented to do the dirty work—great slaves put there for them to use. At least, that's what they told each other. But my brother said that, underneath, he thought they were frightened. It was because they were frightened, he thought, that they had grown so small. Each generation had become smaller and smaller, and more and more hidden. In the olden days, it seems, and in some parts of England, our ancestors talked quite openly about the 'little people.'"

"Yes," said Kate, "I know."

"Nowadays, I suppose," Mrs. May went on slowly, "if they exist at all, you would only find them in houses which are old and quiet and deep in the country—and where the human beings live to a routine. Routine is their safeguard. They must know which rooms are to be used and when. They do not stay long where there are careless people, or unruly children, or certain household pets.

"This particular old house, of course, was ideal—although as far as some of them were concerned, a trifle cold and empty. Great-Aunt Sophy was bedridden, through a hunting accident some twenty years before, and as for other human beings there was only Mrs. Driver the cook, Crampfurl the gardener, and, at rare intervals, an odd housemaid or such. My brother, too, when he went there after rheumatic fever, had to spend long hours in bed, and for those first weeks it seems the Borrowers did not know of his existence.

"He slept in the old night-nursery, beyond the school-

room. The schoolroom, at that time, was sheeted and shrouded and filled with junk—odd trunks, a broken sewing-machine, a desk, a dressmaker's dummy, a table, some chairs, and a disused pianola—as the children who had used it, Great-Aunt Sophy's children, had long since grown up, married, died, or gone away. The night-nursery opened out of the schoolroom and, from his bed, my brother could see the oil painting of the battle of Waterloo which hung above the schoolroom fireplace and, on the wall, a corner cupboard with glass doors in which was set out, on hooks and shelves, a doll's tea-service—very delicate and old. At night, if the schoolroom door was open, he had a view down the lighted passage which led to the head of the stairs, and it would comfort him to see, each evening at dusk, Mrs. Driver appear at the head of the stairs and cross the passage carrying a tray for Aunt Sophy with Bath Oliver biscuits and the tall, cut-glass decanter of Fine

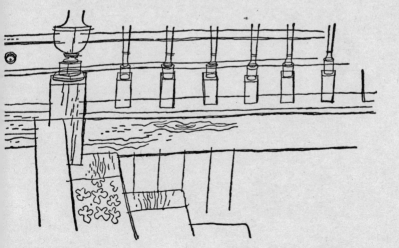

Old Pale Madeira. On her way out Mrs. Driver would pause and lower the gas jet in the passage to a dim, blue flame, and then he would watch her as she stumped away downstairs, sinking slowly out of sight between the banisters.

"Under this passage, in the hall below, there was a clock, and through the night he would hear it strike the hours. It was a grandfather clock and very old. Mr. Frith of Leighton Buzzard came each month to wind it, as his father had come before him and his great-uncle before that. For eighty years, they said (and to Mr. Frith's certain knowledge), it had not stopped and, as far as anyone could tell, for as many years before that. The great thing was—that it must never be moved. It stood against the wainscot, and the stone flags around it had been washed so often that a little platform, my brother said, rose up inside.

"And, under this clock, below the wainscot, there was a hole. . . ."

Chapter Two

It was Pod's hole—the keep of his fortress; the entrance to his home. Not that his home was anywhere near the clock: far from it—as you might say. There were yards of dark and dusty passageway, with wooden doors between the joists and metal gates against the mice. Pod used all kinds of things for these gates—a flat leaf of a folding cheese-grater, the hinged lid of a small cash-box, squares of pierced zinc from an old meat-safe, a wire fly-swatter. . . . "Not that I'm afraid of mice," Homily would say, "but I can't abide the smell." In vain Arrietty had begged for a little mouse of her own, a little blind mouse to bring up by hand—"like Eggletina had had." But Homily would bang with the pan lids and exclaim: "And look what happened to Eggletina!" "What," Arrietty would ask, "what did happen to Eggletina?" But no one would ever say.

It was only Pod who knew the way through the intersecting passages to the hole under the clock. And only Pod could open the gates. There were complicated clasps made of hairpins and safety pins of which Pod alone knew the secret. His wife and child led more sheltered lives in homelike apartments under the kitchen, far removed from the risks and dangers of the dreaded house above. But there was a grating in the brick wall of the house, just below the floor level of the kitchen above, through which Arrietty could see the garden—a piece of graveled path and a bank where crocus bloomed in spring; where blossom drifted from an unseen tree; and where later an azalea bush would flower; and where birds came—and pecked and flirted and sometimes fought. "The hours you waste on them birds," Homily would say, "and when there's a little job to be done you can never find the time. I was brought up in a house," Homily went on, "where there wasn't no grating, and we were all the happier for it. Now go off and get me the potato."

That was the day when Arrietty, rolling the potato before her from the storehouse down the dusty lane under the floor boards, kicked it ill-temperedly so that it rolled rather fast into their kitchen, where Homily was stooping over the stove.

"There you go again," exclaimed Homily, turning angrily; "nearly pushed me into the soup. And when I say 'potato' I don't mean the whole potato. Take the scissor, can't you, and cut off a slice."

"Didn't know how much you wanted," mumbled Arrietty, and Homily, snorting and sniffing, unhooked the blade and handle of half a pair of manicure scissors from a nail on the wall, and began to cut through the peel.

"You've ruined this potato," she grumbled. "You can't roll it back now in all that dust, not once it's been cut open."

"Oh, what does it matter?" said Arrietty. "There are plenty more."

"That's a nice way to talk. Plenty more. Do you realize," Homily went on gravely, laying down the half nail scissor, "that your poor father risks his life every time he borrows a potato?"

"I meant," said Arrietty, "that there are plenty more in the storeroom."

"Well, out of my way now," said Homily, bustling around again, "whatever you meant—and let me get the supper."

Arrietty wandered through the open door into the sitting room. Ah, the fire had been lighted and the room looked bright and cozy. Homily was proud of her sitting room: the walls had been papered with scraps of old letters out of waste-paper baskets, and Homily had arranged the handwriting sideways in vertical stripes which ran from floor to ceiling. On the walls, repeated in various colors, hung several portraits of Queen Victoria as a girl; these were postage stamps, borrowed by Pod some years ago from the stamp box on the desk in the morning room. There was a lacquer trinket box, padded inside and with the lid open, which they used as a settle; and that useful stand-by—a chest of drawers made of match boxes. There was a round table with a red velvet cloth, which Pod had made from the

wooden bottom of a pill box supported on the carved pedestal of a knight from the chess set. (This had caused a great deal of trouble upstairs when Aunt Sophy's eldest son, on a flying mid-week visit, had invited the vicar for "a game after dinner." Rosa Pickhatchet, who was housemaid at the time, gave in her notice. After she had left other things were found to be missing, and no one was engaged in her place. From that time onwards Mrs. Driver ruled supreme.) The knight itself—its bust, so to speak—stood on a column in the corner, where it looked very fine, and lent that air to the room which only statuary can give.

Beside the fire, in a tilted wooden bookcase, stood Arrietty's library. This was a set of those miniature volumes which the Victorians loved to print, but which to Arrietty seemed the size of very large church Bibles. There was Bryce's *Tom Thumb Gazetteer of the World*, including the last census; Bryce's *Tom Thumb Dictionary*, with short explanations of scientific, philosophical, literary, and technical terms; Bryce's *Tom Thumb Edition of the Comedies of William Shakespeare*, including a foreword on the author; another book, whose pages were all blank, called *Memoranda;* and, last but not least, Arrietty's favorite Bryce's *Tom Thumb Diary and Proverb Book*, with a saying for each day of the year and, as a preface, the life story of a little man called General Tom Thumb, who married a girl called Mercy Lavinia Bump. There was an engraving of their carriage and pair, with little horses—

the size of mice. Arrietty was not a stupid girl. She knew that horses could not be as small as mice, but she did not realize that Tom Thumb, nearly two feet high, would seem a giant to a Borrower.

Arrietty had learned to read from these books, and to write by leaning sideways and copying out the writings on the walls. In spite of this, she did not always keep her diary, although on most days she would take the book out for the sake of the saying which sometimes would comfort her. Today it said: "You may go farther and fare worse," and, underneath: "Order of the Garter, instituted 1348." She carried the book to the fire and sat down with her feet on the hob.

"What are you doing, Arrietty?" called Homily from the kitchen.

"Writing my diary."

"Oh," exclaimed Homily shortly.

"What did you want?" asked Arrietty. She felt quite safe; Homily liked her to write; Homily encouraged any form of culture. Homily herself, poor ignorant creature, could not even say the alphabet. "Nothing. Nothing," said Homily crossly, banging away with the pan lids; "it'll do later."

Arrietty took out her pencil. It was a small white pencil, with a piece of silk cord attached, which had come off a dance program, but, even so, in Arrietty's hand, it looked like a rolling-pin.

"Arrietty!" called Homily again from the kitchen.

"Yes?"

"Put a little something on the fire, will you?"

Arrietty braced her muscles and heaved the book off her knees, and stood it upright on the floor. They kept the fuel, assorted slack and crumbled candle-grease, in a pewter mustard-pot, and shoveled it out with the spoon. Arrietty trickled only a few grains, tilting the mustard spoon, not to spoil the blaze. Then she stood there basking in the warmth. It was a charming fireplace, made by Arrietty's grandfather, with a cogwheel from the stables, part of an old cider-press. The spokes of the cogwheel stood out in starry rays, and the fire itself nestled in the center. Above there was a chimney-piece made from a small brass funnel, inverted. This, at one time, belonged to an oil lamp which matched it, and which stood, in the old days, on the hall table upstairs. An arrangement of pipes, from the spout of the funnel, carried the fumes into the kitchen flues above. The fire was laid with match-sticks and fed with assorted slack and, as it burned up, the iron would become hot, and Homily would simmer soup on the spokes in a silver thimble, and Arrietty would broil nuts. How cozy those winter evenings could be. Arrietty, her great book on her knees, sometimes reading aloud; Pod at his last (he was a shoemaker, and made button-boots out of kid gloves—now, alas, only for his family); and Homily, quiet at last, with her knitting.

Homily knitted their jerseys and stockings on black-headed pins, and, sometimes, on darning needles. A great reel of silk or cotton would stand, table high, beside her chair, and sometimes, if she pulled too sharply, the reel would tip up and roll away out of the open door into the dusty passage beyond, and Arrietty would be sent after it, to re-wind it carefully as she rolled it back.

The floor of the sitting room was carpeted with deep red blotting paper, which was warm and cozy, and soaked up the spills. Homily would renew it at intervals when it became available upstairs, but since Aunt Sophy had taken to her bed Mrs. Driver seldom thought of blotting paper unless, suddenly, there were guests. Homily liked things which saved washing because drying was difficult under the floor; water they had in plenty, hot and cold, thanks to Pod's father who had tapped the pipes from the kitchen boiler. They bathed in a small tureen, which once had held *pâté de foie gras.* When you had wiped out your bath you were supposed to put the lid back, to stop people putting things in it. The soap, too, a great cake of it, hung on a nail in the scullery, and they scraped pieces off. Homily liked coal tar, but Pod and Arrietty preferred sandalwood.

"What are you doing now, Arrietty?" called Homily from the kitchen.

"Still writing my diary."

Once again Arrietty took hold of the book and heaved it back on to her knees. She licked the lead of her great pencil, and stared a moment, deep in thought. She allowed herself (when she did remember to write) one little line on each page because she would never—of this she was sure —have another diary, and if she could get twenty lines on each page the diary would last her twenty years. She had kept it for nearly two years already, and today, 22nd March, she read last year's entry: "Mother cross." She thought a while longer then, at last, she put ditto marks under "mother," and "worried" under "cross."

"What did you say you were doing, Arrietty?" called Homily from the kitchen.

Arrietty closed the book. "Nothing," she said.

"Then chop me up this onion, there's a good girl. Your father's late tonight. . . ."

Chapter Three

SIGHING, Arrietty put away her diary and went into the kitchen. She took the onion ring from Homily, and slung it lightly round her shoulders, while she foraged for a piece of razor blade. "Really, Arrietty," exclaimed Homily, "not on your clean jersey! Do you want to smell like a bit-bucket? Here, take the scissor—"

Arrietty stepped through the onion ring as though it were a child's hoop, and began to chop it into segments.

"Your father's late," muttered Homily again, "and it's my fault, as you might say. Oh dear, oh dear, I wish I hadn't—"

"Hadn't what?" asked Arrietty, her eyes watering. She sniffed loudly and longed to rub her nose on her sleeve.

Homily pushed back a thin lock of hair with a worried hand. She stared at Arrietty absently. "It's that tea cup you broke," she said.

"But that was days ago—" began Arrietty, blinking her eyelids, and she sniffed again.

"I know. I know. It's not you. It's me. It's not the breaking that matters, it's what I said to your father."

23

"What did you say to him?"

"Well, I just said—there's the rest of the service, I said—up there, where it always was, in the corner cupboard in the schoolroom."

"I don't see anything bad in that," said Arrietty as, one by one, she dropped the pieces of onion into the soup.

"But it's a high cupboard," exclaimed Homily. "You have to get up by the curtain. And your father at his age—" She sat down suddenly on a metal-topped champagne cork. "Oh, Arrietty, I wish I'd never mentioned it!"

"Don't worry," said Arrietty, "Papa knows what he can do." She pulled a rubber scent-bottle cork out of the hole in the hot-water pipe and let a trickle of scalding drops fall into the tin lid of an aspirin bottle. She added cold and began to wash her hands.

"Maybe," said Homily. "But I went on about it so. What's a tea cup! Your Uncle Hendreary never drank a thing that wasn't out of a common acorn cup, and he's lived to a ripe old age and had the strength to emigrate. My mother's family never had nothing but a little bone thimble which they shared around. But it's once you've *had* a tea cup, if you see what I mean. . . ."

"Yes," said Arrietty, drying her hands on a roller towel made out of surgical bandage.

"It's that curtain," cried Homily. "He can't climb a curtain at his age—not by the bobbles!"

"With his pin he could," said Arrietty.

"His pin! I led him into that one too! Take a hat pin,

I told him, and tie a bit of name-tape to the head, and pull yourself upstairs. It was to borrow the emerald watch from Her bedroom for me to time the cooking." Homily's voice began to tremble. "Your mother's a wicked woman, Arrietty. Wicked and selfish, that's what she is!"

"You know what?" exclaimed Arrietty suddenly.

Homily brushed away a tear. "No," she said wanly, "what?"

"I could climb a curtain."

Homily rose up. "Arrietty, you dare stand there in cold blood and say a thing like that!"

"But I could! I could! I could borrow! I know I could!"

"Oh!" gasped Homily. "Oh, you wicked heathen girl! How can you speak so!" and she crumpled up again on the cork stool. "So it's come to this!" she said.

"Now, Mother, please," begged Arrietty, "now, don't take on!"

"But don't you see, Arrietty . . ." gasped Homily; she stared down at the table at loss for words and then, at last, she raised a haggard face. "My poor child," she said, "don't speak like that of borrowing. You don't know—and, thank goodness, you never will know"—she dropped her voice to a fearful whisper—"what it's like upstairs. . . ."

Arrietty was silent. "What is it like?" she asked after a moment.

Homily wiped her face on her apron and smoothed back her hair. "Your Uncle Hendreary," she began, "Eggletina's father—" and then she paused. "Listen!" she said. "What's that?"

Echoing on the wood was a faint vibration—the sound of a distant click. "Your father!" exclaimed Homily. "Oh, look at me! Where's the comb?"

They had a comb: a little, silver, eighteenth-century eyebrow comb from the cabinet in the drawing room upstairs. Homily ran it through her hair and rinsed her poor red eyes and, when Pod came in, she was smiling and smoothing down her apron.

Chapter Four

POD came in slowly, his sack on his back; he leaned his hat pin, with its dangling name-tape, against the wall and, on the middle of the kitchen table, he placed a doll's tea cup; it was the size of a mixing bowl.

"Why, Pod—" began Homily.

"Got the saucer too," he said. He swung down the sack and untied the neck. "Here you are," he said, drawing out the saucer. "Matches it."

He had a round, currant-bunny sort of face; tonight it looked flabby.

"Oh, Pod," said Homily, "you do look queer. Are you all right?"

Pod sat down. "I'm fair enough," he said.

"You went up the curtain," said Homily. "Oh, Pod, you shouldn't have. It's shaken you—"

Pod made a strange face, his eyes swiveled round toward Arrietty. Homily stared at him, her mouth open, and then she turned. "Come along, Arrietty," she said briskly, "you pop off to bed, now, like a good girl, and I'll bring you some supper."

"Oh," said Arrietty, "can't I see the rest of the borrowings?"

"Your father's got nothing now. Only food. Off you pop to bed. You've seen the cup and saucer."

Arrietty went into the sitting room to put away her diary, and took some time fixing her candle on the up-turned drawing pin which served as a holder.

"Whatever are you doing?" grumbled Homily. "Give it here. There, that's the way. Now off to bed and fold your clothes, mind."

"Good night, Papa," said Arrietty, kissing his flat white cheek.

"Careful of the light," he said mechanically, and watched her with his round eyes until she had closed the door.

"Now, Pod," said Homily, when they were alone, "tell me. What's the matter?"

Pod looked at her blankly. "I been 'seen,' " he said.

Homily put out a groping hand for the edge of the table; she grasped it and lowered herself slowly on to the stool. "Oh, Pod," she said.

There was silence between them. Pod stared at Homily and Homily stared at the table. After a while she raised her white face. "Badly?" she asked.

Pod moved restlessly. "I don't know about badly. I been 'seen.' Ain't that bad enough?"

"No one," said Homily slowly, "hasn't never been 'seen' since Uncle Hendreary and he was the first they say for forty-five years." A thought struck her and she gripped the table. "It's no good, Pod, I won't emigrate!"

"No one's asked you to," said Pod.

"To go and live like Hendreary and Lupy in a badger's set! The other side of the world, that's where they say it is—all among the earthworms."

"It's two fields away, above the spinney," said Pod.

"Nuts, that's what they eat. And berries. I wouldn't wonder if they don't eat mice—"

"You've eaten mice yourself," Pod reminded her.

"All draughts and fresh air and the children growing up wild. Think of Arrietty!" said Homily. "Think of the way she's been brought up. An only child. She'd catch her death. It's different for Hendreary."

"Why?" asked Pod. "He's got four."

"That's why," explained Homily. "When you've got four, they're brought up rough. But never mind that now. . . . Who saw you?"

"A boy," said Pod.

"A what?" exclaimed Homily, staring.

"A boy." Pod sketched out a rough shape in the air with his hands. "You know, a boy."

"But there isn't—I mean, what sort of a boy?"

"I don't know what you mean 'what sort of a boy.' A boy in a night-shirt. A boy. You know what a boy is, don't you?"

"Yes," said Homily, "I know what a boy is. But there hasn't been a boy, not in this house, these twenty years."

"Well," said Pod, "there's one here now."

Homily stared at him in silence, and Pod met her eyes. "Where did he see you?" asked Homily at last.

"In the schoolroom."

"Oh," said Homily, "when you was getting the cup?"

"Yes," said Pod.

"Haven't you got eyes?" asked Homily. "Couldn't you have looked first?"

"There's never nobody in the schoolroom. And what's more," he went on, "there wasn't today."

"Then where was he?"

"In bed. In the night-nursery or whatever it's called. That's where he was. Sitting up in bed. With the doors open."

"Well, you could have looked in the nursery."

"How could I—halfway up the curtain!"

"Is that where you was?"

"Yes."

"With the cup?"

"Yes. I couldn't get up or down."

"Oh, Pod," wailed Homily, "I should never have let you go. Not at your age!"

"Now, look here," said Pod, "don't mistake me. I got up all right. Got up like a bird, as you might say, bobbles or no bobbles. But"—he leaned toward her—"afterwards—with the cup in me hand, if you see what I mean. . . ." He picked it up off the table. "You see, it's heavy like. You can hold it by the handle, like this . . . but it drops or droops, as you might say. You should take a cup like this in your two hands. A bit of cheese off a shelf, or an apple—well, I drop that . . . give it a push and it falls and I climbs down in me own time and picks it up. But with a cup—you see what I mean? And coming down, you got to watch your feet. And, as I say, some of the bobbles was missing. You didn't know what you could hold on to, not safely. . . ."

"Oh, Pod," said Homily, her eyes full of tears, "what did you do?"

"Well," said Pod, sitting back again, "he took the cup."

"What do you mean?" exclaimed Homily, aghast.

Pod avoided her eyes. "Well, he'd been sitting up in bed there watching me. I'd been on that curtain a good ten minutes, because the hall clock had just struck the quarter—"

"But how do you mean—'he took the cup'?"

"Well, he'd got out of bed and there he was standing, looking up. 'I'll take the cup,' he said."

"Oh!" gasped Homily, her eyes staring, "and you give it him?"

"He took it," said Pod, "ever so gentle. And then, when I was down, he give it me." Homily put her face in her hands. "Now don't take on," said Pod uneasily.

"He might have caught you," shuddered Homily in a stifled voice.

"Yes," said Pod, "but he just give me the cup. 'Here you are,' he said."

Homily raised her face. "What are we going to do?" she asked.

Pod sighed. "Well, there isn't nothing we can do. Except—"

"Oh, no," exclaimed Homily, "not that. Not emigrate. Not that, Pod, now I've got the house so nice and a clock and all."

"We could take the clock," said Pod.

32

"And Arrietty? What about her? She's not like those cousins. She can *read*, Pod, and sew a treat—"

"He don't know where we live," said Pod.

"But they look," exclaimed Homily. "Remember Hendreary! They got the cat and—"

"Now, now," said Pod, "don't bring up the past."

"But you've got to think of it! They got the cat and—"

"Yes," said Pod, "but Eggletina was different."

"How different? She was Arrietty's age."

"Well, they hadn't told her, you see. That's where they went wrong. They tried to make her believe that there wasn't nothing but was under the floor. They never told her about Mrs. Driver or Crampfurl. Least of all about cats."

"There wasn't any cat," Homily pointed out, "not till Hendreary was 'seen.'"

"Well, there was, then," said Pod. "You got to tell them, that's what I say, or they try to find out for themselves."

"Pod," said Homily solemnly, "we haven't told Arrietty."

"Oh, she knows," said Pod; he moved uncomfortably. "She's got her grating."

"She doesn't know about Eggletina. She doesn't know about being 'seen.'"

"Well," said Pod, "we'll tell her. We always said we would. There's no hurry."

Homily stood up. "Pod," she said, "we're going to tell her now."

Chapter Five

ARRIETTY had not been asleep. She had been lying under her knitted coverlet staring up at the ceiling. It was an interesting ceiling. Pod had built Arrietty's bedroom out of two cigar boxes, and on the ceiling lovely painted ladies dressed in swirls of chiffon blew long trumpets against a background of blue sky; below there were feathery palm trees and small white houses set about a square. It was a glamorous scene, above all by candlelight, but tonight Arrietty had stared without seeing. The wood of a cigar box is thin and Arrietty, lying straight and still under the quilt, had heard the rise and fall of worried voices. She had heard her own name; she had heard Homily exclaim: "Nuts and berries, that's what they eat!" and she had heard, after a while, the heart-felt cry of "What shall we do?"

So when Homily appeared beside her bed, she wrapped herself obediently in her quilt and, padding in her bare feet along the dusty passage, she joined her parents in the warmth of the kitchen. Crouched on her little stool she sat clasping her knees, shivering a little, and looking from one face to another.

Homily came beside her and, kneeling on the floor, she placed an arm round Arrietty's skinny shoulders. "Arrietty," she said gravely, "you know about upstairs?"

"What about it?" asked Arrietty.

"You know there are two giants?"

"Yes," said Arrietty, "Great-Aunt Sophy and Mrs. Driver."

"That's right," said Homily, "and Crampfurl in the garden." She laid a roughened hand on Arrietty's clasped ones. "You know about Uncle Hendreary?"

Arrietty thought awhile. "He went abroad?" she said.

"Emigrated," corrected Homily, "to the other side of the world. With Aunt Lupy and all the children. To a badger's set—a hole in a bank under a hawthorn hedge. Now why do you think he did this?"

"Oh," said Arrietty, her face alight, "to be out of doors . . . to lie in the sun . . . to run in the grass . . . to swing on twigs like the birds do . . . to suck honey . . ."

"Nonsense, Arrietty," exclaimed Homily sharply, "that's a nasty habit! And your Uncle Hendreary's a rheumatic sort of man. He emigrated," she went on, stressing the word, "because he was 'seen.'"

"Oh," said Arrietty.

"He was 'seen' on the 23rd of April 1892, by Rosa Pickhatchet, on the drawing-room mantelpiece. Of all places . . ." she added suddenly in a wondering aside.

"Oh," said Arrietty.

"I have never heard nor no one has never seen fit to tell

36

why he went on the drawing-room mantelpiece in the first place. There's nothing on it, your father assures me, which cannot be seen from the floor or by standing sideways on the handle of the bureau and steadying yourself on the key. That's what your father does if he ever goes into the drawing room—"

"They said it was a liver pill," put in Pod.

"How do you mean?" asked Homily, startled.

"A liver pill for Lupy." Pod spoke wearily. 'Someone started a rumor," he went on, "that there were liver pills on the drawing-room mantelpiece. . . ."

"Oh," said Homily and looked thoughtful, "I never heard that. All the same," she exclaimed, "it was stupid and foolhardy. There's no way down except by the bell-pull. She dusted him, they say, with a feather duster, and he stood so still, alongside a cupid, that she might never have noticed him if he hadn't sneezed. She was new, you see, and didn't know the ornaments. We heard her screeching right here under the kitchen. And they could never get her to clean anything much after that that wasn't chairs or tables—least of all the tiger-skin rug."

"I don't hardly never bother with the drawing room," said Pod. "Everything's got its place like and they see what goes. There might be a little something left on a table or down the side of a chair, but not without there's been company, and there never is no company—not for the last ten or twelve year. Sitting here in this chair, I can tell you by heart every blessed thing that's in that drawing room, working round from the cabinet by the window to the—"

"There's a mint of things in that cabinet," interrupted Homily, "solid silver some of them. A solid silver violin, they got there, strings and all—just right for our Arrietty."

"What's the good," asked Pod, "of things behind glass?"

"Couldn't you break it?" suggested Arrietty. "Just a corner, just a little tap, just a . . ." Her voice faltered as she saw the shocked amazement on her father's face.

"Listen here, Arrietty," began Homily angrily, and then she controlled herself and patted Arrietty's clasped hands. "She don't know much about borrowing," she explained to Pod. "You can't blame her." She turned again to Arrietty. "Borrowing's a skilled job, an art like. Of all the families who've been in this house, there's only us left, and do you know for why? Because your father, Arrietty, is the best borrower that's been known in these parts since—well, before your grandad's time. Even your Aunt Lupy admitted that much. When he was younger I've seen your father walk the length of a laid dinner table, after the gong was rung, taking a nut or sweet from every dish, and down by a fold in the tablecloth as the first people came

in at the door. He'd do it just for fun, wouldn't you, Pod?"

Pod smiled wanly. "There weren't no sense in it," he said.

"Maybe," said Homily, "but you did it! Who else would dare?"

"I were younger then," said Pod. He sighed and turned to Arrietty. "You don't break things, lass. That's not the way to do it. That's not borrowing. . . ."

"We were rich then," said Homily. "Oh, we did have some lovely things! You were only a tot, Arrietty, and wouldn't remember. We had a whole suite of walnut furniture out of the doll's house and a set of wineglasses in green glass, and a musical snuffbox, and the cousins would come and we'd have parties. Do you remember, Pod? Not only the cousins. The Harpsichords came. Everybody came—except those Overmantels from the morning room. And we'd dance and dance and the young people would sit out by the grating. Three tunes that snuffbox played—*Clementine*, *God Save the Queen*, and the *Post-Chaise Gallop*. We were the envy of everybody— even the Overmantels. . . ."

"Who were the Overmantels?" asked Arrietty.

"Oh, you must've heard me talk of the Overmantels," exclaimed Homily, "that stuck-up lot who lived in the wall high up—among the lath and plaster behind the mantelpiece in the morning room. And a queer lot they were. The men smoked all the time because the tobacco jars were kept there; and they'd climb about and in and out the carvings of the overmantel, sliding down pillars and showing off. The women were a conceited lot too, always admiring themselves in all those bits of overmantel looking-glass. They never asked anyone up there and I, for one, never wanted to go. I've no head for heights, and your father never liked the men. He's always lived steady, your father has, and not only the tobacco jars, but the whisky decanters too, were kept in the morning room and they say those Overmantel men would suck up the dregs in the glasses through those quill pipe-cleaners they keep there on the mantelpiece. I don't know whether it's true but they do say that those Overmantel men used to have a party every Tuesday after the bailiff had been to talk business in the morning room. Laid out, they'd be, dead drunk—or so the story goes—on the green plush tablecloth, all among the tin boxes and the account books—"

"Now, Homily," protested Pod, who did not like gossip, "I never see'd 'em."

"But you wouldn't put it past them, Pod. You said yourself when I married you not to call on the Overmantels."

"They lived so high," said Pod, "that's all."

"Well, they were a lazy lot—that much you can't deny. They never had no kind of home life. Kept themselves warm in winter by the heat of the morning-room fire and ate nothing but breakfast food; breakfast, of course, was the only meal served in the morning room."

"What happened to them?" asked Arrietty.

"Well, when the Master died and She took to her bed, there was no more use for the morning room. So the Overmantels had to go. What else could they do? No food, no fire. It's a bitter cold room in winter."

"And the Harpsichords?" asked Arrietty.

Homily looked thoughtful. "Well, they were different. I'm not saying they weren't stuck-up too, because they were. Your Aunt Lupy, who married your Uncle Hendreary, was a Harpsichord by marriage and we all know the airs she gave herself."

"Now, Homily—" began Pod.

"Well, she'd no right to. She was only a Rain-Pipe from the stables before she married Harpsichord."

"Didn't she marry Uncle Hendreary?" asked Arrietty.

"Yes, later. She was a widow with two children and he was a widower with three. It's no good looking at me like that, Pod. You can't deny she took it out of poor Hendreary: she thought it was a come-down to marry a Clock."

"Why?" asked Arrietty.

"Because we Clocks live under the kitchen, that's why. Because we don't talk fancy grammar and eat anchovy toast. But to live under the kitchen doesn't say we aren't educated. The Clocks are just as old a family as the Harpsichords. You remember that, Arrietty, and don't let anyone tell you different. Your grandfather could count and write down the numbers up to—what was it, Pod?"

"Fifty-seven," said Pod.

"There," said Homily, "fifty-seven! And your father can count, as you know, Arrietty; he can count and write down the numbers, on and on, as far as it goes. How far does it go, Pod?"

"Close on a thousand," said Pod.

"There!" exclaimed Homily, "and he knows the alphabet because he taught you, Arrietty, didn't he? And he would have been able to read—wouldn't you, Pod?—if he hadn't had to start borrowing so young. Your Uncle Hendreary and your father had to go out borrowing at thirteen—your age, Arrietty, think of it!"

"But I should like—" began Arrietty.

"So he didn't have your advantages," went on Homily breathlessly, "and just because the Harpsichords lived in the drawing room—they moved in there, in 1837, to a hole in the wainscot just behind where the harpsichord used to stand, if ever there was one, which I doubt—and were really a family called Linen-Press or some such name and changed it to Harpsichord—"

"What did they live on," asked Arrietty, "in the drawing room?"

"Afternoon tea," said Homily, "nothing but afternoon tea. No wonder the children grew up peaky. Of course, in the old days it was better—muffins and crumpets and such, and good rich cake and jams and jellies. And there was one old Harpsichord who could remember sillabub of an evening. But they had to do their borrowing in such a rush, poor things. On wet days, when the human beings sat all afternoon in the drawing room, the tea would be brought in and taken away again without a chance of the Harpsichords getting near it—and on fine days it might be taken out into the garden. Lupy has told me that, sometimes, there were days and days when they lived on crumbs and on water out of the flower vases. So you can't be too hard on them; their only comfort, poor things, was to show off a bit and wear evening dress and talk like ladies and gentlemen. Did you ever hear your Aunt Lupy talk?"

"Yes. No. I can't remember."

"Oh, you should have heard her say 'Parquet'—that's the stuff the drawing-room floor's made of—'Parkay . . . Parr-r-kay,' she'd say. Oh, it was lovely. Come to think of it, your Aunt Lupy was the most stuck-up of them all. . . ."

"Arrietty's shivering," said Pod. "We didn't get the little maid up to talk about Aunt Lupy."

"Nor we did," cried Homily, suddenly contrite. "You should've stopped me, Pod. There, my lamb, tuck this quilt right round you and I'll get you a nice drop of piping hot soup!"

"And yet," said Pod as Homily, fussing at the stove, ladled soup into the tea cup, "we did in a way."

"Did what?" asked Homily.

"Get her here to talk about Aunt Lupy. Aunt Lupy, Uncle Hendreary, and"—he paused—"Eggletina."

"Let her drink up her soup first," said Homily.

"There's no call for her to stop drinking," said Pod.

Chapter Six

"Your mother and I got you up," said Pod, "to tell you about upstairs."

Arrietty, holding the great cup in both hands, looked at him over the edge.

Pod coughed. "You said a while back that the sky was dark brown with cracks in it. Well, it isn't." He looked at her almost accusingly. "It's blue."

"I know," said Arrietty.

"You know!" exclaimed Pod.

"Yes, of course I know. I've got the grating."

"Can you see the sky through the grating?"

"Go on," interrupted Homily, "tell her about the gates."

"Well," said Pod ponderously, "if you go outside this room, what do you see?"

"A dark passage," said Arrietty.

"And what else?"

"Other rooms."

"And if you go farther?"

"More passages."

"And, if you go walking on and on, in all the passages under the floor, however they twist and turn, what do you find?"

"Gates," said Arrietty.

"Strong gates," said Pod, "gates you can't open. What are they there for?"

"Against the mice?" said Arrietty.

"Yes," agreed Pod uncertainly, as though he gave her half a mark, "but mice never hurt no one. What else?"

"Rats?" suggested Arrietty.

"We don't have rats," said Pod. "What about cats?"

"Cats?" echoed Arrietty, surprised.

"Or to keep you in?" suggested Pod.

"To keep me in?" repeated Arrietty, dismayed.

"Upstairs is a dangerous place," said Pod. "And you, Arrietty, you're all we've got, see? It isn't like Hendreary —he still has two of his own and two of hers. Once," said Pod, "Hendreary had three—three of his own."

"Your father's thinking of Eggletina," said Homily.

"Yes," said Pod, "Eggletina. They never told her about upstairs. And they hadn't got no grating. They told her the sky was nailed up, like, with cracks in it—"

"A foolish way to bring up a child," murmured Homily. She sniffed slightly and touched Arrietty's hair.

"But Eggletina was no fool," said Pod; "she didn't believe them. So one day," he went on, "she went upstairs to see for herself."

"How did she get out?" asked Arrietty, interested.

"Well, we didn't have so many gates then. Just the one under the clock. Hendreary must have left it unlocked or something. Anyway, Eggletina went out . . ."

"In a blue dress," said Homily, "and a pair of button-boots your father made her, yellow kid with jet beads for buttons. Lovely they were."

"Well," said Pod, "any other time it might have been all right. She'd have gone out, had a look around, had a bit of a fright, maybe, and come back—none the worse and no one the wiser . . ."

"But things had been happening," said Homily.

"Yes," said Pod, "she didn't know, as they never told her, that her father had been 'seen' and that upstairs they had got in the cat and—"

"They waited a week," said Homily, "and they waited a month and they hoped for a year but no one ever saw Eggletina no more."

"And that," said Pod after a pause and eyeing Arrietty, "is what happened to Eggletina."

There was silence except for Pod's breathing and the faint bubble of the soup.

"It just broke up your Uncle Hendreary," said Homily at last. "He never went upstairs again—in case, he said, he found the button-boots. Their only future was to emigrate."

Arrietty was silent a moment, then she raised her head. "Why did you tell me?" she asked. "Now? Tonight?"

Homily got up. She moved restlessly toward the stove. "We don't never talk of it," she said, "at least, not much, but, tonight, we felt—" She turned suddenly. "Well, we'll just say it straight out: your father's been 'seen,' Arrietty!"

"Oh," said Arrietty, "who by?"

"Well, by a—something you've never heard of. But that's not the point: the point is—"

"You think they'll get a cat?"

"They may," said Homily.

Arrietty set down the soup for a moment; she stared into the cup as it stood beside her almost knee high on the floor; there was a dreamy, secret something about her lowered face. "Couldn't we emigrate?" she ventured at last, very softly.

Homily gasped and clasped her hands and swung away toward the wall. "You don't know what you're talking about," she cried, addressing a frying pan which hung there. "Worms and weasels and cold and damp and—"

"But supposing," said Arrietty, "that *I* went out, like Eggletina did, and the cat ate *me*. Then you and Papa would emigrate. Wouldn't you?" she asked, and her voice faltered. "Wouldn't you?"

Homily swung round again, this time toward Arrietty; her face looked very angry. "I shall smack you, Arrietty Clock, if you don't behave yourself this minute!"

Arrietty's eyes filled with tears. "I was only thinking," she said, "that I'd like to be there—to emigrate too. Uneaten," she added softly and the tears fell.

"Now," said Pod, "this is enough! You get off to bed, Arrietty, uneaten and unbeaten both—and we'll talk about it in the morning."

"It's not that I'm afraid," cried Arrietty angrily; "I like cats. I bet the cat didn't eat Eggletina. I bet she just ran away because she hated being cooped up . . . day after day . . . week after week . . . year after year. . . . Like I do!" she added on a sob.

"Cooped up!" repeated Homily, astounded.

Arrietty put her face into her hands. "Gates . . ." she gasped, "gates, gates, gates. . . ."

Pod and Homily stared at each other across Arrietty's bowed shoulders. "You didn't ought to have brought it up," he said unhappily, "not so late at night . . ."

Arrietty raised her tear-streaked face. "Late or early, what's the difference?" she cried. "Oh, I know Papa is a wonderful borrower. I know we've managed to stay when all the others have gone. But what has it done for us, in the end? I don't think it's so clever to live on alone, for ever and ever, in a great, big, half-empty house; under the floor, with no one to talk to, no one to play with, nothing to see but dust and passages, no light but candlelight and firelight and what comes through the cracks. Eggletina had brothers and Eggletina had half-brothers; Eggletina had a tame mouse; Eggletina had yellow boots with jet buttons, and Eggletina did get out—just once!"

"Shush," said Pod gently, "not so loud." Above their

heads the floor creaked and heavy footfalls heaved deliberately to and fro. They heard Mrs. Driver's grumbling
voice and the clatter of the fire-irons. "Drat this stove,"
they heard her say, "wind's in the east again." Then they
heard her raise her voice and call, "Crampfurl!"

Pod sat staring glumly at the floor; Arrietty shivered a
little and hugged herself more tightly into the knitted quilt
and Homily drew a long, slow breath. Suddenly she raised
her head.

"The child is right," she announced firmly.

Arrietty's eyes grew big. "Oh, no—" she began. It
shocked her to be right. Parents were right, not children.
Children could say anything, Arrietty knew, and enjoy
saying it—knowing always they were safe and wrong.

"You see, Pod," went on Homily, "it was different for
you and me. There was other families, other children . . .
the Sinks in the scullery, you remember? And those people
who lived behind the knife machine—I forget their names
now. And the Broom-Cupboard boys. And there was that
underground passage from the stables—you know, that the
Rain-Pipes used. We had more, as you might say, freedom."

"Ah, yes," said Pod, "in a way. But where does freedom
take you?" He looked up uncertainly. "Where are they
all now?"

"Some of them may have bettered themselves, I shouldn't
wonder," said Homily sharply. "Times have changed in
the whole house. Pickings aren't what they were. There

were those that went, you remember, when they dug a trench for the gas-pipe. Over the fields, and through the wood, and all. A kind of tunnel it gave them, all the way to Leighton Buzzard."

"And what did they find there?" said Pod unkindly. "A mountain of coke!"

Homily turned away. "Arrietty," she said, in the same firm voice, "supposing one day—we'd pick a special day when there was no one about, and providing they don't get a cat which I have my reasons for thinking they won't—supposing, one day, your father took you out borrowing, you'd be a good girl, wouldn't you? You'd do just what he said, quickly and quietly and no arguing?"

Arrietty turned quite pink; she clasped her hands together. "Oh—" she began in an ecstatic voice, but Pod cut in quickly:

"Now, Homily, we got to think. You can't just say things like that without thinking it out proper. I been 'seen,' remember. This is no kind of time for taking a child upstairs."

"There won't be no cat," said Homily; "there wasn't no screeching. It's not like that time with Rosa Pickhatchet."

"All the same," said Pod uncertainly, "the risk's there. I never heard of no *girl* going borrowing before."

"The way I look at it," said Homily, "and it's only now it's come to me: if you had a son, you'd take him borrowing, now wouldn't you? Well, you haven't got no son—only

Arrietty. Suppose anything happened to you or me, where would Arrietty be—if she hadn't learned to borrow?"

Pod stared down at his knees. "Yes," he said after a moment, "I see what you mean."

"And it'll give her a bit of interest like and stop her hankering."

"Hankering for what?"

"For blue sky and grass and suchlike." Arrietty caught her breath and Homily turned on her swiftly: "It's no good, Arrietty, I'm not going to emigrate—not for you nor any one else!"

"Ah," said Pod and began to laugh, "so that's it!"

"Shush!" said Homily, annoyed, and glanced quickly at the ceiling. "Not so loud! Now kiss your father, Arrietty," she went on briskly, "and pop off back to bed."

As Arrietty snuggled down under the bedclothes she felt, creeping up from her toes, a glow of happiness like a glow of warmth. She heard their voices rising and falling in the next room: Homily's went on and on, measured and confident—there was, Arrietty felt, a kind of conviction behind it; it was the winning voice. Once she heard Pod get up and the scrape of a chair. "I don't like it!" she heard him say. And she heard Homily whisper "Hush!" and there were tremulous footfalls on the floor above and the sudden clash of pans.

Arrietty, half dozing, gazed up at her painted ceiling. "FLOR DE HAVANA," proclaimed the banners proudly.

GARANTIZADOS

SUPERIORES

NON PLUS ULTRA

FLOR DE HAVANA

ESQUISITOS

"Garantizados . . . Superiores . . . Non Plus Ultra . . . Esquisitos . . ." and the lovely gauzy ladies blew their trumpets, silently, triumphantly, on soundless notes of glee. . . .

Chapter Seven

FOR the next three weeks Arrietty was especially "good": she helped her mother tidy the storerooms; she swept and watered the passages and trod them down: she sorted and graded the beads (which they used as buttons) into the screw tops of aspirin bottles; she cut old kid gloves into squares for Pod's shoemaking; she filed fish-bone needles to a bee-sting sharpness; she hung up the washing to dry by the grating so that it blew in the soft air; and at last the day came—that dreadful, wonderful, never-to-be-forgotten day —when Homily, scrubbing the kitchen table, straightened her back and called "Pod!"

He came in from his workroom, last in hand.

"Look at this brush!" cried Homily. It was a fiber brush with a plaited, fiber back.

"Aye," said Pod, "worn down."

"Gets me knuckles now," said Homily, "every time I scrub."

Pod looked worried. Since he had been "seen," they had stuck to kitchen borrowing, the bare essentials of fuel and food. There was an old mousehole under the kitchen stove upstairs which, at night when the fire was out or very low, Pod could use as a chute to save carrying. Since the window-curtain incident they had pushed a match-box chest of drawers below the mousehole, and had stood a wooden stool on the chest of drawers; and Pod, with much help and shoving from Homily, had learned to squeeze up the chute instead of down. In this way he need not venture into the great hall and passages; he could just nip out, from under the vast black stove in the kitchen, for a clove or a carrot or a tasty piece of ham. But it was not a satisfactory arrangement: even when the fire was out, often there was hot ash and cinders under the stove and once, as he emerged, a great brush came at him wielded by Mrs. Driver; and he slithered back, on top of Homily, singed, shaken, and coughing dust. Another time, for some reason, the fire had been in full blaze and Pod had arrived suddenly beneath a glowing inferno, dropping white-hot coals. But usually, at night, the fire was out, and Pod could pick his way through the cinders into the kitchen proper.

"Mrs. Driver's out," Homily went on. "It's her day off. And She"—they always spoke of Aunt Sophy as "She"—"is safe enough in bed."

"It's not them that worries me," said Pod.

"Why," exclaimed Homily sharply, "the boy's not still here?"

"I don't know," said Pod; "there's always a risk," he added.

"And there always will be," retorted Homily, "like when you was in the coal cellar and the coal cart came."

"But the other two," said Pod, "Mrs. Driver and Her, I always know where they are, like."

"As for that," exclaimed Homily, "a boy's even better. You can hear a boy a mile off. Well," she went on after a moment, "please yourself. But it's not like you to talk of risks. . . ."

Pod sighed. "All right," he said and turned away to fetch his borrowing-bag.

"Take the child," called Homily after him.

Pod turned. "Now, Homily," he began in an alarmed voice.

"Why not?" asked Homily sharply. "It's just the day. You aren't going no farther than the front door. If you're nervous you can leave her by the clock, ready to nip underneath and down the hole. Let her just *see* at any rate. Arrietty!"

As Arrietty came running in, Pod tried again. "Now listen, Homily—" he protested.

Homily ignored him. "Arrietty," she said brightly, "would you like to go along with your father and borrow me some brush fiber from the doormat in the hall?"

Arrietty gave a little skip. "Oh," she cried, "could I?"

"Well, take your apron off," said Homily, "and change your boots. You want light shoes for borrowing—better wear the red kid." And then as Arrietty spun away

Homily turned to Pod: "She'll be all right," she said; "you'll see."

As she followed her father down the passage Arrietty's heart began to beat faster. Now the moment had come at last she found it almost too much to bear. She felt light and trembly, and hollow with excitement.

They had three borrowing-bags between the two of them ("In case," Pod had explained, "we pick up something. A

bad borrower loses many a chance for lack of an extra bag") and Pod laid these down to open the first gate, which was latched by a safety pin. It was a big pin, too strongly sprung for little hands to open, and Arrietty watched her father swing his whole weight on the bar and his feet kick loose off the ground. Hanging from his hands, he shifted his weight along the pin toward the curved sheath and, as he moved, the pin sprang open and he, in the same instant, jumped free. "You couldn't do that," he remarked, dusting

his hands; "too light. Nor could your mother. Come along now. Quietly. . . ."

There were other gates; all of which Pod left open ("Never shut a gate on the way out," he explained in a whisper, "you might need to get back quick") and, after a while, Arrietty saw a faint light at the end of the passage. She pulled her father's sleeve. "Is that it?" she whispered.

Pod stood still. "Quietly, now," he warned her. "Yes, that's it: the hole under the clock!" As he said these words, Arrietty felt breathless but, outwardly, she made no sign. "There are three steps up to it," Pod went on, "steep like, so mind how you go. When you're under the clock you just stay there; don't let your mind wander and keep your eyes on me: if all's clear, I'll give you the sign."

The steps were high and a little uneven but Arrietty took them more lightly than Pod. As she scrambled past the jagged edges of the hole she had a sudden blinding glimpse of molten gold: it was spring sunshine on the pale stones of the hall floor. Standing upright, she could no longer see this; she could only see the cave-like shadows in the great case above her and the dim outline of the hanging weights. The hollow darkness around her vibrated with sound; it was a safe sound—solid and regular; and, far above her head, she saw the movement of the pendulum; it gleamed a little in the half light, remote and cautious in its rhythmic swing. Arrietty felt warm tears behind her eyelids and a sudden swelling pride: so this, at last, was The Clock! Their clock . . . after which her family was named! For two hundred years it had stood here, deep-voiced and patient, guarding their threshold, and measuring their time.

But Pod, she saw, stood crouched beneath the carved archway against the light: "Keep your eyes on me," he had said, so Arrietty crouched too. She saw the gleaming golden stone floor of the hall stretching away into distance; she saw the edges of rugs, like richly colored islands in a molten sea, and she saw, in a glory of sunlight—like a dreamed-of gateway to fairyland—the open front door. Beyond she saw grass and, against the clear, bright sky, a waving frond of green.

Pod's eyes slewed round. "Wait," he breathed, "and watch." And then in a flash he was gone.

Arrietty saw him scurry across the sunlit floor. Swiftly he ran—as a mouse runs or a blown dry leaf—and suddenly she saw him as "small." "But," she told herself, "he isn't small. He's half a head taller than Mother. . . ." She watched him run round a chestnut-colored island of doormat into the shadows beside the door. There, it seemed, he became invisible.

Arrietty watched and waited. All was still except for a sudden whirr within the clock. A grinding whirr it was, up high in the hollow darkness above her head, then the sliding grate of slipped metal before the clock sang out its chime. Three notes were struck, deliberate and mellow: "Take it or leave it," they seemed to say, "but that's the time—"

A sudden movement near the shadowed lintel of the front door and there was Pod again, bag in hand, beside the mat; it rose knee deep before him like a field of chestnut corn. Arrietty saw him glance toward the clock and then she saw him raise his hand.

Oh, the warmth of the stone flags as she ran across them . . . the gladdening sunlight on her face and hands . . . the awful space above and around her! Pod caught her and held her at last, and patted her shoulder. "There, there . . ." he said, "get your breath—good girl!"

Panting a little, Arrietty gazed about her. She saw great chair legs rearing up into sunlight; she saw the shadowed undersides of their seats spread above her like canopies; she saw the nails and the strapping and odd tags of silk and string; she saw the terraced cliffs of the stairs, mounting up into the distance, up and up . . . she saw carved table legs and a cavern under the chest. And all the time, in the stillness, the clock spoke—measuring out the seconds, spreading its layers of calm.

And then, turning, Arrietty looked at the garden. She saw a graveled path, full of colored stones—the size of walnuts they were with, here and there, a blade of grass between them, transparent green against the light of the sun. Beyond the path she saw a grassy bank rising steeply to a tangled hedge; and beyond the hedge she saw fruit trees, bright with blossom.

"Here's a bag," said Pod in a hoarse whisper; "better get down to work."

Obediently Arrietty started pulling fiber; stiff it was and full of dust. Pod worked swiftly and methodically, making small bundles, each of which he put immediately in the bag. "If you have to run suddenly," he explained, "you don't want to leave nothing behind."

"It hurts your hands," said Arrietty, "doesn't it?" and suddenly she sneezed.

"Not my hands it doesn't," said Pod; "they're hardened like," and Arrietty sneezed again.

"Dusty, isn't it?" she said.

Pod straightened his back. "No good pulling where it's knotted right in," he said, watching her. "No wonder it hurts your hands. See here," he exclaimed after a moment, "you leave it! It's your first time up like. You sit on the step there and take a peek out of doors."

"Oh, no—" Arrietty began ("If I don't help," she thought, "he won't want me again") but Pod insisted.

"I'm better on me own," he said. "I can choose me bits, if you see what I mean, seeing as it's me who's got to make the brush."

Chapter Eight

THE step was warm but very steep. "If I got down on to the path," Arrietty thought, "I might not get up again," so for some moments she sat quietly. After a while she noticed the shoe-scraper.

"Arrietty," called Pod softly, "where have you got to?"

"I just climbed down the shoe-scraper," she called back.

He came along and looked down at her from the top of the step. "That's all right," he said after a moment's stare, "but never climb down anything that isn't fixed like. Supposing one of them came along and moved the shoe-scraper—where would you be then? How would you get up again?"

"It's heavy to move," said Arrietty.

"Maybe," said Pod, "but it's movable. See what I mean? There's rules, my lass, and you got to learn."

"This path," Arrietty said, "goes round the house. And the bank does too."

"Well," said Pod, "what of it?"

Arrietty rubbed one red kid shoe on a rounded stone. "It's my grating," she explained. "I was thinking that my grating must be just round the corner. My grating looks out on to this bank."

"Your grating!" exclaimed Pod. "Since when has it been your grating?"

"I was thinking," Arrietty went on. "Suppose I just went round the corner and called through the grating to Mother?"

"No," said Pod, "we're not going to have none of that. Not going round corners."

"Then," went on Arrietty, "she'd see I was all right like."

"Well," said Pod, and then he half smiled, "go quickly then and call. I'll watch for you here. Not loud mind!"

Arrietty ran. The stones in the path were firmly bedded and her light, soft shoes hardly seemed to touch them. How glorious it was to run—you could never run under the floor: you walked, you stooped, you crawled—but you never ran. Arrietty nearly ran past the grating. She saw it just in time after she turned the corner. Yes, there it was quite close to the ground, embedded deeply in the old wall of the house; there was moss below it in a spreading, greenish stain.

Arrietty ran up to it. "Mother!" she called, her nose against the iron grille. "Mother!" She waited quietly and, after a moment, she called again.

At the third call Homily came. Her hair was coming down and she carried, as though it were heavy, the screw lid of a pickle jar, filled with soapy water. "Oh," she said in an annoyed voice, "you didn't half give me a turn! What do you think you're up to? Where's your father?"

Arrietty jerked her head sideways. "Just there—by the front door!" She was so full of happiness that, out of Homily's sight, her toes danced on the green moss. Here she was on the other side of the grating—here she was at last, on the outside—looking in!

"Yes," said Homily, "they open that door like that—the first day of spring. Well," she went on briskly, "you run back to your father. And tell him, if the morning-room door happens to be open that I wouldn't say no to a bit of red blotting paper. Mind, out of my way now—while I throw the water!"

"That's what grows the moss," thought Arrietty as she sped back to her father, "all the water we empty through the grating. . . ."

Pod looked relieved when he saw her but frowned at the message. "How's she expect me to climb that desk without me pin? Blotting paper's a curtain-and-chair job and she should know it. Come on now! Up with you!"

"Let me stay down," pleaded Arrietty, "just a bit longer. Just till you finish. They're all out. Except Her. Mother said so."

"She'd say anything," grumbled Pod, "when she wants something quick. How does she know She won't take it into her head to get out of that bed of Hers and come downstairs with a stick? How does she know Mrs. Driver ain't stayed at home today—with a headache? How does she know that boy ain't still here?"

"What boy?" asked Arrietty.

Pod looked embarrassed. "What boy?" he repeated vaguely and then went on: "Or may be Crampfurl—"

"Crampfurl isn't a boy," said Arrietty.

"No, he isn't," said Pod, "not in a manner of speaking. No," he went on as though thinking this out, "no, you wouldn't call Crampfurl a boy. Not, as you might say, a boy—exactly. Well," he said, beginning to move away, "stay down a bit if you like. But stay close!"

Arrietty watched him move away from the step and then she looked about her. Oh, glory! Oh, joy! Oh, freedom!

The sunlight, the grasses, the soft, moving air and halfway up the bank, where it curved round the corner, a flowering cherry tree! Below it on the path lay a stain of pinkish petals and, at the tree's foot, pale as butter, a nest of primroses.

Arrietty threw a cautious glance toward the front doorstep and then, light and dancey, in her soft red shoes, she ran toward the petals. They were curved like shells and rocked as she touched them. She gathered several up and laid them one inside the other . . . up and up . . . like a card castle. And then she spilled them. Pod came again to the top of the step and looked along the path. "Don't you go far," he said after a moment. Seeing his lips move, she smiled back at him: she was too far already to hear the words.

A greenish beetle, shining in the sunlight, came toward her across the stones. She laid her fingers lightly on its shell and it stood still, waiting and watchful, and when she moved her hand the beetle went swiftly on. An ant came hurrying in a busy zigzag. She danced in front of it to tease it and put out her foot. It stared at her, nonplused, waving its antennae; then pettishly, as though put out, it swerved away. Two birds came down, quarreling shrilly, into the grass below the tree. One flew away but Arrietty could see the other among the moving grass stems above her on the slope. Cautiously she moved toward the bank and climbed a little nervously in amongst the green blades.

As she parted them gently with her bare hands, drops of water plopped on her skirt and she felt the red shoes become damp. But on she went, pulling herself up now and again by rooty stems into this jungle of moss and wood-violet and creeping leaves of clover. The sharp-seeming grass blades, waist high, were tender to the touch and sprang back lightly behind her as she passed. When at last she reached the foot of the tree, the bird took fright and flew away and she sat down suddenly on a gnarled leaf of primrose. The air was filled with scent. "But nothing will play with you," she thought and saw the cracks and furrows of the primrose leaves held crystal beads of dew. If she pressed the leaf these rolled like marbles. The bank was warm, almost too warm here within the shelter of the tall grass, and the sandy earth smelled dry. Standing up, she picked a primrose. The pink stalk felt tender and living in her hands and was covered with silvery hairs, and when she held the flower, like a parasol, between her eyes and the sky, she saw the sun's pale light through the veined petals. On a piece of bark she found a wood louse and she struck it lightly with her swaying flower. It curled immediately and became a ball, bumping softly away downhill in amongst the grass roots. But she knew about wood lice. There were plenty of them at home under the floor. Homily always scolded her if she played with them because, she said, they smelled of old knives. She lay back among the stalks of the primroses and they made a coolness between her and the sun, and then, sighing, she turned her head and looked sideways up the bank among the grass stems. Startled, she caught her breath. Something had moved above her on the bank. Something had glittered. Arrietty stared.

Chapter Nine

IT WAS an eye. Or it looked like an eye. Clear and bright like the color of the sky. An eye like her own but enormous. A glaring eye. Breathless with fear, she sat up. And the eye blinked. A great fringe of lashes came curving down and flew up again out of sight. Cautiously, Arrietty moved her legs: she would slide noiselessly in among the grass stems and slither away down the bank.

"Don't move!" said a voice, and the voice, like the eye, was enormous but, somehow, hushed—and hoarse like a surge of wind through the grating on a stormy night in March.

Arrietty froze. "So this is it," she thought, "the worst and most terrible thing of all: I have been 'seen'! Whatever happened to Eggletina will now, almost certainly, happen to me!"

There was a pause and Arrietty, her heart pounding in her ears, heard the breath again drawn swiftly into the vast lungs. "Or," said the voice, whispering still, "I shall hit you with my ash stick."

Suddenly Arrietty became calm. "Why?" she asked.
How strange her own voice sounded! Crystal thin and
harebell clear, it tinkled on the air.

"In case," came the surprised whisper at last, "you ran
toward me, quickly, through the grass . . . in case," it

went on, trembling a little, "you came and scrabbled at me
with your nasty little hands."

Arrietty stared at the eye; she held herself quite still.
"Why?" she asked again, and again the word tinkled—icy
cold it sounded this time, and needle sharp.

"Things do," said the voice. "I've seen them. In India."

Arrietty thought of her Gazetteer of the World. "You're not in India now," she pointed out.

"Did you come out of the house?"

"Yes," said Arrietty.

"From whereabouts in the house?"

Arrietty stared at the eye. "I'm not going to tell you," she said at last bravely.

"Then I'll hit you with my ash stick!"

"All right," said Arrietty, "hit me!"

"I'll pick you up and break you in half!"

Arrietty stood up. "All right," she said and took two paces forward.

There was a sharp gasp and an earthquake in the grass: he spun away from her and sat up, a great mountain in a green jersey. He had fair, straight hair and golden eyelashes. "Stay where you are!" he cried.

Arrietty stared up at him. So this was "the boy"! Breathless, she felt, and light with fear. "I guessed you were about nine," she gasped after a moment.

He flushed. "Well, you're wrong, I'm ten." He looked down at her, breathing deeply. "How old are you?"

"Fourteen," said Arrietty. "Next June," she added, watching him.

There was silence while Arrietty waited, trembling a little. "Can you read?" the boy said at last.

"Of course," said Arrietty. "Can't you?"

"No," he stammered. "I mean—yes. I mean I've just

74

come from India."

"What's that got to do with it?" asked Arrietty.

"Well, if you're born in India, you're bilingual. And if you're bilingual, you can't read. Not so well."

Arrietty stared up at him: what a monster, she thought, dark against the sky.

"Do you grow out of it?" she asked.

He moved a little and she felt the cold flick of his shadow.

"Oh yes," he said, "it wears off. My sisters were bilingual; now they aren't a bit. They could read any of those books upstairs in the schoolroom."

"So could I," said Arrietty quickly, "if someone could hold them, and turn the pages. I'm not a bit bilingual. I can read anything."

"Could you read out loud?"

"Of course," said Arrietty.

"Would you wait here while I run upstairs and get a book now?"

"Well," said Arrietty; she was longing to show off; then a startled look came into her eyes. "Oh—" she faltered.

"What's the matter?" The boy was standing up now. He towered above her.

"How many doors are there to this house?" She squinted up at him against the bright sunlight. He dropped on one knee.

75

"Doors?" he said. "Outside doors?"

"Yes."

"Well, there's the front door, the back door, the gun room door, the kitchen door, the scullery door . . . and the french windows in the drawing room."

"Well, you see," said Arrietty, "my father's in the hall, by the front door, working. He . . . he wouldn't want to be disturbed."

"Working?" said the boy. "What at?"

"Getting material," said Arrietty, "for a scrubbing brush."

"Then I'll go in the side door"; he began to move away but turned suddenly and came back to her. He stood a moment, as though embarrassed, and then he said: "Can you fly?"

"No," said Arrietty, surprised; "can you?"

His face became even redder. "Of course not," he said angrily; "I'm not a fairy!"

"Well, nor am I," said Arrietty, "nor is anybody. I don't believe in them."

He looked at her strangely. "You don't believe in them?"

"No," said Arrietty; "do you?"

"Of course not!"

Really, she thought, he is a very angry kind of boy. "My mother believes in them," she said, trying to appease him. "She thinks she saw one once. It was when she was a girl and lived with her parents behind the sand pile in the

76

potting shed."

He squatted down on his heels and she felt his breath on her face. "What was it like?" he asked.

"About the size of a glowworm with wings like a butterfly. And it had a tiny little face, she said, all alight and moving like sparks and tiny moving hands. Its face was changing all the time, she said, smiling and sort of shimmering. It seemed to be talking, she said, very quickly—but you couldn't hear a word. . . ."

"Oh," said the boy, interested. After a moment he asked: "Where did it go?"

"It just went," said Arrietty. "When my mother saw it, it seemed to be caught in a cobweb. It was dark at the time. About five o'clock on a winter's evening. After tea."

"Oh," he said again and picked up two petals of cherry blossom which he folded together like a sandwich and ate slowly. "Supposing," he said, staring past her at the wall of the house, "you saw a little man, about as tall as a pencil, with a blue patch in his trousers, halfway up a window curtain, carrying a doll's tea cup—would you say it was a fairy?"

"No," said Arrietty, "I'd say it was my father."

"Oh," said the boy, thinking this out, "does your father have a blue patch on his trousers?"

"Not on his best trousers. He does on his borrowing ones."

"Oh," said the boy again. He seemed to find it a safe

77

sound, as lawyers do. "Are there many people like you?"

"No," said Arrietty. "None. We're all different."

"I mean as small as you?"

Arrietty laughed. "Oh, don't be silly!" she said. "Surely you don't think there are many people in the world your size?"

"There are more my size than yours," he retorted.

"Honestly—" began Arrietty helplessly and laughed again. "Do you really think—I mean, whatever sort of a world would it be? Those great chairs . . . I've seen them. Fancy if you had to make chairs that size for everyone? And the stuff for their clothes . . . miles and miles of it . . . tents of it . . . and the sewing! And their great houses, reaching up so you can hardly see the ceilings . . . their great beds . . . the *food* they eat . . . great, smoking mountains of it, huge bogs of stew and soup and stuff."

"Don't you eat soup?" asked the boy.

"Of course we do," laughed Arrietty. "My father had an uncle who had a little boat which he rowed round in the stock-pot picking up flotsam and jetsam. He did bottom-fishing too for bits of marrow until the cook got suspicious through finding bent pins in the soup. Once he was nearly shipwrecked on a chunk of submerged shinbone. He lost his oars and the boat sprang a leak but he flung a line over the pot handle and pulled himself alongside the rim. But all that stock—fathoms of it! And the size of the stock-pot! I mean, there wouldn't be enough stuff in the world to go round after a bit! That's why my father says it's a good thing they're dying out . . . just a few, my father says, that's all we need—to keep us. Otherwise, he says, the whole thing gets"—Arrietty hesitated, trying to remember the word—"exaggerated, he says—"

"What do you mean," asked the boy, " 'to keep us'?"

Chapter Ten

So ARRIETTY told him about borrowing—how difficult it was and how dangerous. She told him about the store-rooms under the floor; about Pod's early exploits, the skill he had shown and the courage; she described those far-off days, before her birth, when Pod and Homily had been rich; she described the musical snuffbox of gold filigree, and the little bird which flew out of it made of kingfisher feathers, how it flapped its wings and sang its song; she described the doll's wardrobe and the tiny green glasses; the little silver teapot out of the drawing-room case; the satin bedcovers and embroidered sheets . . . "those we have still," she told him, "they're Her handkerchiefs. . . ."

"She," the boy realized gradually, was his Great-Aunt Sophy upstairs, bedridden since a hunting accident some twenty years before; he heard how Pod would borrow from Her room, picking his way—in the firelight—among the trinkets on Her dressing table, even climbing Her bed-curtains and walking on Her quilt. And of how She would watch him and sometimes talk to him because, Arrietty explained, every day at six o'clock they brought Her a decanter of Fine Old Pale Madeira, and how before midnight She would drink the lot. Nobody blamed Her, not even Homily, because, as Homily would say, She had so few pleasures, poor soul, but, Arrietty explained, after the first three glasses Great-Aunt Sophy never believed in anything she saw. "She thinks my father comes out of the decanter," said Arrietty, "and one day when I'm older he's going to take me there and She'll think I come out of the decanter too. It'll please Her, my father thinks, as She's used to him now. Once he took my mother, and She perked up like anything and kept asking after her and why didn't she come any more and saying they'd watered the Madeira because once, She says, She saw a little man *and* a little woman and now she only sees a little man. . . ."

"I wish she thought I came out of the decanter," said the boy. "She gives me dictation and teaches me to write. I only see her in the mornings when she's cross. She sends for me and looks behind my ears and asks Mrs. D. if I've learned my words."

"What does Mrs. D. look like?" asked Arrietty. (How delicious it was to say "Mrs. D." like that . . . how careless and daring!)

"She's fat and has a mustache and gives me my bath and hurts my bruise and my sore elbow and says she'll take a slipper to me one of these days. . . ." The boy pulled up a tuft of grass and stared at it angrily and Arrietty saw his lip

tremble. "My mother's very nice," he said. "She lives in India. Why did you lose all your worldly riches?"

"Well," said Arrietty, "the kitchen boiler burst and hot water came pouring through the floor into our house and everything was washed away and piled up in front of the grating. My father worked night and day. First hot, then cold. Trying to salvage things. And there's a dreadful draught in March through that grating. He got ill, you see, and couldn't go borrowing. So my Uncle Hendreary had to do it and one or two others and my mother gave them things, bit by bit, for all their trouble. But the king-fisher bird was spoilt by the water; all its feathers fell off and a great twirly spring came jumping out of its side. My father used the spring to keep the door shut against draughts from the grating and my mother put the feathers in a little moleskin hat. After a while I got born and my father went borrowing again. But he gets tired now and doesn't like curtains, not when any of the bobbles are off. . . ."

"I helped him a bit," said the boy, "with the tea cup. He was shivering all over. I suppose he was frightened."

"My father frightened!" exclaimed Arrietty angrily. "Frightened of you!" she added.

"Perhaps he doesn't like heights," said the boy.

"He loves heights," said Arrietty. "The thing he doesn't like is curtains. I've told you. Curtains make him tired."

The boy sat thoughtfully on his haunches, chewing a

blade of grass. "Borrowing," he said after a while. "Is that what you call it?"

"What else could you call it?" asked Arrietty.

"I'd call it stealing."

Arrietty laughed. She really laughed. "But we *are* Borrowers," she explained, "like you're a—a human bean or whatever it's called. We're part of the house. You might as well say that the fire grate steals the coal from the coal scuttle."

"Then what is stealing?"

Arrietty looked grave. "Don't you know?" she asked. "Stealing is—well, supposing my Uncle Hendreary borrowed an emerald watch from Her dressing-table and my father took it and hung it up on our wall. That's stealing."

"An emerald watch!" exclaimed the boy.

"Well, I just said that because we have one on the wall at home, but my father borrowed it himself. It needn't be a watch. It could be anything. A lump of sugar even. But Borrowers don't steal."

"Except from human beings," said the boy.

Arrietty burst out laughing; she laughed so much that she had to hide her face in the primrose. "Oh dear," she gasped with tears in her eyes, "you are funny!" She stared upward at his puzzled face. "Human beans are *for* Borrowers—like bread's for butter!"

The boy was silent awhile. A sigh of wind rustled the cherry tree and shivered among the blossoms.

"Well, I don't believe it," he said at last, watching the

falling petals. "I don't believe that's what we're for at all and I don't believe we're dying out!"

"Oh, goodness!" exclaimed Arrietty impatiently, staring up at his chin. "Just use your common sense: you're the only real human bean I ever saw (although I do just know of three more—Crampfurl, Her, and Mrs. Driver). But I know lots and lots of Borrowers: the Overmantels and the Harpsichords and the Rain-Barrels and the Linen-Presses and the Boot-Racks and the Hon. John Studdingtons and—"

He looked down. "John Studdington? But he was our grand-uncle—"

"Well, this family lived behind a picture," went on Arrietty, hardly listening, "and there were the Stove-Pipes and the Bell-Pulls and the—"

"Yes," he interrupted, "but did you see them?"

"I saw the Harpsichords. And my mother was a Bell-Pull. The others were before I was born. . . ."

He leaned closer. "Then where are they now? Tell me that."

"My Uncle Hendreary has a house in the country," said Arrietty coldly, edging away from his great lowering face; it was misted over, she noticed, with hairs of palest gold. "And four children, Harpsichords and Clocks."

"But where are the others?"

"Oh," said Arrietty, "they're somewhere." But where? she wondered. And she shivered slightly in the boy's cold shadow which lay about her, slant-wise, on the grass.

He drew back again, his fair head blocking out a great

piece of sky. "Well," he said deliberately after a moment, and his eyes were cold, "I've only seen two Borrowers but I've seen hundreds and hundreds and hundreds and hundreds and hundreds—"

"Oh no—" whispered Arrietty.

"Of human beings." And he sat back.

Arrietty stood very still. She did not look at him. After a while she said: "I don't believe you."

"All right," he said, "then I'll tell you—"

"I still won't believe you," murmured Arrietty.

"Listen!" he said. And he told her about railway stations and football matches and racecourses and royal processions and Albert Hall concerts. He told her about India and China and North America and the British Commonwealth. He told her about the July sales. "Not hundreds," he said, "but thousands and millions and billions and trillions of great, big, enormous people. Now do you believe me?"

Arrietty stared up at him with frightened eyes: it gave her a crick in the neck. "I don't know," she whispered.

"As for you," he went on, leaning closer again, "I don't believe that there are any more Borrowers anywhere in the world. I believe you're the last three," he said.

Arrietty dropped her face into the primrose. "We're not. There's Aunt Lupy and Uncle Hendreary and all the cousins."

"I bet they're dead," said the boy. "And what's more," he went on, "no one will ever believe I've seen *you*. And you'll be the very last because you're the youngest. One day," he told her, smiling triumphantly, "you'll be the only Borrower left in the world!"

He sat still, waiting, but she did not look up. "Now you're crying," he remarked after a moment.

"They're not dead," said Arrietty in a muffled voice; she was feeling in her little pocket for a handkerchief. "They live in a badger's set two fields away, beyond the spinney. We don't see them because it's too far. There are weasels and things and cows and foxes . . . and crows. . . ."

"Which spinney?" he asked.

"I don't KNOW!" Arrietty almost shouted. "It's along by the gas-pipe—a field called Parkin's Beck." She blew her nose. "I'm going home," she said.

"Don't go," he said, "not yet."

"Yes, I'm going," said Arrietty.

His face turned pink. "Let me just get the book," he pleaded.

"I'm not going to read to you now," said Arrietty.

"Why not?"

She looked at him with angry eyes. "Because—"

"Listen," he said, "I'll go to that field. I'll go and find Uncle Hendreary. And the cousins. And Aunt Whatever-she-is. And, if they're alive, I'll tell you. What about that? You could write them a letter and I'd put it down the hole—"

Arrietty gazed up at him. "Would you?" she breathed.

"Yes, I would. Really I would. Now can I go and get the book? I'll go in by the side door."

"All right," said Arrietty absently. Her eyes were shining. "When can I give you the letter?"

"Any time," he said, standing above her. "Where in the house do you live?"

"Well—" began Arrietty and stopped. Why once again did she feel this chill? Could it only be his shadow . . . towering above her, blotting out the sun? "I'll put it somewhere," she said hurriedly, "I'll put it under the hall mat."

"Which one? The one by the front door?"

"Yes, that one."

He was gone. And she stood there alone in the sunshine, shoulder deep in grass. What had happened seemed too big for thought; she felt unable to believe it really had happened: not only had she been "seen" but she had been talked to; not only had she been talked to but she had—

"Arrietty!" said a voice.

She stood up startled and spun round: there was Pod, moon-faced, on the path looking up at her. "Come on down!" he whispered.

She stared at him for a moment as though she did not recognize him; how round his face was, how kind, how familiar!

"Come on!" he said again, more urgently; and obediently because he sounded worried, she slithered quickly toward him off the bank, balancing her primrose. "Put that thing down," he said sharply, when she stood at last beside him on the path. "You can't lug great flowers about—you got to carry a bag. What you want to go up there for?" he grumbled as they moved off across the stones. "I might never have seen you. Hurry up now. Your mother'll have tea waiting!"

Chapter Eleven

HOMILY was there, at the last gate, to meet them. She had tidied her hair and smelled of coal-tar soap. She looked younger and somehow excited. "Well—!" she kept saying. "Well!" taking the bag from Arrietty and helping Pod to fasten the gate. "Well, was it nice? Were you a good girl? Was the cherry tree out? Did the clock strike?" She seemed, in the dim light, to be trying to read the expression on Arrietty's face. "Come along now. Tea's all ready. Give me your hand. . . ."

Tea was indeed ready, laid on the round table in the sitting room with a bright fire burning in the cogwheel. How familiar the room seemed, and homely, but, suddenly, somehow strange: the firelight flickering on the wallpaper —the line which read: ". . . it would be so charming if—" If what? Arrietty always wondered. If our house were less dark, she thought, that would be charming. She looked at the homemade dips set in upturned drawing pins which Homily had placed as candle-holders among the tea things; the old teapot, a hollow oak-apple, with its quill spout and wired-on handle—burnished it was now and hard with age; there were two roast sliced chestnuts which they would eat like toast with butter and a cold boiled chestnut which Pod would cut like bread; there was a plate of hot dried currants, well plumped before the fire; there were cinnamon breadcrumbs, crispy golden, and lightly dredged with sugar, and in front of each place, oh, delight of delights, a single potted shrimp. Homily had put out the silver plates—the florin ones for herself and Arrietty and the half-crown one for Pod.

"Come along, Arrietty, if you've washed your hands," exclaimed Homily, taking up the teapot, "don't dream!"

Arrietty drew up a cotton spool and sat down slowly. She watched her mother pulling on the spout of the teapot; this was always an interesting moment. The thicker end of the quill being inside the teapot, a slight pull just before pouring would draw it tightly into the hole and thus prevent a leak. If, as sometimes happened, a trace of dampness appeared about the join, it only meant a rather harder pull and a sudden gentle twist.

"Well?" said Homily, gingerly pouring. "Tell us what you saw!"

"She didn't see so much," said Pod, cutting himself a slice of boiled chestnut to eat with his shrimp.

"Didn't she see the overmantel?"

"No," said Pod, "we never went in the morning room."

"What about my blotting paper?"

"I never got it," said Pod.

"Now that's a nice thing—" began Homily.

"Maybe," said Pod, munching steadily, "but I had me feeling. I had it bad."

"What's that?" asked Arrietty. "His feeling?"

"Up the back of his head and in his fingers," said Homily. "It's a feeling your father gets when"—she dropped her voice—"there's someone about."

"Oh," said Arrietty and seemed to shrink.

"That's why I brought her along home," said Pod.

"And was there anyone?" asked Homily anxiously.

Pod took a mouthful of shrimp. "Must have been," he said, "but I didn't see nothing."

Homily leaned across the table. "Did you have any feeling, Arrietty?"

Arrietty started. "Oh," she said, "do we all have it?"

"Well, not in the same place," said Homily. "Mine starts at the back of me ankles and then me knees go. My mother —hers used to start just under her chin and run right round her neck—"

"And tied in a bow at the back," said Pod, munching.

"No, Pod," protested Homily, "it's a fact. No need to be sarcastic. All the Bell-Pulls were like that. Like a collar, she said it was—"

"Pity it didn't choke her," said Pod.

"Now, Pod, be fair; she had her points."

"Points!" said Pod. "She was all points!"

Arrietty moistened her lips; she glanced nervously from Pod to Homily. "I didn't feel anything," she said.

"Well," said Homily, "perhaps it was a false alarm."

"Oh no," began Arrietty, "it wasn't—" and, as Homily glanced at her sharply, she faltered: "I mean if Papa felt something—I mean— Perhaps," she went on, "I don't have it."

"Well," said Homily, "you're young. It'll come, all in good time. You go and stand in our kitchen, just under the chute, when Mrs. Driver's raking out the stove upstairs. Stand right up on a stool or something—so's you're fairly near the ceiling. It'll come—with practice."

After tea, when Pod had gone to his workbench and Homily was washing up, Arrietty rushed to her diary: "I'll just open it," she thought, trembling with haste, "anywhere." It fell open at the 9th and 10th of July: "Talk of Camps but Stay at Home. Old Cameronian Colors in Glasgow Cathedral, 1885"—that's what it said for the 9th. And on the 10th the page was headed: "Make Hay while the Sun Shines. Snowdon Peak sold for £5,750, 1889." Arrietty tore out this last page. Turning it over she read on the reverse side: "July 11th: Make Not a Toil of your Pleasure. Niagara passed by C. D. Graham in a cask, 1886." No, she thought, I'll choose the 10th, "Make Hay while the Sun Shines," and, crossing out her last entry ("Mother out of sorts"), she wrote below it:

Dear Uncle Hendreary,

    I hope you are quite well and the cousins are well and Aunt Lupy. We are very well and I am learning to borrow,

your loving neice,

Arrietty Clock

Write a letter on the back please

"What are you doing, Arrietty?" called Homily from the kitchen.

"Writing in my diary."

"Oh," said Homily shortly.

"Anything you want?" asked Arrietty.

"It'll do later," said Homily.

Arrietty folded the letter and placed it carefully between the pages of Bryce's *Tom Thumb Gazetteer of the World* and, in the diary, she wrote: "Went borrowing. Wrote to H. Talked to B." After that Arrietty sat for a long time staring into the fire, and thinking and thinking and thinking. . . .

Chapter Twelve

But it was one thing to write a letter and quite another to find some means of getting it under the mat. Pod, for several days, could not be persuaded to go borrowing: he was well away on his yearly turn-out of the storerooms, mending partitions, and putting up new shelves. Arrietty usually enjoyed this spring sorting, when half-forgotten treasures came to light and new uses were discovered for old borrowings. She used to love turning over the scraps of silk or lace; the odd kid gloves; the pencil stubs; the rusty razor blades; the hairpins and the needles; the dried figs, the hazel nuts, the powdery bits of chocolate, and the scarlet stubs of sealing wax. Pod, one year, had made her a hairbrush from a toothbrush and Homily had made her a small pair of Turkish bloomers from two glove fingers for "knocking about in the mornings." There were spools and spools of colored silks and cottons and small variegated balls of odd wool, penpoints which Homily used as flour scoops, and bottle tops galore.

But this year Arrietty banged about impatiently and stole

away whenever she dared, to stare through the grating, hoping to see the boy. She now kept the letter always with her, stuffed inside her jersey, and the edges became rubbed. Once he did run past the grating and she saw

his woolen stockings; he was making a chugging noise in his throat like some kind of engine, and as he turned the corner he let out a piercing "Ooooo—oo" (it was a train whistle, he told her afterwards) so he did not hear her call. One evening, after dark, she crept away and tried to open the first gate, but swing and tug as she might she could not budge the pin.

Homily, every time she swept the sitting room, would

grumble about the carpet. "It may be a curtain-and-chair job," she would say to Pod, "but it wouldn't take you not a quarter of an hour, with your pin and name-tape, to fetch me a bit of blotting paper from the desk in the morning room . . . anyone would think, looking at this floor, that we lived in a toad hole. No one could call me house-proud," said Homily. "You couldn't be, not with my kind of family, but I do like," she said, "to keep 'nice things nice.'" And at last, on the fourth day, Pod gave in. He laid down his hammer (a small electric-bell clapper) and said to Arrietty: "Come along. . . ."

Arrietty was glad to see the morning room; the door luckily had been left ajar and it was fascinating to stand at last in the thick pile of the carpet gazing upward at the shelves and pillars and towering gables of the famous over-mantel. So that's where they had lived, she thought, those pleasure-loving creatures, remote and gay and self-sufficient. She imagined the Overmantel women—a little "tweedy," Homily had described them, with wasp waists and piled Edwardian hair—swinging carelessly outwards on the pilas-ters, lissom and laughing; gazing at themselves in the inset looking-glass which reflected back the tobacco jars, the cut-glass decanters, the bookshelves, and the plush-covered table. She imagined the Overmantel men—fair, they were said to be, with long mustaches and nervous, slender hands —smoking and drinking and telling their witty tales. So they had never asked Homily up there! Poor Homily with her bony nose and never tidy hair. . . . They would have looked at her strangely, Arrietty thought, with their long, half-laughing eyes, and smiled a little and, humming, turned away. And they had lived only on breakfast food—on toast and egg and tiny snips of mushroom; sausage they'd have had and crispy bacon and little sips of tea and coffee. Where were they now? Arrietty wondered. Where could such creatures go?

Pod had flung his pin so it stuck into the seat of the chair and was up the leg in a trice, leaning outwards on his tape; then, pulling out the pin, he flung it like a javelin, above his head, into a fold of curtain. This is the moment, Arrietty thought, and felt for her precious letter. She slipped into the hall. It was darker, this time, with the front door closed, and she ran across it with a beating heart. The mat was heavy, but she lifted up the corner and slid the letter under by pushing with her foot. "There!" she said, and looked about her . . . shadows, shadows, and the ticking clock. She looked across the great plain of floor to where, in the distance, the stairs mounted. "Another world above," she thought, "world on world . . ." and shivered slightly.

"Arrietty," called Pod softly from the morning room, and she ran back in time to see him swing clear of the chair seat and pull himself upward on the name-tape, level with the desk. Lightly he came down feet apart and she saw him, for safety's sake, twist the name-tape lightly round his wrist. "I wanted you to see that," he said, a little breathless. The blotting paper, when he pushed it, floated down quite softly, riding lightly on the air, and lay at last some feet beyond the desk, pink and fresh, on the carpet's dingy pile.

"You start rolling," whispered Pod. "I'll be down," and Arrietty went on her knees and began to roll the blotting paper until it grew too stiff for her to hold. Pod soon finished it off and lashed it with his name-tape, through which he ran his hat pin, and together they carried the long cylinder, as two house painters would carry a ladder, under the clock and down the hole.

Homily hardly thanked them when, panting a little, they dropped the bundle in the passage outside the sitting room door. She looked alarmed. "Oh, there you are," she said. "Thank goodness! That boy's about again. I've just heard Mrs. Driver talking to Crampfurl."

"Oh!" cried Arrietty. "What did she say?" and Homily glanced sharply at her and saw that she looked pale. Arrietty realized she should have said: "What boy?" It was too late now.

"Nothing real bad," Homily went on, as though to reassure her. "It's just a boy they have upstairs. It's nothing at all, but I heard Mrs. Driver say that she'd take a slipper to him, see if she wouldn't, if he had the mats up once again in the hall."

"The mats up in the hall!" echoed Arrietty.

"Yes. Three days running, she said to Crampfurl, he'd had the mats up in the hall. She could tell, she said, by the dust and the way he'd put them back. It was the hall

part that worried me, seeing as you and your father—
What's the matter, Arrietty? There's no call for that sort
of face! Come on now, help me move the furniture and
we'll get down the carpet."

"Oh dear, oh dear," thought Arrietty miserably, as she
helped her mother empty the match-box chest of drawers.
"Three days running he's looked and nothing there. He'll
give up hope now . . . he'll never look again."

That evening she stood for hours on a stool under the
chute in their kitchen, pretending she was practicing to get
"a feeling" when really she was listening to Mrs. Driver's
conversations with Crampfurl. All she learned was that
Mrs. Driver's feet were killing her, and that it was a pity
that she hadn't given in her notice last May, and would
Crampfurl have another drop, considering there was more
in the cellar than anyone would drink in Her lifetime, and
if they thought she was going to clean the first-floor windows singlehanded they had better think again. But on
the third night, just as Arrietty had climbed down off the
stool before she overbalanced with weariness, she heard
Crampfurl say: "If you ask me, I'd say he had a ferret."
And quickly Arrietty climbed back again, holding her
breath.

"A ferret!" she heard Mrs. Driver exclaim shrilly.
"Whatever next? Where would he keep it?"

"That I wouldn't like to say," said Crampfurl in his
rumbling earthy voice; "all I know is he was up beyond

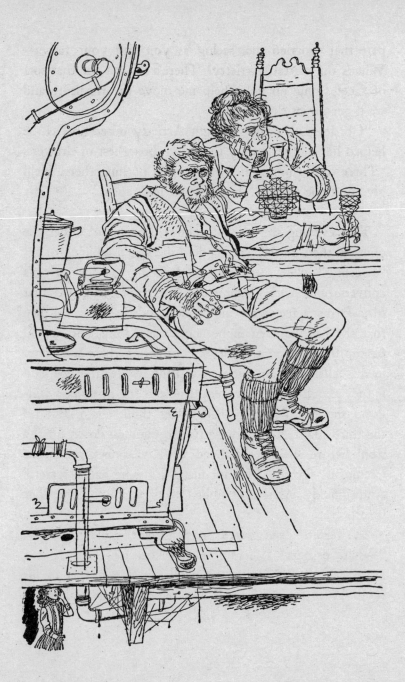

Parkin's Beck, going round all the banks and calling-like down all the rabbit holes."

"Well, I never," said Mrs. Driver. "Where's your glass?"

"Just a drop," said Crampfurl. "That's enough. Goes to your liver, this sweet stuff—not like beer, it isn't. Yes," he went on, "when he saw me coming with a gun he pretended to be cutting a stick like from the hedge. But I'd see'd him all right and heard him. Calling away, his nose down a rabbit hole. It's my belief he's got a ferret." There was a gulp, as though Crampfurl was drinking. "Yes," he said at last, and Arrietty heard him set down the glass, "a ferret called Uncle something."

Arrietty made a sharp movement, balanced for one moment with arms waving, and fell off the stool. There was a clatter as the stool slid sideways, banged against a chest of drawers and rolled over.

"What was that?" asked Crampfurl.

There was silence upstairs and Arrietty held her breath.

"I didn't hear nothing," said Mrs. Driver.

"Yes," said Crampfurl, "it was under the floor like, there by the stove."

"That's nothing," said Mrs. Driver. "It's the coals falling. Often sounds like that. Scares you sometimes when you're sitting here alone. . . . Here, pass your glass, there's only a drop left—might as well finish the bottle. . . ."

They're drinking Fine Old Madeira, thought Arrietty, and very carefully she set the stool upright and stood quietly beside it, looking up. She could see light through the crack, occasionally flicked with shadow as one person or another moved a hand or arm.

"Yes," went on Crampfurl, returning to his story, "and when I come up with m'gun he says, all innocent like—to put me off, I shouldn't wonder: 'Any old badgers' sets round here?'"

"Artful," said Mrs. Driver; "the things they think of . . . badgers' sets . . ." and she gave her creaking laugh.

"As a matter of fact," said Crampfurl, "there did used to be one, but when I showed him where it was like, he didn't take no notice of it. Just stood there, waiting for me to go." Crampfurl laughed. "Two can play at that game, I thought, so I just sits m'self down. And there we were the two of us."

"And what happened?"

"Well, he had to go off in the end. Leaving his ferret. I waited a bit, but it never came out. I poked around a bit and whistled. Pity I never heard properly what he called it. Uncle something it sounded like—" Arrietty heard the sudden scrape of a chair. "Well," said Crampfurl, "I'd better get on now and shut up the chickens—"

The scullery door banged and there was a sudden clatter overhead as Mrs. Driver began to rake the stove. Arrietty replaced the stool and stole softly into the sitting room, where she found her mother alone.

Chapter Thirteen

HOMILY was ironing, bending and banging and pushing the hair back out of her eyes. All round the room underclothes hung airing on safety pins which Homily used like coathangers.

"What happened?" asked Homily. "Did you fall over?"

"Yes," said Arrietty, moving quietly into her place beside the fire.

"How's the feeling coming?"

"Oh, I don't know," said Arrietty. She clasped her knees and laid her chin on them.

"Where's your knitting?" asked Homily. "I don't know what's come over you lately. Always idle. You don't feel seedy, do you?"

"Oh," exclaimed Arrietty, "let me be!" And Homily for once was silent. "It's the spring," she told herself. "Used to take me like that sometimes at her age."

"I must see that boy," Arrietty was thinking—staring blindly into the fire. "I must hear what happened. I must hear if they're all right. I don't want us to die out. I don't want to be the last Borrower. I don't want"—and here Arrietty dropped her face on to her knees—"to live for ever and ever like this . . . in the dark . . . under the floor. . . ."

"No good getting supper," said Homily, breaking the silence; "your father's gone borrowing. To Her room. And you know what that means!"

Arrietty raised her head. "No," she said, hardly listening; "what does it mean?"

"That he won't be back," said Homily sharply, "for a good hour and a half. He likes it up there, gossiping with Her and poking about on the dressing table. And it's safe enough once that boy's in bed. Not that there's anything we want special," she went on. "It's just these new shelves he's made. They look kind of bare, he says, and he might, he says, just pick up a little something . . ."

Arrietty suddenly was sitting bolt upright: a thought had struck her, leaving her breathless and a little shaky at the knees. "A good hour and a half," her mother had said and the gates would be open!

"Where are you going?" asked Homily as Arrietty moved toward the door.

"Just along to the storerooms," said Arrietty, shading with one hand her candle-dip from the draught. "I won't be long."

"Now don't you untidy anything!" Homily called out after her. "And be careful of that light!"

As Arrietty went down the passage she thought: "It is

true. I am going to the storerooms—to find another hat pin. And if I do find a hat pin (and a piece of string—there won't be any name-tape) I still 'won't be long' because I'll have to get back before Papa. And I'm doing it for their sakes," she told herself doggedly, "and one day they'll thank me." All the same she felt a little guilty. "Artful"—that's what Mrs. Driver would say she was.

There was a hat pin—one with a bar for a top—and she tied on a piece of string, very firmly, twisting it back and forth like a figure of eight and, as a crowning inspiration, she sealed it with sealing wax.

The gates were open and she left the candle in the middle of the passage where it could come to no harm, just below the hole by the clock.

The great hall when she had climbed out into it was dim with shadows. A single gas jet, turned low, made a pool of light beside the locked front door and another faintly flickered on the landing halfway up the stairs. The ceiling sprang away into height and darkness and all around was space. The night-nursery, she knew, was at the end of the upstairs passage and the boy would be in bed—her mother had just said so.

Arrietty had watched her father use his pin on the chair, and single stairs, in comparison, were easier. There was a kind of rhythm to it after a while: a throw, a pull, a scramble, and an upward swing. The stair rods glinted coldly, but the pile of the carpet seemed soft and warm and delicious to fall back on. On the half-landing she paused to get her breath. She did not mind the semi-darkness; she lived in darkness; she was at home in it and, at a time like this, it made her feel safe.

On the upper landing she saw an open door and a great square of golden light which like a barrier lay across the passage. "I've got to pass through that," Arrietty told herself, trying to be brave. Inside the lighted room a voice was talking, droning on. ". . . And this mare," the voice said, "was a five-year-old which really belonged to my brother in Ireland, not my elder brother but my younger brother, the one who owned Stale Mate and Oh My Darling. He had entered her for several point-to-points . . . but when I say 'several' I mean three or at least two. . . . Have you ever seen an Irish point-to-point?"

"No," said another voice, rather absent-mindedly. "That's my father," Arrietty realized with a start, "my father talking to Great-Aunt Sophy or rather Great-Aunt Sophy talking to my father." She gripped her pin with its loops of string, and ran into the light and through it to the passage beyond. As she passed the open door she had a glimpse of firelight and lamplight and gleaming furniture and dark-red silk brocade.

Beyond the square of light the passage was dark again and she could see, at the far end, a half-open door. "That's the day-nursery," she thought, "and beyond that is the night-nursery."

"There are certain differences," Aunt Sophy's voice went on, "which would strike you at once. For instance . . ."

Arrietty liked the voice. It was comforting and steady, like the sound of the clock in the hall, and as she moved off the carpet on to the strip of polished floor beside the skirting-board, she was interested to hear there were walls in Ireland instead of hedges. Here by the skirting she could run and she loved running. Carpets were heavy going—thick and clinging, they held you up. The boards were smooth and smelled of beeswax. She liked the smell.

The schoolroom, when she reached it, was shrouded in dust sheets and full of junk. Here too a gas jet burned, turned low to a bluish flame. The floor was linoleum, rather worn, and the rugs were shabby. Under the table was a great cavern of darkness. She moved into it, feeling about, and bumped into a dusty hassock higher than her head. Coming out again, into the half light, she looked up and saw the corner cupboard with the doll's tea service, the painting above the fireplace, and the plush curtain where her father had been "seen." Chair legs were everywhere and chair seats obscured her view. She found her way among them to the door of the night-nursery and there she saw, suddenly, on a shadowed plateau in the far corner, the boy in bed. She saw his great face, turned toward her on the edge of the pillow; she saw the gaslight reflected in his open eyes; she saw his hand gripping the bedclothes, holding them tightly pressed against his mouth.

She stopped moving and stood still. After a while, when she saw his fingers relax, she said softly: "Don't be frightened. . . . It's me, Arrietty."

He let the bedclothes slide away from his mouth and said: "Arri-*what*-y?" He seemed annoyed.

"Etty," she repeated gently. "Did you take the letter?"

He stared at her for a moment without speaking, then he said: "Why did you come creeping, creeping, into my room?"

"I didn't come creeping, creeping," said Arrietty. "I even ran. Didn't you see?"

He was silent, staring at her with his great, wide-open eyes.

"When I brought the book," he said at last, "you'd gone."

"I had to go. Tea was ready. My father fetched me."

He understood this. "Oh," he said matter-of-factly, and did not reproach her.

"Did you take the letter?" she asked again.

"Yes," he said, "I had to go back twice. I shoved it down the badger's hole. . . ." Suddenly he threw back the bedclothes and stood up in bed, enormous in his pale flannel night-shirt. It was Arrietty's turn to be afraid. She half turned, her eyes on his face, and began backing slowly toward the door. But he did not look at her; he was feeling behind a picture on the wall. "Here it is," he said, sitting down again, and the bed creaked loudly.

"But I don't want it back!" exclaimed Arrietty, coming forward again. "You should have left it there! Why did you bring it back?"

He turned it over in his fingers. "He's written on it," he said.

"Oh, please," cried Arrietty excitedly, "show me!" She ran right up to the bed and tugged at the trailing sheet. "Then they are alive! Did you see him?"

"No," he said, "the letter was there, just down the hole where I'd put it." He leaned toward her. "But he's written on it. Look!"

She made a quick dart and almost snatched the letter out of his great fingers, but was careful to keep out of range of his hand. She ran with it to the door of the schoolroom where the light, though dim, was a little brighter. "It's very faint," she said, holding it close to her eyes. "What's he written it with? I wonder. It's all in capitals—" She turned suddenly. "Are you sure you didn't write it?" she asked.

"Of course not," he began. "I write small—" But she had seen by his face that he spoke the truth and began to spell out the letters. "T—e—double l," she said. "Tell y—o—r—e." She looked up. "Yore?" she said.

"Yes," said the boy, "your."

"Tell your a—n—t, ant?" said Arrietty. "Ant? My ant?" The boy was silent, waiting. "Ant L—u— Oh, Aunt Lupy!" she exclaimed. "He says—listen, this is what he says: 'Tell your Aunt Lupy to come home'!"

There was silence. "Then tell her," said the boy after a moment.

"But she isn't here!" exclaimed Arrietty. "She's never been here! I don't even remember what she looked like!"

"Look," said the boy, staring through the door, "someone's coming!"

Arrietty whipped round. There was no time to hide: it was Pod, borrowing-bag in one hand and pin in the other. He stood in the doorway of the schoolroom. Quite still he stood, outlined against the light in the passage, his little shadow falling dimly in front of him. He had seen her.

"I heard your voice," he said, and there was a dreadful quietness about the way he spoke, "just as I was coming out of Her room." Arrietty stared back at him, stuffing the letter up her jersey. Could he see beyond her into the shadowed room. Could he see the tousled shape in bed?

"Come on home," said Pod, and turned away.

Chapter Fourteen

Pod did not speak until they reached the sitting room. Nor did he look at her. She had had to scramble after him as best she might. He had ignored her efforts to help him shut the gates, but once, when she tripped, he had waited until she had got up again, watching her, it seemed, almost without interest while she brushed the dust off her knees.

Supper was laid and the ironing put away and Homily came running in from the kitchen, surprised to see them together.

Pod threw down his borrowing-bag. He stared at his wife.

"What's the matter?" faltered Homily, looking from one to the other.

"She was in the night-nursery," said Pod quietly, "talking to that boy!"

Homily moved forward, her hands clasped tremblingly against her apron, her startled eyes flicking swiftly to and fro. "Oh, no—" she breathed.

Pod sat down. He ran a tired hand over his eyes and forehead; his face looked heavy like a piece of dough. "Now what?" he said.

Homily stood quite still, bowed over her clasped hands, and stared at Arrietty. "Oh, you never—" she whispered.

"They are frightened," Arrietty realized; "they are not angry at all—they are very, very frightened." She moved forward. "It's all right—" she began.

Homily sat down suddenly on the cotton spool; she had begun to tremble. "Oh," she said, "whatever shall we do?" She began to rock herself, very slightly, to and fro.

"Oh, Mother, don't!" pleaded Arrietty. "It isn't so bad as that. It really isn't." She felt up the front of her jersey; at first she could not find the letter—it had slid round her side to the back—but at last she drew it out, very crumpled. "Look," she said, "here's a letter from Uncle Hendreary. I wrote to him and the boy took the letter—"

"You wrote to him!" cried Homily on a kind of suppressed shriek. "Oh," she moaned, and closed her eyes, "whatever next! Whatever shall we do?" and she fanned herself limply with her bony hand.

"Get your mother a drink of water, Arrietty," said Pod sharply. Arrietty brought it in a sawed-off hazel shell—it had been sawed off at the pointed end and was shaped like a brandy glass.

"But whatever made you do such a thing, Arrietty?" said Homily more calmly, setting the empty cup down on the table. "Whatever came over you?"

So Arrietty told them about being "seen"—that day under the cherry tree. And how she had kept it from them not to worry them. And what the boy said about "dying out." And how—more than important—how imperative it had seemed to make sure the Hendrearys were alive. "Do understand," pleaded Arrietty, "please understand! I'm trying to save the race!"

"The expressions she uses!" said Homily to Pod under her breath, not without pride.

But Pod was not listening. "Save the race!" he repeated grimly. "It's people like you, my girl, who do things sudden like with no respect for tradition, who'll finish us Borrowers once for all. Don't you see what you've done?"

Arrietty met his accusing eyes. "Yes," she said falteringly, "I've—I've got in touch with the only other ones still alive. So that," she went on bravely, "from now on we can all stick together. . . ."

"All stick together!" Pod repeated angrily. "Do you think Hendreary's lot would ever come to live back here? Can you see your mother emigrating to a badger's set, two fields away, out in the open and no hot water laid on?"

"Never!" cried Homily in a full, rich voice which made them both turn and look at her.

"Or do you see your mother walking across two fields and a garden," went on Pod, "two fields full of crows and cows and horses and what-not, to take a cup of tea with your Aunt Lupy whom she never liked much anyway? But wait," he said as Arrietty tried to speak, "that's not the point—as far as all that goes we're just where we was—the point," he went on, leaning forward and speaking with great solemnity, "is this: that boy knows now where we live!"

"Oh no," said Arrietty, "I never told him that. I—"

"You told him," interrupted Pod, "about the kitchen pipe bursting; you told him how all our stuff got washed away to the grating." He sat back again glaring at her. "He's only got to think," he pointed out. Arrietty was silent and Pod went on: "That's a thing that has never happened before, never, in the whole long history of the Borrowers. Borrowers have been 'seen'—yes; Borrowers have been caught—maybe: but no human being has ever known where any Borrower lived. We're in very grave danger, Arrietty, and you've put us there. And that's a fact."

"Oh, Pod," whimpered Homily, "don't frighten the child."

"Nay, Homily," said Pod more gently, "my poor old girl! I don't want to frighten no one, but this is serious. Suppose I said to you pack up tonight, all our bits and pieces, where would you go?"

"Not to Hendreary's," cried Homily, "not there, Pod! I couldn't never share a kitchen with Lupy—"

"No," agreed Pod, "not to Hendreary's. And don't you see for why? The boy knows about that too!"

"Oh!" cried Homily in real dismay.

"Yes," said Pod, "a couple of smart terriers or a well-trained ferret and that'd be the end of that lot."

117

"Oh, Pod . . ." said Homily and began again to tremble. The thought of living in a badger's set had been bad enough, but the thought of not having even that to go to seemed almost worse. "And I dare say I could have got it nice in the end," she said, "providing we lived quite separate—"

"Well, it's no good thinking of it now," said Pod. He turned to Arrietty: "What does your Uncle Hendreary say in his letter?"

"Yes," exclaimed Homily, "where's this letter?"

"It doesn't say much," said Arrietty, passing over the paper; "it just says 'Tell your Aunt Lupy to come home.' "

"What?" exclaimed Homily sharply, looking at the letter upside-down. "Come home? What can he mean?"

"He means," said Pod, "that Lupy must have set off to come here and that she never arrived."

"Set off to come here?" repeated Homily. "But when?"

"How should I know?" said Pod.

"It doesn't say when," said Arrietty.

"But," exclaimed Homily, "it might have been weeks ago!"

"It might," said Pod. "Long enough anyway for him to want her back."

"Oh," cried Homily, "all those poor little children!"

"They're growing up now," said Pod.

"But something must have happened to her!" exclaimed Homily.

"Yes," said Pod. He turned to Arrietty. "See what I mean, Arrietty, about those fields?"

"Oh, Pod," said Homily, her eyes full of tears, "I don't suppose none of us'll ever see poor Lupy again!"

"Well, we wouldn't have anyway," said Pod.

"Pod," said Homily soberly, "I'm frightened. Everything seems to be happening at once. What are we going to do?"

"Well," said Pod, "there's nothing we can do tonight. That's certain. But have a bit of supper and a good night's rest." He rose to his feet.

"Oh, Arrietty," wailed Homily suddenly, "you naughty wicked girl! How could you go and start all this? How could you go and talk to a human bean? If only—"

"I was 'seen,'" cried Arrietty. "I couldn't help being 'seen.' Papa was 'seen.' I don't think it's all as awful as you're trying to make out. I don't think human beans are all that bad—"

"They're bad and they're good," said Pod; "they're honest and they're artful—it's just as it takes them at the moment. And animals, if they could talk, would say the same. Steer clear of them—that's what I've always been told. No matter what they promise you. No good never really came to no one from any human bean."

Chapter Fifteen

THAT night, while Arrietty lay straight and still under her cigar-box ceiling, Homily and Pod talked for hours. They talked in the sitting room, they talked in the kitchen, and later, much later, she heard them talk in their bedroom. She heard drawers shutting and opening, doors creaking, and boxes being pulled out from under beds. "What are they doing?" she wondered. "What will happen next?" Very still she lay in her soft little bed with her familiar belongings about her: her postage stamp view of Rio harbor; her silver pig off a charm bracelet; her turquoise ring which sometimes, for fun, she would wear as a crown, and, dearest of all, her floating ladies with the golden trumpets, tooting above their peaceful town. She did not want to lose these, she realized suddenly, lying there straight and still in bed, but to have all the other things as well, adventure and safety mixed—that's what she wanted. And that (the restless bangings and whisperings told her) is just what you couldn't do.

As it happened, Homily was only fidgeting: opening

drawers and shutting them, unable to be still. And she ended up, when Pod was already in bed, by deciding to curl her hair. "Now, Homily," Pod protested wearily, lying there in his night-shirt, "there's really no call for that. Who's going to see you?"

"That's just it," exclaimed Homily, searching in a drawer for her curl-rags; "in times like these one never knows. I'm not going to be caught out," she said irritably, turning the drawer upside-down and picking over the spilled contents, "with me hair like this!"

She came to bed at last, looking spiky, like a washed-out golliwog, and Pod with a sigh turned over at last and closed his eyes.

Homily lay for a long time staring at the oil lamp; it was the silver cap of a perfume bottle with a tiny, floating wick. She felt unwilling, for some reason, to blow it out. There were movements upstairs in the kitchen and it was late for movements—the household should be asleep—and the lumpy curlers pressed uncomfortably against her neck. She gazed—just as Arrietty had done—about the familiar room (too full, she realized, with little bags and boxes and makeshift cupboards) and thought: "What now? Perhaps nothing will happen after all; the child perhaps is right, and we are making a good deal of fuss about nothing very much; this boy, when all's said and done, is only a guest; perhaps," thought Homily, "he'll go away again quite soon, and that," she told herself drowsily, "will be that."

Later (as she realized afterwards) she must have dozed off because it seemed she was crossing Parkin's Beck; it was night and the wind was blowing and the field seemed very steep; she was scrambling up it, along the ridge by the gas-pipe, sliding and falling in the wet grass. The trees, it seemed to Homily, were threshing and clashing, their branches waving and sawing against the sky. Then (as she told them many weeks later) there was a sound of splintering wood. . . .

And Homily woke up. She saw the room again and the oil lamp flickering, but something, she knew at once, was different: there was a strange draught and her mouth felt dry and full of grit. Then she looked up at the ceiling: "Pod!" she shrieked, clutching his shoulder.

Pod rolled over and sat up. They both stared at the ceiling: the whole surface was on a steep slant and one side of it had come right away from the wall—this was what had caused the draught—and down into the room, to within an inch of the foot of the bed, protruded a curious object: a huge bar of gray steel with a flattened, shining edge.

"It's a screwdriver," said Pod.

They stared at it, fascinated, unable to move, and for a moment all was still. Then slowly the huge object swayed upward until the sharp edge lay against their ceiling and Homily heard a scrape on the floor above and a sudden human gasp. "Oh, my knees," cried Homily, "oh, my feeling—" as, with a splintering wrench, their whole roof flew off and fell down with a clatter, somewhere out of sight.

Homily screamed then. But this time it was a real scream, loud and shrill and hearty; she seemed almost to settle down in her scream, while her eyes stared up, half interested, into empty lighted space. There was another ceiling, she realized, away up above them—higher, it seemed, than the sky; a ham hung from it and two strings of onions. Arrietty appeared in the doorway, scared and trembling, clutching her nightgown. And Pod slapped Homily's back. "Have done," he said, "that's enough," and Homily, suddenly, was quiet.

A great face appeared then between them and that distant height. It wavered above them, smiling and terrible: there was silence and Homily sat bolt upright, her mouth open. "Is that your mother?" asked a surprised voice after a moment, and Arrietty from the doorway whispered: "Yes."

It was the boy.

Pod got out of bed and stood beside it, shivering in his night-shirt. "Come on," he said to Homily, "you can't stay there!"

But Homily could. She had her old nightdress on with the patch in the back and nothing was going to move her. A slow anger was rising up in Homily: she had been caught in her hair-curlers; Pod had raised his hand to her; and she remembered that, in the general turmoil and for once in her life, she had left the supper washing-up for morning,

and there it would be, on the kitchen table, for all the world to see!

She glared at the boy—he was only a child after all. "Put it back!" she said, "put it back at once!" Her eyes flashed and her curlers seemed to quiver.

He knelt down then, but Homily did not flinch as the great face came slowly closer. She saw his under lip, pink and full—like an enormous exaggeration of Arrietty's—and she saw it wobble slightly. "But I've got something for you," he said.

Homily's expression did not change and Arrietty called out from her place in the doorway: "What is it?"

The boy reached behind him and very gingerly, careful to keep it upright, he held a wooden object above their heads. "It's this," he said, and very carefully, his tongue out and breathing heavily, he lowered the object slowly into their hole: it was a doll's dresser, complete with plates. It had two drawers in it and a cupboard below; he adjusted its position at the foot of Homily's bed. Arrietty ran round to see better.

"Oh," she cried ecstatically. "Mother, look!"

Homily threw the dresser a glance—it was dark oak and the plates were hand-painted—and then she looked quickly away again. "Yes," she said coldly, "it's very nice."

There was a short silence which no one knew how to break.

"The cupboard really opens," said the boy at last, and the great hand came down all amongst them, smelling of bath soap. Arrietty flattened herself against the wall and Pod exclaimed, nervous: "Now then!"

"Yes," agreed Homily after a moment, "I see it does."

Pod drew a long breath—a sigh of relief as the hand went back.

"There, Homily," he said placatingly, "you've always wanted something like that!"

"Yes," said Homily—she still sat bolt upright, her hands clasped in her lap. "Thank you very much. And now," she went on coldly, "will you please put back the roof?"

"Wait a minute," pleaded the boy. Again he reached behind him; again the hand came down; and there, beside the dresser, where there was barely room for it, was a very small doll's chair; it was a Victorian chair, upholstered in red velvet. "Oh!" Arrietty exclaimed again and Pod said shyly: "Just about fit me, that would."

"Try it," begged the boy, and Pod threw him a nervous glance. "Go on!" said Arrietty, and Pod sat down—in his night-shirt, his bare feet showing. "That's nice," he said after a moment.

"It would go by the fire in the sitting room," cried Arrietty; "it would look lovely on red blotting paper!"

"Let's try it," said the boy, and the hand came down again. Pod sprang up just in time to steady the dresser as the red velvet chair was whisked away above his head and placed presumably in the next room but one. Arrietty ran out of the door and along the passage to see. "Oh," she called out to her parents, "come and see. It's lovely!"

But Pod and Homily did not move. The boy was leaning over them, breathing hard, and they could see the middle buttons of his night-shirt. He seemed to be examining the farther room.

"What do you keep in that mustard-pot?" he asked.

"Coal," said Arrietty's voice. "And I helped to borrow this new carpet. Here's the watch I told you about, and the pictures. . . ."

"I could get you some better stamps than those," the boy said. "I've got some jubilee ones with the Taj Mahal."

"Look," cried Arrietty's voice again, and Pod took Homily's hand, "these are my books—"

Homily clutched Pod as the great hand came down once more in the direction of Arrietty. "Quiet," he whispered; "sit still. . . ." The boy, it seemed, was touching the books.

"What are they called?" he asked, and Arrietty reeled off the names.

"Pod," whispered Homily, "I'm going to scream—"

"No," whispered Pod. "You mustn't. Not again."

"I feel it coming on," said Homily.

Pod looked worried. "Hold your breath," he said, "and count ten."

The boy was saying to Arrietty: "Why couldn't you read me those?"

"Well, I could," said Arrietty, "but I'd rather read something new."

"But you never come," complained the boy.

"I know," said Arrietty, "but I will."

127

"Pod," whispered Homily, "did you hear that? Did you hear what she said?"

"Yes, yes," Pod whispered; "keep quiet—"

"Do you want to see the storerooms?" Arrietty suggested next and Homily clapped a hand to her mouth as though to stifle a cry.

Pod looked up at the boy. "Hey," he called, trying to attract his attention. The boy looked down. "Put the roof back now," Pod begged him, trying to sound matter of fact and reasonable; "we're getting cold."

"All right," agreed the boy, but he seemed to hesitate: he reached across them for the piece of board which formed their roof. "Shall I nail you down?" he asked, and they saw him pick up the hammer; it swayed above them, very dangerous looking.

"Of course nail us down," said Pod irritably.

"I mean," said the boy, "I've got some more things upstairs—"

Pod looked uncertain and Homily nudged him. "Ask him," she whispered, "what kind of things?"

"What kind of things?" asked Pod.

"Things from an old doll's house there is on the top shelf of the cupboard by the fireplace in the schoolroom."

"I've never seen no doll's house," said Pod.

"Well, it's in the cupboard," said the boy, "right up by the ceiling; you can't see it—you've got to climb on the lower shelves to get to it."

"What sort of things *are* there in the doll's house?" asked Arrietty from the sitting room.

"Oh, everything," the boy told her; "carpets and rugs and beds with mattresses, and there's a bird in a cage—not a real one—of course, and cooking pans and tables and five gilt chairs and a pot with a palm in it—a dish of plaster tarts and an imitation leg of mutton—"

Homily leaned across to Pod. "Tell him to nail us down lightly," she whispered. Pod stared at her and she nodded vigorously, clasping her hands.

Pod turned to the boy. "All right," he said, "you nail us down. But lightly, if you see what I mean. Just a tap or two here and there. . . ."

Chapter Sixteen

THEN began a curious phase in their lives: borrowings beyond all dreams of borrowing—a golden age. Every night the floor was opened and treasures would appear: a real carpet for the sitting room, a tiny coal-scuttle, a stiff little sofa with damask cushions, a double bed with a round bolster, a single ditto with a striped mattress, framed pictures instead of stamps, a kitchen stove which didn't work but which looked "lovely" in the kitchen; there were oval tables and square tables and a little desk with one drawer; there were two maple wardrobes (one with a looking-glass) and a bureau with curved legs. Homily grew not only accustomed to the roof coming off but even went so far as to suggest to Pod that he put the board on hinges. "It's just the hammering I don't care for," she explained; "it brings down the dirt."

When the boy brought them a grand piano Homily begged Pod to build a drawing room. "Next to the sitting room," she said, "and we could move the storerooms farther down. Then we could have those gilt chairs he talks about and the palm in a pot. . . ." Pod, however, was a little tired of furniture removing; he was looking forward to the quiet evenings when he could doze at last beside the fire in his new red velvet chair. No sooner had he put a chest of drawers in one place when Homily, coming in and out at the door—"to get the effect"—made him "try" it somewhere else. And every evening, at about his usual bedtime, the roof would fly up and more stuff would arrive. But Homily was tireless; bright-eyed and pink-cheeked, after a long day's pushing and pulling, she still would leave nothing until morning. "Let's just *try* it," she would beg, lifting up one end of a large doll's sideboard, so that Pod would have to lift the other; "it won't take a minute!" But as Pod well knew, in actual fact it would be several hours before, disheveled and aching, they finally dropped into bed. Even then Homily would sometimes hop out "to have one last look."

In the meantime, in payment for these riches, Arrietty would read to the boy—every afternoon in the long grass beyond the cherry tree. He would lie on his back and she would stand beside his shoulder and tell him when to turn the page. They were happy days to look back on afterwards, with the blue sky beyond the cherry boughs, the grasses softly stirring, and the boy's great ear listening beside her. She grew to know that ear quite well, with its curves and shadows and sunlit pinks and golds. Sometimes, as she grew bolder, she would lean against his shoulder. He was very still while she read to him and always grateful.

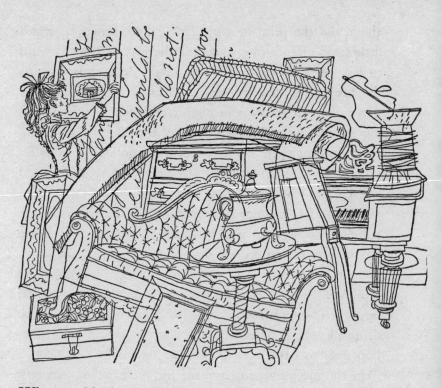

What worlds they would explore together—strange worlds to Arrietty. She learned a lot and some of the things she learned were hard to accept. She was made to realize once and for all that this earth on which they lived turning about in space did not revolve, as she had believed, for the sake of little people. "Nor for big people either," she reminded the boy when she saw his secret smile.

In the cool of the evening Pod would come for her—a rather weary Pod, disheveled and dusty—to take her back for tea. And at home there would be an excited Homily

and fresh delights to discover. "Shut your eyes!" Homily would cry. "Now open them!" and Arrietty, in a dream of joy, would see her home transformed. All kinds of surprises there were—even, one day, lace curtains at the grating, looped up with pink string.

Their only sadness was that there was no one there to see: no visitors, no casual droppers-in, no admiring cries and envious glances! What would Homily have not given for an Overmantel or a Harpsichord? Even a Rain-Barrel would have been better than no one at all. "You write to your Uncle Hendreary," Homily suggested, "and tell *him*. A nice long letter, mind, and don't leave anything out!" Arrietty began the letter on the back of one of the discarded pieces of blotting-paper, but it became as she wrote it just a dull list, far too long, like a sale catalogue or the inventory of a house to let; she would have to keep jumping up to count spoons or to look up words in the dictionary, and after a while she laid it aside: there was so much else to do, so many new books to read, and so much, now, that she could talk of with the boy.

"He's been ill," she told her mother and father; "he's been here for the quiet and the country air. But soon he'll go back to India. Did you know," she asked the amazed Homily, "that the Arctic night lasts six months, and that the distance between the two poles is less than that between the two extremities of a diameter drawn through the equator?"

Yes, they were happy days and all would have been well, as Pod said afterwards, if they had stuck to borrowing from the doll's house. No one in the human household seemed to remember it was there and consequently nothing was missed. The drawing room, however, could not help but be a temptation: it was so seldom used nowadays; there were so many knick-knack tables which had been out of Pod's reach, and the boy, of course, could turn the key in the glass doors of the cabinet.

The silver violin he brought them first and then the silver harp; it stood no higher than Pod's shoulder and

Pod restrung it with horse-hair from the sofa in the morning room. "A musical conversazione, that's what we could have!" cried the exulting Homily as Arrietty struck a tiny, tuneless note on a horse-hair string. "If only," she went on fervently, clasping her hands, "your father would start on the drawing room!" (She curled her hair nearly every evening nowadays and, since the house was more or less straight, she would occasionally change for dinner into a satin dress; it hung like a sack, but Homily called it "Grecian.") "We could use your painted ceiling," she explained to Arrietty, "and there are quite enough of those toy builders' bricks to make a parquet floor." ("Parkay," she would say. "Par-r-r-kay . . . ," just like a Harpsichord.)

Even Great-Aunt Sophy, right away upstairs in the littered grandeur of her bedroom, seemed distantly affected by a spirit of endeavor which seemed to flow, in gleeful whorls and eddies, about the staid old house. Several times lately Pod, when he went to her room, had found her out of bed. He went there nowadays not to borrow, but to rest: the room, one might almost say, had become his club; a place to which he could go "to get away from things." Pod was a little irked by his riches; he had never visualized, not in his wildest dreams, borrowing such as this. Homily, he felt, should call a halt; surely, now, their home was grand enough; these jeweled snuffboxes and diamond-encrusted miniatures, these filigree vanity cases and Dresden figurines—all, as he knew, from the drawing-room cabinet—were not really necessary: what was the good of a shepherdess nearly as tall as Arrietty or an outsize candle-snuffer? Sitting just inside the fender, where he could warm his hands at the fire, he watched Aunt Sophy hobble slowly round the room on her two sticks. "She'll be downstairs soon, I shouldn't wonder," he thought glumly, hardly listening to her oft-told tale about a royal luncheon aboard a Russian yacht, "then she'll miss these things. . . ."

It was not Aunt Sophy, however, who missed them first. It was Mrs. Driver. Mrs. Driver had never forgotten the trouble over Rosa Pickhatchet. It had not been, at the time, easy to pin-point the guilt. Even Crampfurl had felt under suspicion. "From now on," Mrs. Driver had said, "I'll manage on me own. No more strange maids in *this* house—not if I'm to stay on meself!" A drop of Madeira here, a pair of old stockings there, a handkerchief or so, an odd vest, or an occasional pair of gloves—these, Mrs. Driver felt, were different; these were within her rights. But trinkets out of the drawing-room cabinet—that, she told herself grimly, staring at the depleted shelves, was a different story altogether!

She felt tricked. Standing there, on that fateful day, in the spring sunshine, feather duster in hand, her little black eyes had become slits of anger and cunning. It was, she calculated, as though someone, suspecting her dishonesty, were trying to catch her out. But who could it be? Crampfurl? That boy? The man who came to wind the clocks? These things had disappeared gradually, one by one: it was someone, of that she felt sure, who knew the house—and someone who wished her ill. Could it, she wondered suddenly, be the old lady herself? The old girl had been out of bed lately and walking about her room. Might she not have come downstairs in the night, poking about with her stick, snooping and spying. (Mrs. Driver remembered suddenly the empty Madeira bottle and the two glasses which, so often, were left on the kitchen table.) Ah, thought Mrs. Driver, was not this just the sort of thing she might do—the sort of thing she would cackle over, back upstairs again among her pillows, watching and waiting for Mrs. Driver to report the loss? "Everything all right downstairs, Driver?"—that's what she'd always say and she would look at Mrs. Driver sideways out of those wicked old eyes of hers. "I wouldn't put it past her!" Mrs. Driver exclaimed aloud, gripping her feather duster as though it were a club. "And a nice merry-andrew she'd look if I caught her at it—creeping about the downstairs rooms in the middle of the night. All right, my lady," muttered Mrs. Driver grimly, "pry and potter all you want—two can play at that game!"

Chapter Seventeen

MRS. DRIVER was short with Crampfurl that evening; she would not sit down and drink with him as usual, but stumped about the kitchen, looking at him sideways every now and again out of the corners of her eyes. He seemed uneasy—as indeed he was: there was a kind of menace in her silence, a hidden something which no one could ignore. Even Aunt Sophy had felt it when Mrs. Driver brought up her wine; she heard it in the clink of the decanter against the glass as Mrs. Driver set down the tray and in the rattle of the wooden rings as Mrs. Driver drew the curtains; it was in the tremble of the floorboards as Mrs. Driver crossed the room and in the click of the latch as Mrs. Driver closed the door. "What's the matter with her now?" Aunt Sophy wondered vaguely as delicately, ungreedily, she poured the first glass.

The boy had felt it too. From the way Mrs. Driver had stared at him as he sat hunched in the bath; from the way she soaped the sponge and the way she said: "And now!" She had scrubbed him slowly, with a careful, angry steadiness, and all through the bathing time she did not say a word. When he was in bed she had gone through all his things, peering into cupboards and opening his drawers. She had pulled his suitcase out from under the wardrobe and found his dear dead mole and his hoard of sugar lumps and her best potato knife. But even then she had not spoken. She had thrown the mole into the waste-paper basket and had made angry noises with her tongue; she pocketed the potato knife and all the sugar lumps. She had stared at him a moment before she turned the gas low —a strange stare it had been, more puzzled than accusing.

Mrs. Driver slept above the scullery. She had her own backstairs. That night she did not undress. She set the alarm clock for midnight and put it, where the tick would not disturb her, outside her door; she unbuttoned her tight shoes and crawled, grunting a little, under the eiderdown. She had "barely closed her eyes" (as she told Crampfurl afterwards) when the clock shrilled off—chattering and rattling on its four thin legs on the bare boards of the passageway. Mrs. Driver tumbled herself out of bed and fumbled her way to the door. "Shush!" she said to the clock as she felt for the catch, "Shush!" and clasped it to her bosom. She stood there, in her stockinged feet, at the head of the scullery stairs: something, it seemed, had flickered below—a hint of light. Mrs. Driver peered down the dark curve of the narrow stairway. Yes, there it was again— a moth-wing flutter! Candlelight—that's what it was! A moving candle—beyond the stairs, beyond the scullery, somewhere within the kitchen.

Clock in hand, Mrs. Driver creaked down the stairs in her stockinged feet, panting a little in her eagerness. There seemed a sigh in the darkness, an echo of movement. And it seemed to Mrs. Driver, standing there on the cold stone flags of the scullery, that this sound that was barely a sound could only mean one thing: the soft swing-to of the green baize door—that door which led out of the kitchen into the main hall beyond. Hurriedly Mrs. Driver felt her way into the kitchen and fumbled for matches along the ledge above the stove; she knocked off a pepper-pot and a paper bag of cloves, and glancing quickly downwards saw a filament of light; she saw it in the second before she struck a match—a thread of light, it looked like, on the floor beside her feet; it ran in an oblong shape, outlining a rough square. Mrs. Driver gasped and lit the gas and the room leapt up around her: she glanced quickly at the baize door; there seemed to her startled eye a quiver of movement in it, as though it had just swung to; she ran to it and pushed it open, but the passage beyond was still and dark—no flicker of shadow nor sound of distant footfall. She let the door fall to again and watched it as it swung back, slowly, regretfully, held by its heavy spring. Yes, that was the sound she had heard from the scullery—that sighing whisper—like an indrawn breath.

Cautiously, clutching back her skirts, Mrs. Driver moved toward the stove. An object lay there, something pinkish, on the floor beside the jutting board. Ah, she realized, that board—that was where the light had come from! She hesitated and glanced about the kitchen: everything else looked normal and just as she had left it—the plates on the dresser, the saucepans on the wall, and the row of tea-towels hanging symmetrically on their string above the stove. The pinkish object, she saw now, was a heart-shaped cachou-box—one that she knew well—from the glassed-in tray-table beside the fireplace in the drawing room. She picked it up; it was enamel and gold and set with tiny brilliants. "Well, I'm—" she began, and stooping swiftly with a sudden angry movement, she wrenched back the piece of floor.

And then she shrieked, loud and long. She saw movement: a running, a scrambling, a fluttering! She heard a squeaking, a jabbering, and a gasping. Little people, they looked like, with hands and feet . . . and mouths opening. That's what they looked like . . . but they couldn't *be* that, of course! Running here, there, and everywhere. "Oh! oh! oh!" she shrieked and felt behind her for a chair. She clambered on to it and it wobbled beneath her and she climbed, still shrieking, from the chair to the table. . . .

And there she stood, marooned, crying and gasping, and calling out for help, until, after hours it seemed, there was a rattling at the scullery door. Crampfurl it was, roused at last by the light and the noise. "What is it?" he called. "Let me in!" But Mrs. Driver would not leave the table. "A nest! A nest!" she shouted. "Alive and squeaking!"

Crampfurl threw his weight against the door and burst

open the lock. He staggered, slightly dazed, into the kitchen, his corduroy trousers pulled on over his nightshirt. "Where?" he cried, his eyes wide beneath his tousled hair. "What sort of a nest?"

Mrs. Driver, sobbing still with fright, pointed at the floor. Crampfurl walked over in his slow, deliberate way and stared down. He saw a hole in the floor, lined and cluttered with small objects—children's toys, they looked like, bits of rubbish—that was all. "It's nothing," he said after a moment; "it's that boy, that's what it is." He stirred the contents with his foot and all the partitions fell down. "There ain't nothing alive in there."

"But I saw them, I tell you," gasped Mrs. Driver, "little people like with hands—or mice dressed up. . . ."

Crampfurl stared into the hole. "Mice dressed up?" he repeated uncertainly.

"Hundreds of them," went on Mrs. Driver, "running and squeaking. I saw them, I tell you!"

"Well, there ain't nothing there now," said Crampfurl, and he gave a final stir round with his boot.

"Then they've run away," she cried, "under the floor . . . up inside the walls . . . the place is alive with them."

"Well," said Crampfurl stolidly, "maybe. But if you ask me, I think it's that boy—where he hides things." His eye brightened and he went down on one knee. "Where he's got the ferret, I shouldn't wonder."

"Listen," cried Mrs. Driver, and there was a despairing note in her voice, "you've got to listen. This wasn't no

142

boy and it wasn't no ferret." She reached for the back of the chair and lowered herself clumsily on to the floor; she came beside him to the edge of the hole. "They had hands and faces, I tell you. Look," she said, pointing, "see that? It's a bed. And now I come to think of it one of 'em was in it."

"Now you come to think of it," said Crampfurl.

"Yes," went on Mrs. Driver firmly, "and there's something else I come to think of. Remember that girl, Rosa Pickhatchet?"

"The one that was simple?"

"Well, simple or not, she saw one—on the drawing-room mantelpiece, with a beard."

"One what?" asked Crampfurl.

Mrs. Driver glared at him. "What I've been telling you about—one of these—these—"

"Mice dressed up?" said Crampfurl.

"Not mice!" Mrs. Driver almost shouted. "Mice don't have beards."

"But you said—" began Crampfurl.

"Yes, I know I said it. Not that these had beards. But what would you call them? What could they be but mice?"

"Not so loud!" whispered Crampfurl. "You'll wake the house up."

"They can't hear," said Mrs. Driver, "not through the baize door." She went to the stove and picked up the fire tongs. "And what if they do? We ain't done nothing. Move over," she went on, "and let me get at the hole."

One by one Mrs. Driver picked things out—with many shocked gasps, cries of amazement, and did-you-evers. She made two piles on the floor—one of valuables and one of what she called "rubbish." Curious objects dangled from the tongs: "Would you believe it—her best lace handkerchiefs! Look, here's another . . . and another! And my big mattress needle—I knew I had one—my silver thimble, if you please, and one of hers! And look, oh my, at the wools . . . the cottons! No wonder you can never find a spool of white cotton if you want one. Potatoes . . . nuts . . . look at this, a pot of caviar—CAVIAR! No, it's too much, it really is. Doll's chairs . . . tables . . . and look at all this blotting paper—so that's where it goes! Oh, my goodness gracious!" she cried suddenly, her eyes staring. "What's this?" Mrs. Driver laid down the tongs and leaned over the hole—tentatively and fearfully as though afraid of being stung. "It's a watch—an emerald watch—her watch! And she's never missed it!" Her voice rose. "And it's going! Look, you can see by the kitchen clock! Twenty-five past twelve!" Mrs. Driver sat down suddenly on a hard chair; her eyes were staring and her face looked white and flabby, as though deflated. "You know what this means?" she said to Crampfurl.

"No?" he said.

"The police," said Mrs. Driver, "that's what this means —a case for the police."

Chapter Eighteen

THE boy lay, trembling a little, beneath the bed-clothes. The screwdriver was under his mattress. He had heard the alarm clock; he had heard Mrs. Driver exclaim on the stairs and he had run. The candle on the table beside his bed still smelt a little and the wax must still be warm. He lay there waiting, but they did not come upstairs. After hours, it seemed, he heard the hall clock strike one. All seemed quiet below, and at last he slipped out of bed and crept along the passage to the head of the stairway. There he sat for a while, shivering a little, and gazing downwards into the darkened hall. There was no sound but the steady tick of the clock and occasionally that shuffle or whisper which might be wind, but which, as he knew, was the sound of the house itself—the sigh of the tired floors and the ache of knotted wood. So quiet it was that at last he found courage to move and to tiptoe down the staircase and along the kitchen passage. He listened awhile outside the baize door, and at length, very gently, he pushed it open. The kitchen was silent and filled with grayish darkness. He felt, as Mrs. Driver had done, along the shelf for the matches and he struck a light. He saw the gaping hole in the floor and the objects piled beside it and, in the same flash, he saw a candle on the shelf. He lit it clumsily, with trembling hands. Yes, there they lay—the contents of the little home—higgledy-piggledy on the boards and the tongs lay beside them. Mrs. Driver had carried away all she considered valuable and had left the "rubbish." And rubbish it looked thrown down like this—balls of wool, old potatoes, odd pieces of doll's furniture, match boxes, cotton spools, crumpled squares of blotting paper. . . .

He knelt down. The "house" itself was a shambles—partitions fallen, earth floors revealed (where Pod had dug down to give greater height to the rooms), match-sticks, an old cogwheel, onion skins, scattered bottle tops. . . . The boy stared, blinking his eyelids and tilting the candle so that the grease ran hot on his hand. Then he got up from his knees and, crossing the kitchen on tiptoe, he closed the scullery door. He came back to the hole and, leaning down, he called softly: "Arrietty . . . Arrietty!" After a while he called again. Something else fell hot on his hand: it was a tear from his eye. Angrily he brushed it away, and, leaning farther into the hole, he called once more. "Pod," he whispered. "Homily!"

They appeared so quietly that at first, in the wavering light of the candle, he did not see them. Silent they stood, looking up at him with scared white faces from what had been the passage outside the storerooms.

147

"Where have you been?" asked the boy.

Pod cleared his throat. "Up at the end of the passage. Under the clock."

"I've got to get you out," said the boy.

"Where to?" asked Pod.

"I don't know. What about the attic?"

"That ain't no good," said Pod. "I heard them talking They're going to get the police and a cat and the sanitary inspector and the rat-catcher from the town hall at Leighton Buzzard."

They were all silent. Little eyes stared at big eyes. "There won't be nowhere in the house that's safe," Pod said at last. And no one moved.

"What about the doll's house on the top shelf in the schoolroom?" suggested the boy. "Even a cat can't get there."

Homily gave a little moan of assent. "Yes," she said, "the doll's house. . . ."

"No," said Pod in the same expressionless voice, "you can't live on a shelf. Maybe the cat can't get up, but no more can't you get down. You're stuck. You got to have water."

"I'd bring you water," said the boy. "And there are beds and things here." He touched the pile of "rubbish."

"No," said Pod, "a shelf ain't no good. Besides, you'll be going soon, or so they say."

"Oh, Pod," pleaded Homily in a husky whisper, "there's stairs in the doll's house, and two bedrooms, and a dining room, and a kitchen. And a bathroom," she said.

"But it's up by the ceiling," Pod explained wearily. "You got to eat, haven't you," he asked, "and drink?"

"Yes, Pod, I know. But—"

"There ain't no buts," said Pod. He drew a long breath. "We got to emigrate," he said.

"Oh," moaned Homily softly and Arrietty began to cry.

"Now don't take on," said Pod in a tired voice.

Arrietty had covered her face with her hands and her tears ran through her fingers; the boy, watching, saw them glisten in the candlelight. "I'm not taking on," she gasped, "I'm so happy . . . happy."

"You mean," said the boy to Pod, but with one eye on Arrietty, "you'll go to the badger's set?" He too felt a mounting excitement.

"Where else?" asked Pod.

"Oh, my goodness gracious!" moaned Homily, and sat down on the broken match-box chest of drawers.

"But you've got to go somewhere tonight," said the boy. "You've got to go somewhere before tomorrow morning."

"Oh, my goodness gracious!" moaned Homily again.

"He's right at that," said Pod. "Can't cross them fields in the dark. Bad enough getting across them in daylight."

"I know," cried Arrietty. Her wet face glistened in the candlelight; it was alight and tremulous and she raised her arms a little as though about to fly, and she swayed as she balanced on her toe-tips. "Let's go to the doll's house just for tonight and tomorrow—" she closed her eyes against the brightness of the vision—"tomorrow the boy will take us—take us—" and she could not say to where.

"Take us?" cried Homily in a strange hollow voice. "How?"

"In his pockets," chanted Arrietty; "won't you?" Again she swayed, with lighted upturned face.

"Yes," he said, "and bring the luggage up afterwards—in a fish basket."

"Oh, my goodness!" moaned Homily.

"I'll pick all the furniture out of this pile here. Or most of it. They'll hardly notice. And anything else you want."

"Tea," murmured Homily. "Enough for our lifetimes."

"All right," said the boy. "I'll get a pound of tea. And coffee too if you like. And cooking pots. And matches. You'll be all right," he said.

"But what do they eat?" wailed Homily. "Caterpillars?"

"Now, Homily," said Pod, "don't be foolish. Lupy was always a good manager."

"But Lupy isn't there," said Homily. "Berries. Do they eat berries? How do they cook? Out of doors?"

"Now, Homily," said Pod, "we'll see all that when we get there."

"I couldn't light a fire of sticks," said Homily, "not in

the wind. What if it rains?" she asked. "How do they cook in the rain?"

"Now, Homily—" began Pod—he was beginning to lose patience—but Homily rushed on.

"Could you get us a couple of tins of sardines to take?" she asked the boy. "And some salt? And some candles? And matches? And could you bring us the carpets from the doll's house?"

"Yes," said the boy, "I could. Of course I could. Anything you want."

"All right," said Homily. She still looked wild, partly because some of her hair had rolled out of the curlers, but she seemed appeased. "How are you going to get us upstairs? Up to the schoolroom?"

The boy looked down at his pocketless night-shirt. "I'll carry you," he said.

"How?" asked Homily. "In your hands?"

"Yes," said the boy.

"I'd rather die," said Homily. "I'd rather stay right here and be eaten by the rat-catcher from the town hall at Leighton Buzzard."

The boy looked round the kitchen; he seemed bewildered. "Shall I carry you in the clothespin bag?" he asked at last, seeing it hanging in its usual place on the handle of the scullery door.

"All right," said Homily. "Take out the clothespins first."

But she walked into it bravely enough when he laid it

out on the floor. It was soft and floppy and made of woven raffia. When he picked it up Homily shrieked and clung to Pod and Arrietty. "Oh," she gasped as the bag swayed a little, "oh, I can't! Stop it! Put me out! Oh! Oh!" And, clutching and slipping, they fell into a tangle at the bottom.

"Be quiet, Homily, can't you!" exclaimed Pod angrily, and held her tightly by the ankle. It was not easy to control her as he was lying on his back with his face pushed forward on his chest and one leg, held upright by the side of the bag, somewhere above his head. Arrietty climbed up, away from them, clinging to the knots of raffia, and looked out over the edge.

"Oh, I can't! I can't!" cried Homily. "Stop it, Pod. I'm dying. Tell him to put us down."

"Put us down," said Pod in his patient way, "just for a moment. That's right. On the floor," and, as once again the bag was placed beside the hole, they all ran out.

"Look here," said the boy unhappily to Homily, "you've got to try."

"She'll try all right," said Pod. "Give her a breather, and take it slower, if you see what I mean."

"All right," agreed the boy, "but there isn't much time. Come on," he said nervously, "hop in."

"Listen!" cried Pod sharply, and froze.

The boy, looking down, saw their three upturned faces catching the light—like pebbles they looked, still and stony, against the darkness within the hole. And then in a flash they were gone—the boards were empty and the hole was bare. He leaned into it. "Pod!" he called in a frantic whisper. "Homily! Come back!" And then he too became frozen, stooped and rigid above the hole. The scullery door creaked open behind him.

It was Mrs. Driver. She stood there silent, this time in her nightdress. Turning, the boy stared up at her. "Hallo," he said, uncertainly, after a moment.

She did not smile, but something lightened in her eyes —a malicious gleam, a look of triumph. She carried a candle which shone upwards on her face, streaking it strangely with light and shadow. "What are you doing down here?" she asked.

He stared at her, but he did not speak.

"Answer me," she said. "And what are you doing with the clothespin bag?"

Still he stared at her, almost stupidly. "The clothespin bag?" he repeated and looked down as though surprised to see it in his hand. "Nothing," he said.

"Was it you who put the watch in the hole?"

"No," he said, staring up at her again, "it was there already."

"Ah," she said and smiled, "so you knew it was there?"

"No," he said; "I mean yes."

"Do you know what you are?" asked Mrs. Driver, watching him closely. "You are a sneaking, thieving, noxious little dribbet of no-good!"

His face quivered. "Why?" he said.

"You know why. You're a wicked, black-hearted,

fribbling little pickpocket. That's what you are. And so are they. They're nasty little crafty, scampy, scurvy, squeaking little—"

"No, they're not," he put in quickly.

"And you're in league with them!" She came across to him and, taking him by the upper arm, she jerked him to his feet. "You know what they do with thieves?" she asked.

"No," he said.

"They lock them up. That's what they do with thieves. And that's what's going to happen to you!"

"I'm not a thief," cried the boy, his lips trembling, "I'm a borrower."

"A what?" She swung him round by tightening the grip on his arm.

"A borrower," he repeated; there were tears on his eyelids; he hoped they would not fall.

"So that's what you call it!" she exclaimed (as he had done—so long ago, it seemed now—that day with Arrietty).

"That's their name," he said. "The kind of people they are—they're Borrowers."

"Borrowers, eh?" repeated Mrs. Driver wonderingly. She laughed. "Well, they've done all the borrowing they're ever going to do in this house!" She began to drag him toward the door.

The tears spilled over his eyelids and ran down his cheeks. "Don't hurt them," he begged. "I'll move them. I promise. I know how."

Mrs. Driver laughed again and pushed him roughly through the green baize door. "They'll be moved all right," she said. "Don't worry. The rat-catcher will know how. Crampfurl's old cat will know how. So will the sanitary inspector. And the fire brigade, if need be. The police'll know how, I shouldn't wonder. No need to worry about moving them. Once you've found the nest," she went on, dropping her voice to a vicious whisper as they passed Aunt Sophy's door, "the rest is easy!"

She pushed him into the schoolroom and locked the door and he heard the boards of the passage creak beneath her tread as, satisfied, she moved away. He crept into bed then, because he was cold, and cried his heart out under the blankets.

Chapter Nineteen

"AND that," said Mrs. May, laying down her crochet hook, "is really the end."

Kate stared at her. "Oh, it can't be," she gasped, "oh, please . . . *please.* . . ."

"The last square," said Mrs. May, smoothing it out on her knee, "the hundred and fiftieth. Now we can sew them together—"

"Oh," said Kate, breathing again, "the quilt! I thought you meant the story."

"It's the end of the story too," said Mrs. May absently, "or the beginning. He never saw them again," and she began to sort out the squares.

"But," stammered Kate, "you can't—I mean— It's not fair," she cried, "it's cheating. It's—" Tears sprang to her eyes; she threw her work down on the table and her crochet hook after it, and she kicked the bag of wools which lay beside her on the carpet.

"Why, Kate, why?" Mrs. May looked genuinely surprised.

"Something more must have happened," cried Kate angrily. "What about the rat-catcher? And the policeman? And the—"

"But something more did happen," said Mrs. May, "a lot more happened. I'm going to tell you."

"Then why did you say it was the end?"

"Because," said Mrs. May (she still looked surprised), "he never saw them again."

"Then how can there be more?"

"Because," said Mrs. May, "there is more. A lot more."

Kate glared at her. "All right," she said, "go on."

Mrs. May looked back at her. "Kate," she said after a moment, "stories never really end. They can go on and on and on. It's just that sometimes, at a certain point, one stops telling them."

"But not at this kind of point," said Kate.

"Well, thread your needle," said Mrs. May, "with gray wool, this time. And we'll sew these squares together. I'll start at the top and you can start at the bottom. First a gray square, then an emerald, then a pink, and so on—"

"Then you didn't really mean it," said Kate irritably, trying to push the folded wool through the narrow eye of the needle, "when you said he never saw them again?"

"But I did mean it," said Mrs. May. "I'm telling you just what happened. He had to leave suddenly—at the end of the week—because there was a boat for India and a family who could take him. And for the three days before he left they kept him locked up in those two rooms."

"For three days!" exclaimed Kate.

"Yes. Mrs. Driver, it seemed, told Aunt Sophy that he had a cold. She was determined, you see, to keep him out of the way until she'd got rid of the Borrowers."

"And did she?" asked Kate. "I mean—did they all come? The policeman? And the rat-catcher? And the—"

"The sanitary inspector didn't come. At least, not while my brother was there. And they didn't have the rat-catcher from the town hall, but they had the local man. The policeman came—" Mrs. May laughed. "During those three days Mrs. Driver used to give my brother a running commentary on what was going on below. She loved to grumble, and my brother, rendered harmless and shut away upstairs, became a kind of neutral. She used to bring his meals up, and, on that first morning, she brought all the doll's furniture up on the breakfast tray and made my brother climb the shelves and put it back in the doll's house. It was then she told him about the policeman. Furious he said she was."

"Why?" asked Kate.

"Because the policeman turned out to be Nellie Runacre's son Ernie, a boy Mrs. Driver had chased many a time for stealing russet apples from the tree by the gate—'A nasty, thieving, good-for-nothing dribbet of no-good,' she told my brother. 'Sitting down there he is now, in the kitchen, large as life with his notebook out, laughing fit to bust . . . twenty-one, he says he is now, and as cheeky as you make 'em. . . .' "

"And was he," asked Kate, round-eyed, "a dribbet of no-good?"

"Of course not. Any more than my brother was. Ernie Runacre was a fine, upstanding young man and a credit to the police force. And he did not actually laugh at Mrs. Driver when she told him her story, but he gave her what Crampfurl spoke of afterwards as 'an old-fashioned look' when she described Homily in bed—'Take more water with it,' it seemed to say."

"More water with what?" asked Kate.

"The Fine Old Pale Madeira, I suppose," said Mrs. May. "And Great-Aunt Sophy had the same suspicion: she was furious when she heard that Mrs. Driver had seen several little people when she herself on a full decanter had only risen to one or, at most, two. Crampfurl had to bring all the Madeira up from the cellar and stack the cases against the wall in a corner of Aunt Sophy's bedroom where, as she said, she could keep an eye on it."

"Did they get a cat?" asked Kate.

"Yes, they did. But that wasn't much of a success either. It was Crampfurl's cat, a large yellow tom with white streaks in it. According to Mrs. Driver, it had only two ideas in its head—to get out of the house or into the larder. 'Talk of borrowers,' Mrs. Driver would say as she slammed down the fish pie for my brother's luncheon, 'that cat's a borrower, if ever there was one; borrowed the fish, that cat did, and a good half-bowl of egg sauce!' But the cat wasn't there long. The first thing the rat-catcher's terriers did was to chase it out of the house. There was a dreadful set-to, my brother said. They chased it everywhere—upstairs and downstairs, in and out all the rooms, barking their heads off. The last glimpse my brother had of the cat was streaking away through the spinney and across the fields with the terriers after it."

"Did they catch it?"

"No." Mrs. May laughed. "It was still there when I went, a year later. A little morose, but as fit as a fiddle."

"Tell about when *you* went."

"Oh, I wasn't there long," said Mrs. May rather hastily, "and after that the house was sold. My brother never went back."

Kate stared at her suspiciously, pressing her needle against the center of her lower lip. "So they never caught the little people?" she said at last.

Mrs. May's eyes flicked away. "No, they never actually caught them, but"—she hesitated—"as far as my poor brother was concerned, what they did do seemed even worse."

"What did they do?"

Mrs. May laid down her work and stared for a moment, thoughtfully, at her idle hands. "I hated the rat-catcher," she said suddenly.

"Why, did you know him?"

"Everybody knew him. He had a wall eye and his name was Rich William. He was also the pig-killer, and, well —he did other things as well—he had a gun, a hatchet, a spade, a pick-ax, and a contraption with bellows for smoking things out. I don't know what the smoke was exactly —poison fumes of some kind which he made himself from herbs and chemicals. I only remember the smell of it; it clung round the barns or wherever he'd been. You can imagine what my brother felt on that third day, the day he was leaving, when suddenly he smelled that smell. . . .

"He was all dressed and ready to go. The bags were packed and down in the hall. Mrs. Driver came and unlocked the door and took him down the passage to Aunt Sophy. He stood there, stiff and pale, in gloves and overcoat beside the curtained bed. 'Seasick already?' Aunt Sophy mocked him, peering down at him over the edge of the great mattress.

" 'No,' he said, 'it's that smell.'

"Aunt Sophy lifted her nose. She sniffed. 'What smell is it, Driver?'

" 'It's the rat-catcher, my lady,' explained Mrs. Driver, reddening, 'down in the kitchen.'

" 'What!' exclaimed Aunt Sophy, 'are you smoking them out?' and she began to laugh. 'Oh dear . . . oh dear!' she gasped, 'but if you don't like them, Driver, the remedy's simple.'

" 'What is that, my lady?' asked Mrs. Driver coldly, but even her chins were red.

"Helpless with mirth Aunt Sophy waved a ringed hand toward her, her eyes were screwed up and her shoulders shaking: 'Keep the bottle corked,' she managed at last and motioned them weakly away. They heard her laughing still as they went on down the stairs.

" 'She don't believe in them,' muttered Mrs. Driver, and she tightened her grip on my brother's arm. 'More fool her! She'll change her tune, like enough, when I take them up afterwards, laid out in sizes, on a clean piece of newspaper . . .' and she dragged him roughly across the hall.

"The clock had been moved, exposing the wainscot, and, as my brother saw at once, the hole had been blocked and sealed. The front door was open as usual and the sunshine streamed in. The bags stood there beside the fiber mat, cooking a little in the golden warmth. The fruit trees beyond the bank had shed their petals and were lit with tender green, transparent in the sunlight. 'Plenty of time,' said Mrs. Driver, glancing up at the clock, 'the cab's not due 'til three-thirty—'

" 'The clock's stopped,' said my brother.

"Mrs. Driver turned. She was wearing her hat and her best black coat, ready to take him to the station. She looked strange and tight and chapel-going—not a bit like 'Driver.' 'So it has,' she said; her jaw dropped and her cheeks became heavy and pendulous. 'It's moving it,' she decided after a moment. 'It'll be all right,' she went on, 'once we get it back. Mr. Frith comes on Monday,' and she dragged again at his arm above the elbow.

" 'Where are we going?' he asked, holding back.

" 'Along to the kitchen. We've got a good ten minutes. Don't you want to see them caught?'

" 'No,' he said, 'no!' and pulled away from her.

"Mrs. Driver stared at him, smiling a little. 'I do,' she said; 'I'd like to see 'em close. He puffs this stuff in and they come running out. At least, that's how it works with rats. But first, he says, you block up all the exits . . .' and her eyes followed his to the hole below the wainscot.

" 'How did they find it?' the boy asked (puttied it looked, and with a square of brown paper pasted on crooked).

" 'Rich William found it. That's his job.'

" 'They could unstick that,' said the boy after a moment.

"Mrs. Driver laughed. 'Oh no they couldn't! Cemented, that is. A great block of it, right inside, with a sheet of iron across from the front of that old stove in the outhouse. He and Crampfurl had to have the morning-room floor up to get at it. All Tuesday they was working, up till tea-time. We aren't going to have no more capers of that kind. Not under the clock. Once you get that clock back, it can't be moved again in a hurry. Not if you want it to keep time, it can't. See where it's stood—where the floor's washed away like?' It was then my brother saw, for the first and last time, that raised platform of unscrubbed stone. 'Come on now,' said Mrs. Driver and took him by the arm. 'We'll hear the cab from the kitchen.'

"But the kitchen, as she dragged him past the baize door, seemed a babel of sound. No approaching cab could be heard here—what with yelps and barks and stampings and excited voices. 'Steady, steady, steady, steady, steady . . .'

164

Crampfurl was saying, on one loud note, as he held back the rat-catcher's terriers which shrilled and panted on the leash. The policeman was there, Nellie Runacre's son Ernie. He had come out of interest and stood back from the others a little, in view of his calling, with a cup of tea in his hand and his helmet pushed off his forehead. But his face was pink with boyish excitement and he stirred the teaspoon round and round. 'Seeing's believing!' he said cheerfully to Mrs. Driver when he saw her come in at the door. A boy from the village was there with a ferret. It kept sort of pouring out of his pocket, my brother said, and the boy kept pushing it back. Rich William himself was crouched on the floor by the hole. He had lighted something beneath a piece of sacking and the stench of its smoldering eddied about the room. He was working the bellows now, with infinite care, stooping over them—rapt and tense.

"My brother stood there as though in a dream ('Perhaps it was a dream,' he said to me later—much later, after we were all grown up). He gazed round the kitchen. He saw the sunlit fruit trees through the window and a bough of the cherry tree which stood upon the bank; he saw the empty tea cups on the table, with spoons stuck in them and one without a saucer; he saw, propped against the wall close beside the baize door, the rat-catcher's belongings—a frayed coat, patched with leather; a bundle of rabbit snares; two sacks; a spade, a gun, and a pick-ax. . . .

" 'Stand by now,' Rich William was saying; there was

165

a rising note of excitement in his voice, but he did not turn his head. 'Stand by. Ready now to slip the dogs.'

"Mrs. Driver let go my brother's arm and moved toward the hole. 'Keep back,' said the rat-catcher, without turning. 'Give us room—' and Mrs. Driver backed nervously toward the table. She put a chair beside it and half raised one knee, but lowered it again when she caught Ernie Runacre's mocking glance. 'All right, ma,' he said, cocking one eyebrow, 'we'll give you a leg up when the time comes,' and Mrs. Driver threw him a furious look; she snatched up the three cups from the table and stumped away with them, angrily, into the scullery. 'Seemingless smutch of something-or-other . . .' my brother heard her mutter as she brushed past him. And at those words, suddenly, my brother came to life. . . .

"He threw a quick glance about the kitchen: the men were absorbed; all eyes were on the rat-catcher—except those of the village boy who was getting out his ferret. Stealthily my brother drew off his gloves and began to move backwards . . . slowly . . . slowly . . . toward the green baize door; as he moved, gently stuffing his gloves into his pocket, he kept his eyes on the group around the hole. He paused a moment beside the rat-catcher's tools, and stretched out a wary, groping hand; his fingers closed at last on a wooden handle—smooth it was and worn with wear; he glanced down quickly to make sure—yes, it was, as he hoped, the pick-ax. He leaned back a little and pushed—almost imperceptibly—against the door

168

with his shoulders: it opened sweetly, in its silent way. Not one of the men had looked up. 'Steady now,' the rat-catcher was saying, stooping closely over the bellows, 'it takes a moment like to go right through . . . there ain't much ventilation, not under a floor. . . .'

"My brother slid through the barely opened door and it sighed to behind him, closing out the noise. He took a few steps on tiptoe down the dark kitchen passage and then he ran.

"There was the hall again, steeped in sunshine, with his bags beside the door. He bumped against the clock and it struck a note, a trembling note—urgent and deep. He raised the pick-ax to the height of his shoulder and aimed a sideways blow at the hole below the wainscot. The paper tore, a few crumbs of plaster fell out, and the pick-ax rebounded sharply, jarring his hands. There was indeed iron behind the cement—something immovable. Again he struck. And again and again. The wainscot above the hole became split and scratched, and the paper hung down in strips, but still the pick-ax bounced. It was no good; his hands, wet with sweat, were sliding and slipping on the wood. He paused for breath and, looking out, he saw the cab. He saw it on the road, beyond the hedge on the far side of the orchard; soon it would reach the russet apple tree beside the gate; soon it would turn into the drive. He glanced up at the clock. It was ticking steadily—the result, perhaps, of his knock. The sound gave him comfort and steadied his thumping heart; time, that's what he needed, a little more time. 'It takes a moment like,' the rat-catcher had said, 'to go right through . . . there ain't much ventilation, not under a floor. . . .'

" 'Ventilation'—that was the word, the saving word. Pick-ax in hand my brother ran out of the door. He

stumbled once on the gravel path and nearly fell; the pick-ax handle came up and struck him a sharp blow on the temple. Already, when he reached it, a thin filament of smoke was eddying out of the grating and he thought, as he ran toward it, that there was a flicker of movement against the darkness between the bars. And that was where they would be, of course, to get the air. But he did not stop to make sure. Already he heard behind him the crunch of wheels on the gravel and the sound of the horse's hoofs. He was not, as I have told you, a very strong little boy, and he was only nine (not ten, as he had boasted to Arrietty) but, with two great blows on the brickwork, he dislodged one end of the grating. It fell down sideways, slightly on a slant, hanging—it seemed—by one nail. Then he clambered up the bank and threw the pick-ax with all his might into the long grass beyond the cherry tree. He remembered thinking as he stumbled back, sweaty and breathless, toward the cab, how that too—the loss of the pick-ax—would cause its own kind of trouble later."

Chapter Twenty

"But," exclaimed Kate, "didn't he see them come out?"

"No. Mrs. Driver came along then, in a flurry of annoyance, because they were late for the train. She bustled him into the cab because she wanted to get back again, she said, as fast as she could to be 'in at the death.' Driver was like that."

Kate was silent a moment, looking down. "So that *is* the end," she said at last.

. "Yes," said Mrs. May, "it could be. Or the beginning."

"But"—Kate raised a worried face—"perhaps they didn't escape through the grating?"

"Oh, they escaped all right," said Mrs. May lightly.

"But how do you know?"

"I just know," said Mrs. May.

"But how did they get across those fields? With the cows and things? And the crows?"

"They walked, I suppose. The Hendrearys did it. People can do anything when they have a mind to."

"But poor Homily! She'd be so upset."

"Yes, she was upset," said Mrs. May.

"And how would they know the way?"

"By the gas-pipe," said Mrs. May. "There's a kind of ridge all along, through the spinney and across the fields. You see, when men dig a trench and put a pipe in it all the earth they've dug out doesn't quite fit when they've put it back. The ground looks different."

"But poor Homily—she didn't have her tea or her furniture or her carpets or anything. Do you suppose they took anything?"

"Oh, people always grab something," said Mrs. May shortly, "the oddest things sometimes—if you've read about shipwrecks." She spoke hurriedly, as though she were tired of the subject. "Do be careful, child—not gray next to pink. You'll have to unpick it."

"But," went on Kate in a despairing voice as she picked up the scissors, "Homily would hate to arrive there all poor and dessitute in front of Lupy."

"Destitute," said Mrs. May patiently, "and Lupy wasn't there remember. Lupy never came back. And you know what Homily would do? Can't you see her—she'd be in her element. She would tie on her apron at once and cry '. . . these poor silly men,' and she'd bustle and fuss and cook and clean and make them wipe their feet when they came in."

"On what?" asked Kate.

"On a piece of moss, of course, laid down at the door."

"Were they all boys?" Kate asked, after a moment.

"Yes, Harpsichords and Clocks. And they'd spoil Arrietty dreadfully."

"What did they eat? *Did* they eat caterpillars, do you think?"

"Oh, goodness, child, of course they didn't. They had a wonderful life—all that Arrietty had ever dreamed of. They could live very well. Badgers' sets are almost like villages—full of passages and chambers and storehouses. They could gather hazel nuts and beechnuts and chestnuts; they could gather corn—which they could store and grind into flour, just as humans do—it was all there for them: they didn't even have to plant it. They had honey. They could make elderflower tea and lime tea. They had hips and haws and blackberries and sloes and wild strawberries. The boys could fish in the stream and a minnow to them would be as big as a mackerel is to you. They had birds' eggs—any amount of them—for custards and cakes and omelettes. You see, they would know where to look for things. And they had greens and salads, of course. Think of a salad made of those tender shoots of young hawthorn —bread and cheese we used to call it—with sorrel and dandelion and a sprinkling of thyme and wild garlic. Homily was a good cook remember. It wasn't for nothing that the Clocks had lived under the kitchen."

"But the danger," cried Kate; "the weasels and the crows and the stoats and all those things?"

"Yes," agreed Mrs. May, "of course there was danger. There's danger everywhere, but no more for them than for many human beings. At least, they didn't have *wars*. And what about the early settlers in America? And those people who farm in the middle of the big game country in Africa and on the edge of the jungles in India? They get to know the habits of the animals. Few animals kill for the sake of killing. Even rabbits know when a fox isn't hunting; they will run quite near him when he's full fed and lazing in the sun. These were boys remember; they would learn to hunt for the pot and how to protect themselves. I don't suppose Arrietty and Homily would wander far afield."

"Arrietty would," said Kate.

"Yes," agreed Mrs. May, laughing, "I suppose Arrietty might."

"So they'd have meat?" said Kate.

"Yes, sometimes. But Borrowers are Borrowers; not killers. I think," said Mrs. May, "that if a stoat, say, killed a partridge they would borrow a leg!"

"And if a fox killed a rabbit they'd use the fur?"

"Yes, for rugs and things."

"Supposing," said Kate, "when they had a little roast, they skinned haws and baked them, would they taste like browned potatoes?"

"Perhaps," said Mrs. May.

"But they couldn't cook in the badger's set. I suppose they cooked out of doors. How would they keep warm then in winter?"

"Do you know what I think?" said Mrs. May; she laid

down her work and leaned forward a little. "I think that they didn't live in the badger's set at all. I think they used it, with all its passages and storerooms, as a great honeycomb of an entrance hall. None but they would know the secret way through the tunnels which led at last to their home. Borrowers love passages and they love gates; and they love to live a long way from their own front doors."

"Where *would* they live then?"

"I was wondering," said Mrs. May, "about the gas-pipe—"

"Oh yes," cried Kate, "I see what you mean!"

"The soil's all soft and sandy up there. I think they'd go right through the badger's set and dig out a circular chamber, level with the gas-pipe. And off this chamber, all around it, there'd be little rooms, like cabins. And I think," said Mrs. May, "that they'd bore three little pin-holes in the gas-pipe. One would be so tiny that you could hardly see it and that one would be always alight. The other two would have stoppers in them which, when they wanted to light the gas, they would pull out. They would light the bigger ones from the small burner. That's where they'd cook and that would give them light."

"But would they be so clever?"

"But they are clever," Mrs. May assured her, "very clever. Much too clever to live near a gas-pipe and not use it. They're Borrowers remember."

"But they'd want a little airhole?"

176

"Oh," said Mrs. May quickly, "they did have one."

"How do you know?" asked Kate.

"Because once when I was up there I smelled hot-pot."

"Oh," cried Kate excitedly; she twisted round and knelt up on the hassock, "so you did go up there? So that's how you know! You saw them too!"

"No, no," said Mrs. May, drawing back a little in her chair, "I never saw them. Never."

"But you went up there? You know something! I can see you know!"

"Yes, I went up there." Mrs. May stared back into Kate's eager face; hesitant, she seemed, almost a little guilty. "Well," she conceded at last, "I'll tell you. For what it's worth. When I went to stay in that house it was just before Aunt Sophy went into the nursing home. I knew the place was going to be sold, so I"—again Mrs. May hesitated, almost shyly—"well, I took all the furniture out of the doll's house and put it in a pillowcase and took it up there. I bought things too out of my pocket money—tea and coffee beans and salt and pepper and cloves and a great packet of lump sugar. And I took a whole lot of little pieces of silk which were over from making a patchwork quilt. And I took them some fish bones for needles. I took the tiny thimble I had got in a Christmas pudding and a whole collection of scraps and cracker things I'd had in a chocolate box—"

"But you never saw them!"

"No. I never saw them. I sat for hours against the

177

bank below the hawthorn hedge. It was a lovely bank, twined with twisted hawthorn roots and riddled with sandy holes and there were wood-violets and primroses and early campion. From the top of the bank you could see for miles across the fields: you could see the woods and the valleys and the twisting lanes; you could see the chimneys of the house."

"Perhaps it was the wrong place."

"I don't think so. Sitting there in the grass, half dreaming and watching beetles and ants, I found an oak-apple; it was smooth and polished and dry and there was a hole bored in one side of it and a slice off the top—"

"The teapot!" exclaimed Kate.

"I think so. I looked everywhere, but I couldn't find the quill spout. I called then, down all the holes—as my brother had done. But no one answered. Next day, when I went up there, the pillowcase had gone."

"And everything in it?"

"Yes, everything. I searched the ground for yards around, in case there might be a scrap of silk or a coffee bean. But there was nothing. Of course, somebody passing might just have picked it up and carried it away. That was the day," said Mrs. May, smiling, "that I smelled hot-pot."

"And which was the day," asked Kate, "that you found Arrietty's diary?"

Mrs. May laid down her work. "Kate," she began in a startled voice, and then, uncertainly, she smiled, "what makes you say that?" Her cheeks had become quite pink.

"I guessed," said Kate. "I knew there was something—something you wouldn't tell me. Like—like reading somebody else's diary."

"It wasn't the diary," said Mrs. May hastily, but her cheeks had become even pinker. "It was the book called 'Memoranda,' the book with blank pages. That's where she'd written it. And it wasn't on that day I found it, but three weeks later—the day before I left."

Kate sat silent, staring at Mrs. May. After a while she drew a long breath. "Then that proves it," she said finally, "underground chamber and all."

"Not quite," said Mrs. May.

"Why not?" asked Kate.

"Arrietty used to make her 'e's' like little half-moons with a stroke in the middle—"

"Well?" said Kate.

Mrs. May laughed and took up her work again. "My brother did too," she said.

Cinda's
Surprise

Mary Davis

Heartsong Presents

To Zola who planted the thought in me to get published, then watched it grow. Thanks mom! To my sister who graciously plucked the weeds in my writing. And to my husband who encouraged my writing into full bloom!

A note from the author:
I love to hear from my readers! You may correspond with me by writing:

Mary Davis
Author Relations
PO Box 719
Uhrichsville, OH 44683

ISBN 1-58660-026-5

CINDA'S SURPRISE

All Scripture quotations are taken from the King James Version of the Bible.

Cover illustration by Chris Cocozza.

PRINTED IN THE U.S.A.

one

South of Chicago, 1883

"Smile, Cinda."

Cinda stopped just short of running into David Swan in his own front yard. In her worry, her gaze had been focused on the ground and not on where she was going. Now, she looked up at her best friend's new husband with an apologetic smile.

"Oh, hi, David. Is Allison inside?"

Cinda had rushed over to see her friend as soon as the mail had arrived. Normally, she strolled along, enjoying whatever pleasures the day had to offer; however, today in her haste, she had heard nothing but her own rushing thoughts and had seen even less. She hadn't even seen David until he spoke to her.

David was six-feet one-inch tall, broad across the shoulders but lean in build, with a kind face and thin and sandy blond hair. He stood firmly in her path. "I won't tell you until you smile. You'll never get a husband with that scowl."

Cinda gave him a quick, forced smile. The last thing she felt like doing today was smiling.

"You're a pretty girl, Cinda. If you smiled more often and looked up once in awhile, you'd catch a husband in no time."

Her cheeks warmed at his compliment. She could see that look in his eyes—*help poor, shy Cinda, so she doesn't become an unhappy old maid.* Why were all old maids assumed to be miserable? Wasn't it possible for a spinster to be happy? "Now, who said I was fishing for one, anyway?" she asked him.

5

"Aren't all young ladies looking for a man to put a ring on their finger?"

Here he was playing big brother again; she was irritated by his teasing, but if she could choose a brother, he would be David. She could see now he was amused. Putting her hands on her hips, she stood up to her full five-feet eleven and one-half-inches. Like this, she could intimidate most men unless they were young, handsome, and unmarried—then it was Cinda who was intimidated. She was tall, but she never felt she could measure up in the eyes of a potential suitor.

Less than two inches shorter than David, she was almost eye to eye with him, as she was with most men. "No, David. Some of us are independent souls and don't need marriage to feel complete." Her own words hurt her because she wasn't so sure she was one of the independent souls.

David opened his mouth as if to counter, but Cinda spoke quickly. "Allison? Is she inside?"

David's hesitation made her uncomfortable. She hoped he wouldn't harass her further. She had had enough for one day. "Yes. She's in the kitchen," David said finally with half a grin.

❧

Allison glanced up at her friend lurking in the doorway and smiled. "Don't just stand there. Peel me some apples." Allison stood at the kitchen worktable stirring the ingredients for a piecrust. "You can help me make these pies for supper."

Cinda had no siblings while Allison was the only girl of five children; the two had developed a special sisterly bond rooted in friendship.

"I'll just spoil it. You know I can't cook," Cinda countered, staying out of the way by the door.

"Nonsense. That's your aunt talking." Allison set a paring knife on the table next to a bowl of last year's apples she had brought up from the cellar.

Cinda sat down in one of the kitchen chairs. She thought Allison painted the perfect picture with her white apron over her light blue blouse and navy skirt and her blond curls pulled back with just a wisp dangling beside the smudge of flour on her cheek. She obviously enjoyed being a wife and mother-to-be.

Cinda forcefully pushed the thoughts away. She picked up an apple and started peeling. "How are you and the baby doing?"

Allison patted her growing stomach. "Great. He's an active one." Allison put a glob of dough on the floured end of the table. "David fusses over us already. He's going to be a great father."

"It's hard to believe you are six months along. You hardly show."

"Seven. It's this skirt and the apron over top." She smoothed the layers of fabric tightly at the top and bottom of her rounded tummy. She was definitely pregnant.

Cinda peeled apple after apple.

When Allison had the crusts rolled out, she sat down and sliced the peeled apples. "Out with it."

"What?" Cinda looked up from the apple she was peeling, surprised.

"You're frettin' over something. You might as well tell me before it spoils these pies." Allison waved her knife in the air.

"I'm sorry. I don't mean to bring my troubles down on you, but I'm in an awful fix. I don't know who else to turn to." Cinda let out a heavy sigh.

"What has your aunt Ginny done now?"

"It's not her this time, but I hate to think what she will say when she finds out." Cinda wiped her hands on the dish towel and laid it back on the table, then pulled a letter from her pocket. "It's this letter."

"Who's it from?"

Cinda lowered the letter to her lap and looked down. "A man."

"A man? Who?"

"I don't know."

"Didn't he sign it? Are you sure it's from a man then?" Allison picked up another apple and sliced it.

"Mr. Rawlings is definitely a man!"

"How do you know this Mr. Rawlings?"

"I don't," Cinda exclaimed. "That's just it. I've never heard of him until today when I opened this letter." She waved the letter in the air.

"It's probably just a mistake then. Take it back to the post office and tell them to return it to Mr. Rawlings." Allison let out a sigh of relief.

"I can't do that." Cinda could tell her friend was brushing this off as inconsequential.

"Then write to Mr. Rawlings yourself and tell him he made a mistake."

"I can't do that either."

"Why not?" Exasperation coated Allison's heavy sigh. "It would be the proper way to deal with it. Honestly, Cinda, when there's a man concerned, you can make a problem where there is none."

"He's coming here—today." Cinda's voice squeaked. "He's coming for me!"

When Allison's eyes widened, Cinda's stomach flipped. Cinda could tell her friend was trying to hide her surprise.

"Now, why would this Mr. Rawlings, whom you don't even know, be comin' after you?"

"I don't know." Cinda twisted her hands together in her lap. Her aunt had convinced her she was no good for any man; her tall stature had confirmed it in her own mind.

"It can't be all that bad." Allison patted Cinda's hand. "Read the letter aloud and let's see what Mr. Rawlings has to say."

Cinda unfolded the letter and drew in a deep breath. " 'Dear Miss Harrison,' " Cinda started calmly. "That's me. There is no mistaking that. I'm the only unmarried Harrison in town. In fact, I'm the *only* Harrison in town."

"Just read on."

" 'I have enjoyed your letters and feel I know you well.' " She stopped and looked at her friend. "Did you hear that? Letters. With an *s*, meaning more than one. He has *letters* from me! *I* didn't write any letters. How can he know me?"

"Go on," Allison said.

Cinda looked back to the letter. " 'After these months of correspondence, I look forward to finally meeting you.' *These months!*" Cinda choked out the words and looked wide-eyed at Allison. "He says he has been corresponding with me for months!"

"So far, there is nothing so terrible to have you so worked up."

"Oh, it gets worse. A lot worse."

"Just finish the letter. Or I'll be havin' this baby before I find out what all the fuss is about."

Fuss? Allison thought she was making a fuss over nothing. Well, she would soon see there was a great deal to fuss over. Cinda's hands shook as she continued.

> *Since we have come to know each other through our letters, and due to a deficiency of time, if it's all right with you, we will need to be married immediately and return for the spring planting.*

Cinda's voice was fairly shaking by now.

I will arrive in the afternoon on the second of April.

Yours truly,
Lucas Rawlings

Cinda meticulously refolded the letter. "That's what all the *fuss* is about."

The two women sat in silence for a few moments.

"The postman simply delivered it to the wrong house."

"No!" Cinda showed her the address. There was no mistake; the letter was meant for Cinda. "I'm a mail-order bride! What am I going to do?" This kind of thing might happen up north in Chicago—but not in their sleepy little town.

"There has to be a good explanation for all this," Allison said as she put the tops on the two pies and trimmed the edges. "Someone must have been writing to Mr. Rawlings using your name. Would you open the oven for me?" She picked up the pies and slid them into the oven.

Cinda closed the oven door. "Who would do that to me?"

The women fretted over that question while the pies baked. Finally, Allison jotted down something on a piece of paper and sent it off with the freckle-faced boy next door.

two

An hour after the note was sent, Vivian and Eve came prancing up onto the porch in a fit of giggles. Cinda and Allison were sitting in wooden rocking chairs on the front porch. Allison was knitting some booties for the baby, and Cinda was working on a half-sewn baby shirt. This was the first spring day warm enough to be outside, and despite their anxiety, they were enjoying the fresh air.

"Allison, it's good to see you looking so fit," Vivian said cordially.

"Yes. You do look fit, Allison," Eve echoed.

Eve wore a low-cut green velour walking dress with her shawl hanging around her elbows. Her black hair was pulled back in the front with ringlets cascading down behind. Vivian's tawny hair was done up in a stylish chignon with jeweled combs. She was dressed in a peach walking dress with a mass of ruffled lace about the neck, upper chest, and sleeves. Vivian could wear all that flounce because she was small, as were Eve and Allison. Cinda seemed to be the only one inflicted with height; she could never get away with all that frill on her tall frame. Suddenly, she drooped her shoulders and pulled her head down between them, feeling overly large.

Vivian and Eve turned simultaneously to Cinda. "How do you do, Cinda?" Eve said in greeting. She turned to Vivian and giggled again. A mischievous smile played on Vivian's lips.

"Sit down you two, and tell us all about Mr. Lucas Rawlings." Allison's irritation was evident in her tone.

11

The chastised Vivian and Eve sat down dutifully, one on a wooden bench and the other on a straight-back chair. "How did you find out about Lucas?" Vivian asked.

So these two are behind the mysterious letter. Had they written to Cinda pretending to be this man—or was there really a Lucas Rawlings? Cinda pulled out the letter. "I received this from him this morning."

"Vivian!" Eve scolded. "How did that get past you?"

"I haven't been at the post office much lately. My wedding is only two weeks off." Vivian folded her hands in her lap.

"Vivian, maybe you should tell us the whole story," Allison said.

"Oh, do let me tell it. It really is quite amusing," Eve jumped in, eager to tell all. "You remember when we stayed over at your parents' house the night before your wedding, Allison?" She paused until the others nodded, then continued. "Remember that advertisement in the ladies' magazine for finding a husband? Remember the letter we wrote? We sent the letter, Viv and I."

"It was just for fun. You said you weren't going to really mail it. *I* threw that letter away." Cinda was trying to convince herself that this couldn't be happening. Marry a stranger? The thought was appalling.

"I was the one who took it out of the trash. Viv and I rewrote it." Eve's grin widened as she pointed to herself. "We improved it."

Cinda felt the blood drain from her face. "I knew something bad would happen. I never should have agreed to let you use my name." She slumped in the chair and put her head back.

"Who else was there?" Vivian said. "Allison was getting married the next day. I had just gotten engaged. And Eve already had three beaus buzzing around her. It wouldn't have been fair to add another one to her hive when you had none."

"What happened after you sent the letter?" Allison's voice was tinged with annoyance.

"We didn't send it right away," Eve went on. "But about a month after we did send it, we received the first letter from Lucas. We wrote back to him, and before we knew it, we had a regular correspondence with the man."

"Regular correspondence!" Cinda gasped, confirming her fear. Her stomach knotted and lodged in her throat.

Allison gave Cinda a sorrowful look. "Where are the other letters?" Allison demanded.

Eve pulled a bundle of letters out of her reticule. "There are four of them." She handed them to Cinda.

Cinda stared at the stack, too paralyzed to take them from Eve. If she didn't touch them, they weren't real. It was all a bad dream, a nightmare.

Allison reached over and relieved Eve of the collection. "Shall I read them aloud, or do you want to read them in private?" she asked Cinda.

Cinda found it difficult to speak. All she could do was shake her head. She didn't want to know any more about the man. She wanted it not to be true. This couldn't be happening.

Allison took the top letter and opened it.

Dear Miss Harrison,
   I acquired your name through the Matrimonial Agency.

Cinda grimaced. She closed her eyes to block out Eve's and Vivian's excited faces.

Allison hesitated a moment then continued.

   I would very much like to begin correspondence with
you. Since we live some distance apart, I'll have to court

you by mail. If this arrangement is satisfactory with you,
I will expect to receive your correspondence.

Sincerely,
Lucas Rawlings

Cinda shook her head. No, it wasn't satisfactory.

"He's not very verbose," Vivian acknowledged, "but he does sound educated and refined."

"Educated and refined! He could be a desperado for all you know," Cinda shot at them.

Allison opened the next letter.

Dear Miss Harrison,

I'm sorry to say that I don't have a way with words as you do, but I will do my best to answer your many questions. I live on a prosperous farm outside a small town called Buckskin. Montana is the most beautiful country you will ever see. Majestic mountains that reach clear up to the big blue sky. Sparkling rivers and fertile ground. A man could grow just about anything here he put his mind to.

I am twenty-eight years old and share your love for the Lord. Life has not always been easy but God has been good to me.

I have never been married and so I have no children of my own. I do like children and hope to have some one day. Family is very important to me. It is the backbone of this country, God's own design.

I anxiously await your next letter.

Respectfully,
Lucas Rawlings

Cinda could feel Vivian's and Eve's eyes on her. Allison

opened the next letter.

No, no, Cinda wanted to shout. She didn't want to hear any more, but all she could do was sit there.

Dear Miss Harrison,

I do so enjoy your letters. To answer your further questions, most folks in town consider me tall, though I am not overly so. I have dark hair and blue eyes. Buckskin has a population of two hundred people, more or less, mostly cattle ranchers spread out across the rolling hills. We have a general store, telegraph-post office, church, and we even have a local doctor.

My farm lies to the south of town and supports six horses, twenty-five laying hens, a rooster, a milking cow, and a sow with nine piglets. There are also five apple trees, two peach trees, two cherry trees, and one plum tree, a large garden area, and even a water pump in the kitchen as well as one outside.

The house is two stories with four bedrooms and a large front porch with two rocking chairs. Not far from the house are wild blackberries and huckleberries. The farm does quite well and provides a good life.

I look forward to your next letter.

Cordially,
Lucas Rawlings

He sounded like a peddler selling his wares. Cinda sucked in a small, quick breath as Allison unfolded the last letter. Wouldn't she ever stop this torture? Cinda bit her bottom lip, knowing that this was the one where he asked *the question*.

Dear Miss Harrison,

I feel as if I know you so well from your letters and

*have come to the conclusion that we would be most com-
patible. I can provide well for you and give you a good
life.*

Cinda buried her face in her hands and shook her head as
Allison went on.

*I hope you don't think it improper of me to ask without
our ever having met, but as I said, I feel as if I know you.
Would you do me the honor of accepting my proposal of
marriage?*

*Warm regards,
Lucas Rawlings*

Cinda heard Allison fold the last letter and heard the shuffle
of papers as she added it to the others. The silence hung
heavy in the air.

Eve impatiently broke the silence. "So, what does our—or
should I say your dear Lucas have to say in his latest letter?"
she crooned.

"How could you two accept his marriage proposal?" Allison
scolded.

"Don't get huffy with us, Allison." Vivian preened the ruffles on her sleeves. "You want to see Cinda happily married
as much as anybody. We were only trying to do a favor for a
friend. She is our friend, too."

"I'm going to get hysterical if someone doesn't tell me
what is in that last letter," Eve said, coming off her seat.

Cinda heaved a sigh and relinquished the letter as Eve
plucked it from her hand. Cinda moved her lips to the words
as Eve read the dismal letter aloud. "Why, isn't today the second of April?" Eve's cheery tone settled a cloud of gloom and
doom over Cinda.

"Yes," Cinda moaned. It was true then. She was expected to marry a stranger whose arrival was imminent.

"We certainly didn't expect this." Eve's eyes brightened with excitement. "For him to rush out here as soon as he got a positive reply, I mean. I can't wait to finally meet him."

"Just what did you expect?" Cinda snapped.

Vivian shifted in her seat. "We expected to break the news to you first. . .slowly. . .gently. Then we'd giggle over wedding plans."

"He must be pretty desperate to rush out here, grab his bride, and vamoose." Eve's thoughtless words were out before she could stop them. She quickly gave Cinda a wide-eyed look. "I'm sorry. I didn't mean. . .oh." She stopped before she made things worse.

Is that what my friends really think of me? Cinda wondered. *That I could only be the wife of a desperate man?*

"You heard what he said in the letter. He has to get back for spring planting." Vivian sat rigid as she tried to smooth things over. "If he is desperate, it's only to be a good provider. He's being a perfect gentleman by coming all this way to escort you safely back to his home. He could have simply sent you train fare and let you travel all by yourself out to the wilds of Montana. That's the way it's usually done."

"Why are you pushing this, Viv?" Allison asked, eyeing her suspiciously.

"Because," Vivian said tightly, "because I want to believe Lucas is the right man for Cinda." She straightened the skirt of her dress, then her voice softened. "I don't want her to turn into an unhappy old maid. There! I've said it. I've said the terrible words we have been all thinking. . .old maid."

"Vivian, I had no idea you cared so much!" Allison said with surprise.

"Well, I do." Vivian looked off across the lawn, but Cinda

could see the sincerity on her face.

"I don't have to be married to be happy, Viv." Cinda stood and laid a hand on Vivian's shoulder. She could tell there was more to this for Vivian than a practical joke. Vivian placed her hand on Cinda's. "I don't even want to get married, ever."

Allison sputtered behind her, and Cinda turned to her. "What?"

Allison's mouth hung open in disbelief. "What do you mean 'what'?"

"Not every woman wants a husband."

Allison straightened in her chair. "Ever since the day we met, we've dreamed of getting married. When we were fourteen, we even planned our weddings. Remember?"

"That was *your* dream, Allison, not mine," Cinda interrupted before Allison could go on with any more unpleasant truths. "I just went along to make you happy."

She knew it was a lie, and she felt a rush of shame. Her whole life she had wanted a man to love her more than life itself, the way her father had loved her mother. But she knew now she would never have a love like that; she had given up that unattainable dream several years ago. Now, an inch and a half taller, the dream was even more impossible.

"I don't believe you. I know you better than that." Allison was near tears.

"I don't believe you either," Vivian stated matter-of-factly.

"I believe it. Give her a stack of dusty old books, and she'd be happy," Eve said.

"Eve!" Vivian scolded.

"If we are being honest here, then let's be honest," Eve said, a little indignantly. "This is the first time in three years I've seen her without a book in her hand."

Eve wasn't normally so blunt, but Cinda knew she never had understood Cinda's reluctance with men. Cinda walked to the end of the porch so no one would see the tears welling in her eyes.

"Didn't you ever think all that reading was to cover the pain?" Allison whispered, but Cinda could still hear.

"What pain?" Eve asked innocently.

"Eve, sometimes you are so impossible. You are so caught up in yourself you can't see anyone else," Allison said.

"Well, how do you like that. You try to be honest and this is the thanks you get," Eve said.

"Eve, hush!" Vivian said.

Cinda wiped her cheeks as Allison came over to where she leaned on the rail. "Is everything all right?"

"Fine. I just had something in my eye."

"Did you get it?" Allison asked. Cinda nodded. If her friend knew there was nothing in her eye except tears, she didn't say anything. For that Cinda was grateful. The two returned to the rocking chairs.

"Cinda, Eve and I are sorry." The sincerity in Vivian's voice touched Cinda. "We never meant to hurt you. We just wanted to make you happy."

"I am happy, just the way I am," Cinda said.

"You should at least give him a chance, after coming all this way," Eve said. "You never know, he may be your Prince Charming."

Cinda could tell Eve was trying to be encouraging, but her stomach was too knotted for her to respond.

three

As the four women continued their conversation on the porch, Cinda tried focusing on the beautiful spring weather. Vivian and Eve went on about the virtues of Lucas Rawlings and what they thought he was really like. "I think he's quite tall. Certainly tall enough for Cinda," Vivian said.

"He said he didn't consider himself tall. I think he could be short. He just didn't want to say so in his letters. Even if he is average, you know most men like a small—" Eve tried to soften the blow. "I mean a shorter woman for a wife."

"It doesn't matter one way or the other. We have it in writing, his offer of marriage. That's almost as good as a contract," Vivian said.

Cinda's stomach reeled and flipped. Some stranger was going to show up at her house to claim her. Fortunately, she would not be at home and Aunt Ginny would send him away. Still, she would have to face him sooner or later. How would she tell him she couldn't—she wouldn't—marry him, and that it was all a big mistake? What would he do when he found out he came all this way for nothing? She hoped he didn't have a violent temper. What if he insisted on her sticking to their agreement? But *she* hadn't agreed to anything; it was Eve and Viv who had done it all. A terrifying thought popped into her head. What if he forced her to marry him? He, too, had it in writing.

Cinda looked at Allison. Allison was shaking her head at something Eve had said. Cinda wanted to ask if she thought Mr. Rawlings could actually force her into marriage when a

20

tall figure crossing the lawn caught her attention.

His dark hair curled up from under the back of his bowler. He wore a white linen shirt, a faded green waistcoat, and a dark brown suit that looked like it had been years since it fit properly. If he moved too fast, the stitches would likely pop for the coat stretched taut across his wide shoulders. She couldn't help but think he was handsome, in an odd sort of way, even if he did look out of place in his old clothes and the stylish new bowler perched on his head.

"Good afternoon ladies," the tall man said, tipping his hat. "I was told I could find Miss Harrison here."

Cinda drew in a quick breath. *Me? Why would he want to see me? I don't know this man.*

"Who is it that wants to know?" Eve cooed, leaning on the porch rail.

"Lucas Rawlings, Ma'am." He removed his bowler, revealing his unfashionably long hair.

Cinda's eyes grew large. For a moment she forgot how to breathe. She couldn't help but notice his clear blue eyes even from a distance. But what was he doing there?

Cinda and Allison exchanged glances. Allison patted her arm as she rose and went down the steps to greet him. "Mr. Rawlings, it's nice to finally meet you."

❧

Lucas looked at the blond, bewildered. He was expecting a redhead instead of this delightful blond smiling up at him. She'd probably blow away in a good strong wind. He smiled back. "Miss Harrison?"

He took her hand and was about to kiss it when he felt a hand clamp down hard on his shoulder. He whirled around and caught the first punch in the palm of his right hand. His hand engulfed the other man's fist and held it firmly. "I don't think you want to do that," Lucas said through gritted teeth. A muscle in his jaw twitched. He clenched his left fist still at his side.

A fight would not make a good impression on his bride-to-be. He would avoid it if possible. He stared at the smaller man in front of him, willing him to back down.

"David, stop it!" the blond practically screamed. "I can explain everything—later. Now let him go."

David yanked his hand free and stepped backward. "Keep your hands off my wife." David ground out each word.

"I understood that *Miss* Harrison wasn't married," Lucas said while his focus never left the smaller man. He didn't come for a fight, but he could certainly finish one if necessary.

David wrapped a possessive arm around the woman and said, "This is Mrs. David Swan."

"My mistake, Mrs. Swan." Lucas gave the woman a nod and slight smile.

Two other women slid up next to Mrs. Swan. "Ooo, you're a tall one," the black-haired woman cooed.

An elegant smile slid into place on the other woman's face, and she held out her hand to him. "I'm Miss Vivian Van Dornick." Her tawny hair was pulled up in a sophisticated twist.

Lucas declined the offer of her hand. He dipped his head as he said, "Pleased to meet you, Miss Van Dornick."

"Soon to be Mrs. Alvin Pratt," the black-haired woman said, slipping in front of her. "I'm Miss Eve Weston. Do call me Eve." She held out his hat that he had flung to the ground when David had abruptly arrived.

Lucas's blue eyes flashed to the immodestly dressed Eve. He slowly shrank away from her as he reached for his hat. "Thank you, Miss Weston." Lucas had a little difficulty getting it from her grasp. She had offered it to him but now seemed to be reluctant to give it up. He was relieved she hadn't introduced herself as Miss Harrison. He couldn't imagine spending his life with her purring around.

"I came to see Miss Harrison." Lucas raised his hat to his head. "If she's not here, I'll be on my way."

"She's here," Mrs. Swan said quickly and turned to call her down from the porch. But the porch was empty. She turned back around slowly and said with a polite smile, "Miss Harrison is indisposed at the moment."

Lucas looked toward the house. He remembered there had been four ladies on the porch when he arrived. He couldn't recall what the fourth woman looked like; everything happened so fast. He did recall her letter said she had auburn hair.

"Mr. Rawlings, would you be so kind as to come back for supper? Miss Harrison would be glad to see you then," Mrs. Swan offered.

Lucas glanced at David who still had his arm wrapped protectively around his wife. His piercing glare continued to drill Lucas. "I don't think your husband would approve of that, Ma'am."

"David, tell Mr. Rawlings he's welcome in our home." When David remained silent, the little blond jabbed her husband in the ribs with her elbow and said through a forced smile, "David! Tell him."

David let out a gust of air. "You're welcome to come for supper." David's glare never wavered.

Lucas could tell by the man's look he didn't want him to return. "Until then." He dipped his head. "Ladies. Mr. Swan, Mrs. Swan. Good day."

"We eat at seven," Mrs. Swan called after him.

"I'll be here." Lucas walked down the street.

❧

Cinda had watched in disbelief as Allison went down the steps and greeted Mr. Rawlings on the lawn. David seemed to appear out of nowhere, and the two men were instantly locked in a confrontation, David's hand engulfed by the tall stranger's. Cinda's hand flew to her mouth as she gasped. *That brute is going to hit sweet David,* she thought. He could easily whip poor David.

But after a verbal reprimand from Allison, the men disengaged. Everyone was safe. Now if he would only leave, Cinda could breathe easily. She hoped Allison would just send him away. She watched as Vivian and Eve got up. *Where are they going?*

Mr. Rawlings's rich, deep voice reverberated up to the porch, though she couldn't hear what he or anyone was saying. But she knew it was only a matter of time before she was called down to join the group gathered on the grass. That was one trip she was not ready to make. She slipped inside the door and hoped no one noticed her unladylike escape.

She leaned against the wall next to the door. With her hands clenched at her chest, she held her breath and waited for someone to call after her. No one called her name. She let out her breath but stood frozen to the wall, listening to the muffled voices outside, unable to hear what they were saying. Curious as to what was going on, she peered around the edge of the front window, being careful to remain unseen. Mr. Rawlings said something, then left. *Good, the ruffian has gone.* She couldn't help but watch and wonder about him as he walked away.

Cinda hoped and prayed Allison, Vivian, and Eve had the good sense to tell Mr. Rawlings it was all a mistake. Then she would never even have to face the man or explain the unfortunate situation to him.

four

Cinda had barely stepped through the door before her aunt started in on her. "Where have you been all day?" Cinda's aunt Ginny dried her hands on her apron. Her tone was accusing, her lips pinched. "I've been working all day by myself while you have been off doing who knows what."

"But you don't like anyone in your kitchen," Cinda said, her nerves still frayed from the day's events. She hung up her hat and shawl on the wall pegs by the door.

"Well, you could have done a little fetch and carry for me. I can't be expected to do everything around here. With all the cooking, there is so little time left to do the other house chores." Aunt Ginny liked making elaborate meals that kept her busy in the kitchen, far busier than she needed to be.

Cinda had come to live with her aunt and uncle eleven years ago when she was twelve. Her father had just died and her mother had died three years earlier. Uncle Barney and Aunt Ginny, being her only relatives, took her in. Uncle Barney welcomed her warmly with open arms, but Aunt Ginny had always kept a cool distance.

Cinda knew if she had been home today her aunt would have found fault with her, saying she was in the way and useless. It didn't matter what she did, it was always wrong in her aunt's eyes. "I would be happy to help you with the cooking if you would only—"

Her aunt cut her off. "Do you know how to knead bread dough so it rises properly for baking?"

"No, but—"

"Can you mix up piecrust and roll it out even and make up a pie so the crust is flaky?"

"No." Cinda sighed. It was the same old argument, over and over.

"What about roast a chicken tender so it almost falls from the bone and isn't scorched and shriveled?"

"No, but—"

"Then what use would you be in my kitchen?"

"I could learn if you would teach me." Cinda spoke quickly so she wouldn't be overridden again.

"I have too much work to do to be wasting time teaching you what your mother should have." Aunt Ginny straightened her apron and headed back to the kitchen. "You could at least set the table for supper," she said over her shoulder.

Cinda walked into the dining area just off the kitchen. "I'm glad to help in any way I can." She automatically removed three plates from the cupboard, then put one back. There would be one less for supper tonight. What would her aunt have to say about that?

"You say that now; but put hard work in front of you, you will crumble," her aunt called from the kitchen. "Mark my words. No man wants to marry a girl who can't cook and keep a house."

No man? Cinda sighed, dropping her shoulders and head simultaneously. The strong, dark-haired stranger who came to claim her as his bride flashed before her eyes. He wanted her, or at least he thought he did.

"Stand up straight," her aunt said, strolling into the room. "Ladies don't slouch. Haven't you learned anything?"

Cinda snapped to attention

"A man stopped by this afternoon. A very tall man."

Cinda's eyes got large. That was how Mr. Rawlings had found her. He came there first. What had he said to Aunt

Ginny? What had she said to him?

"I didn't like the looks of him. He's not from around here. But then it's none of my business what you do."

Cinda rolled her eyes.

"I told him you were probably over at Allison's. But then how was I to know where you were, you went flying out of here so fast this morning." She waved her hand as if shooing a fly. "Did he find you over at Allison's?" She turned to face Cinda with her hands perched on her hips.

"Yes," was all Cinda could manage. She wasn't sure what to say. How much did her aunt know?

"Who is he?"

"I really don't know. It was all some sort of mistake." Cinda hoped her aunt wouldn't grill her any further.

"He seemed sure he knew you." Her aunt pointed at the table. "You forgot a plate."

Cinda decided to ignore her aunt's prodding and take advantage of the opportunity to change the subject. "Allison invited me over for supper. I hope you don't mind."

"Why should I mind? You spend more time at her house than you do here. I don't know why you even bother to come home at all sometimes."

Cinda dropped her head and turned to leave the room.

"Stand up straight!" her aunt called after her.

Cinda snapped up straight and went to her room to slouch in solitude. She pulled out the green dress Allison had suggested she wear. Allison said it would enhance her green eyes, but Cinda didn't want to enhance her eyes. She wanted to calm the fluttering in her stomach by backing out. She still couldn't believe her best friend had betrayed her, but she had promised she would have supper with Mr. Rawlings at Allison and David's, so she would go and be perfectly miserable.

꿍

Cinda stood in the kitchen doorway. Even though she wasn't sure what to do, she wanted to be in the kitchen doing something to keep busy. David was even put to work, but Allison wouldn't let Cinda help with supper because she might spill something. "Allison, I thought you were on my side."

"I am." Allison paused from her work at the stove. "You just haven't realized yet that this *is* your side."

"He nearly hit your husband, and you want him inside your home?" Cinda hoped she could talk her friend out of this.

"No. David nearly hit him." Allison waved a wooden spoon in Cinda's direction. "He was only defending himself, and nobody got hurt."

"Did you see his clothes? They weren't well tailored and they are out of style. And what about his hair?"

"Give the poor man a chance. He came all this way. The least you can do is talk with him a little. If he is completely repulsive, I'll have David throw him out."

"Just say the word and I'll throw him out before he steps inside," David said with a smile on his face.

"David, you wouldn't."

Cinda stood back, nearly forgotten as the two argued over her future.

"If Cinda doesn't want to see him, he's not coming in." David's words were stern and not to be questioned.

"This is no different than your inviting over suitors for Cinda," Allison said, her attention focused on her husband.

"Except this man expects a little more than supper conversation. He's planning on a wedding!" David was clearly irritated at what his wife had roped him into.

"This is better. The hard part is done. They already know each other, so to speak. Cinda just has to carry on polite conversation. We'll have a nice meal and learn a little about him.

If Cinda decides she doesn't want to marry him, she can tell him about the little misunderstanding." Allison turned her pleading eyes on Cinda. "Please."

❧

Lucas stood outside the gate at the Swans' residence. He pulled out his pocket watch and looked at the time once again, one minute to seven. He had come early to make sure he wasn't late and ended up wandering around to kill time. He didn't want to be early and seem overly eager.

He looked down at his ash gray suit and shifted his coat. This suit fit almost as poorly as the one he had worn that afternoon. On the farm he didn't have much use for a suit. He was going to save it for the wedding, but he had decided making a good first impression was more important. Now he wished he had bought a new suit.

He strode up to the door. His hands felt oddly empty as he looked at them. *Flowers!* Women liked flowers. He fisted his hands. Why didn't he think of it before? Or candy. He could have gotten candy. It was too late now. He swallowed hard and knocked on the door. He wasn't sure what kind of a reception he would get after this afternoon.

The door opened. The moment of truth. Mrs. Swan's friendly smile greeted him. She graciously invited him in. At least one person was glad to see him.

Lucas shook David Swan's outstretched hand and met his disapproving stare. Mr. Swan's words and actions were welcoming, but his glare told Lucas he wasn't. Obviously, Mr. Swan was cordial for his wife's sake, but Lucas refused to be intimidated. He backed down once to a man much less threatening than this David Swan when he was young, and he had regretted it ever since. Never again.

Allison drew his attention away from David. "This is who you really came to see," she said, motioning toward Cinda.

"Mr. Rawlings, this is Miss Harrison."

Before him stood a beautiful woman in a modest green dress. Her dark, auburn hair was neatly pulled back and swept up on her head. She was the picture of femininity and not at all too short either. He wouldn't spend the rest of his life looking down at the top of her head. Why would this stunning woman need to be a mail-order bride? Surely she had several beaus. He had expected a homely, somewhat plump, unmarriageable woman.

"Pleased to meet you," Cinda said with a slight nod of her head but her gaze didn't quite meet his.

"The pleasure is mine." Lucas watched as her cheeks flushed.

He was glad to see his intended was modestly dressed—not like Miss Weston with her low-cut dress and forward manner.

Allison kept the meal from being eaten in complete silence by plying him with question after question. He answered attentively, but his attention kept drifting back to the quiet young woman across from him.

"Miss Harrison told us about all your animals and that large house. It all sounds really nice. I would love to have all those fruit trees," Allison said, filling the silence. Lucas wished she had used his fiancée's first name, but everyone was acting stiff and formal.

"A mighty big house for just one man," David said skeptically, insinuation in his tone. He had remained silent until now, but Lucas figured he was about to do a lot more talking before the meal was over. "And an awful lot of livestock and fruit."

Lucas shifted uncomfortably, looking down at his plate to take another bite. "I took the place over from the previous owner, lock, stock, and barrel." He raised his eyes in time to see Allison admonish her husband with a scolding look.

At that moment he caught Miss Harrison looking at him. He had guessed her eyes would be brown and he couldn't have been more pleased to be wrong. She had the most brilliant green eyes he had ever seen. They were greener than any emerald. He had never seen a real emerald, but no gem could be as beautiful as those sparkling green depths. She quickly diverted her gaze back to her plate.

"So, Mr. Rawlings, do you run that big farm of yours all by yourself?" Allison asked.

He cleared his throat. "I have help. We hire extra hands when it gets busy."

"We?" David said, clearly looking for anything to question.

Lucas looked him squarely in the eyes. "I have a couple of guys who are pretty regular out at the place."

"Sorta like family?" David said in a condescending tone.

"I suppose you could say that." He swallowed hard. "This is delicious beef, Mrs. Swan." He turned back to his plate and took another bite. He hoped that would terminate Mr. Swan's accusing questions. He much preferred Mrs. Swan's polite, dignified ones.

"I thought Montana was cattle country." David said.

Lucas had to give Mr. Swan credit for his persistence. "Most of it is." Before he could elaborate, Mrs. Swan, bless her soul, jumped back in the conversation.

"We aren't interested in cows and farming. We want to know more about you, your family."

Family? That was a subject he would like to avoid for the time being. Thankfully his mouth was full and he had a moment to think while he chewed slowly.

"Where are they from?"

"Virginia," he said upon swallowing.

"It must be really lonesome in Montana for you," she said, giving a sly sideways peek at his intended.

Lucas stole a glance, too. His bride-to-be sat staring at her plate with flushed cheeks. "It's not so bad," he said.

"Then why come all this way to get a wife?" David folded his arms across his chest, a challenge in his eyes. "Aren't there any women in Montana?"

"David."

He ignored his wife and went on. "Certainly there must be one that would want all you have to offer? This is all a little too good to be true. Maybe the Montana women know something we don't?"

"David!"

"What's wrong?" David leaned forward across the table. "What aren't you telling us?"

"Dessert anyone?" Miss Harrison's voice cracked as she pushed away from the table, successfully terminating the conversation. Allison cleared the dinner plates and served dessert.

"This pie is delicious, Mrs. Swan," Lucas said, breaking the long silence.

"Your fiancée helped," she said, indicating Miss Harrison. He looked at her and saw her blush. Again her first name wasn't used.

He had hoped to get to talk with her, but she kept her eyes on her plate and said nothing unless she was directly asked. Even then, her answers were short and to the point.

She wasn't at all like her letters. Her letters had been lengthy, flowing from one subject to another. But then he supposed he wasn't much like his letters either. He glanced at David, who glared back at him. What kind of a hold did this David Swan have on his fiancée? Once away from him, it would be easier to talk with her; he was sure of that.

But David drilled him with a menacing stare all night. What was his problem?

"May I escort you home, Miss Harrison?" Lucas asked

after dessert. Maybe she would open up more when not under Mr. Swan's scrutiny.

Lucas didn't like how protective David was over *his* soon-to-be wife. She seemed to be shy with David around. She didn't seem so shy in her letters, but confident and self-assured.

❧

Cinda didn't know what to say. She dreaded the thought of being alone with Mr. Rawlings, but how could she gracefully decline? Fortunately, David came to her rescue. "A walk sounds nice. We'll all go." He reached for his wife's coat.

Cinda was relieved she wouldn't be left alone with him.

"David, I'm not feeling well." Allison lowered herself to the sofa and rested her hands on her stomach. "We'll have to pass on that walk tonight."

"If you're not feeling well, I can stay," Cinda offered, seating herself next to Allison. She wanted to stay as much for herself as for her friend.

"Nonsense. You go on home. I'm just a little tired. We've got David to look after us." She patted her belly.

Cinda reluctantly accepted Lucas's offered arm. She didn't know what to say to this stranger. Should she tell him flat out what Vivian and Eve had done? He would think she was childish and backward. She could always tell him she changed her mind. Then he would think she was fickle and petty.

❧

Lucas and his betrothed walked along in silence. The first half of the walk he tried to decide the best way to bring up the wedding. This wasn't as easy as he had thought. He had imagined strolling into town, getting hitched, and hopping on the next train out of town with a bride in tow. He had proposed. She had accepted. Everything had been settled. Hadn't it? Now he felt like he was starting all over—courting! If marriage weren't necessary, he would call the whole thing off and hightail it home.

She shivered in the cool night air. Lucas quickly shed his coat and draped it around her shoulders. When she looked up at him, he thought she might refuse it, but instead she pulled it around her more tightly. "Thank you." She spoke so softly he almost couldn't understand her.

The silence was finally broken. Lucas decided to take advantage of it and start a conversation. "You know I don't even know your first name." He succeeded in making his question light and inoffensive.

"You don't?" She looked up at him, startled.

He smiled down at her, seeing her face clearly in the moon light; long dark lashes framed her green eyes. "Your letters were all signed Miss Harrison," he said in a musing tone.

"Oh." She looked away. "I didn't realize."

"You do have a name, don't you?" he teased.

"Yes," she said, smiling. "Cinda."

"Cindy. That's pretty. I like it." He was making headway; at least she was talking to him. She looked at him sideways as if to say something, but she remained silent.

He was considering bringing up the wedding when they reached her house. He held the gate open for her. Cindy whisked through the gate and turned, closing it behind her. "Thank you for walking me home." She held out his coat to him.

He took the coat and looked down at the gate that was obviously meant to keep him away. "My pleasure." His bride-to-be was more reserved than her letters. She was a nice blend of grace and dignity, a real lady. Just what he was looking for.

Unsure of what he had done to make her skittish, he decided to take it slow. He wanted this to work. He would wait until tomorrow to broach the subject of the wedding. That gate wasn't the only barrier between them. "Until tomorrow," he said, tipped his hat, and left.

When Lucas got a little way down the street, he noticed the figure of a man leaning against a maple tree. *David Swan!* Lucas was furious. He strode up to David and stopped. "You followed us?"

David stood silent against the tree with his arms folded, suspicion etched on his face.

Lucas shook his head and walked on. He knew David didn't trust him. It didn't really matter. Once he and Cindy were married, the man would be out of their lives for good.

❧

Cinda leaned against the porch rail and let out a sigh of relief when Mr. Rawlings disappeared into the night. Even though he had been polite all evening, she was uncomfortable. If she hadn't closed the gate on him, she was sure he would have insisted on coming up to the door, or worse, wanted to come inside.

Cinda crept into the house, careful to close the door without a sound. She wanted to slip upstairs undetected.

"That's the same man who was here this afternoon," her aunt called from the parlor when she was only three steps up the staircase.

She couldn't avoid her aunt now. Cinda put on a smile and glided into the parlor. Her uncle sat in a winged chair, puffing on his pipe, She greeted him with a kiss on the cheek. "Good evening, Uncle Barney." She turned to her aunt and said formally, "Aunt Ginny."

Aunt Ginny nodded as she poked at her sewing. "I didn't see a chaperone." Her words were clipped. "It's not proper for a young lady to be escorted without a chaperone."

Aunt Ginny usually referred to her as a lady but treated her like a child. Cinda knew her aunt wouldn't give up until she explained Lucas Rawlings. Cinda took a deep breath. "Allison invited Mr. Rawlings to supper. He's visiting."

"Does he have relatives in town? Who is he visiting?" her aunt asked, prying as usual.

How was she going to answer that question without lying? She certainly couldn't tell her aunt he was here to marry her. "He has friends in town." In a way, he did.

"I don't like this. I don't like this one bit," her aunt said between pinched lips.

"Oh, leave the poor girl alone," Uncle Barney said, waving his pipe in the air. "So she has a beau." Her uncle popped his pipe back in his mouth and sucked on it.

"Umph." Her aunt went back to jabbing at her sewing.

Thank you, Uncle Barney. He often stood up for her when her aunt got difficult.

Cinda retreated to her bedroom and readied herself for bed. She found sleep elusive and needed desperately to talk about the sufferings of the day. The stress-filled day swirled in her mind. She closed her eyes and lifted her ordeal up to her heavenly Father. A calm settled around her. She got out the letters from Mr. Rawlings and reread them with curiosity. Her fears renewed, she prayed again until she finally succumbed to sleep.

five

Cinda sprang out of bed. The sun had been up for some time. She rushed about, trying to dress as quickly as possible. She wanted to visit Allison and be back before Mr. Rawlings came to call. If her aunt got hold of him again, there was no telling what she would get the unsuspecting man to confess. She skipped breakfast, giving herself enough time for a quick visit with Allison.

When she heard her aunt's voice outside, Cinda peered out her bedroom window. She sucked in a quick breath and blinked several times. This couldn't be happening—Aunt Ginny and Lucas Rawlings. . .talking! Cinda quickly pinned her hat on and rushed down the stairs with her shawl draped over her arm.

When Cinda came up to the pair, Lucas was speaking. "Mrs. Crawford, I assure you, your niece and I had chaperones all evening. Mr. Swan was kind enough to accompany us and remain a distance back when I escorted Miss Harrison home."

David had followed them! Cinda wanted to turn around and hide in the house, but it would be more embarrassing if Lucas Rawlings stated his real reason for being there and her aunt said she knew nothing about it. Cinda didn't think their conversation had gotten around to it—yet. Her fear of her aunt finding out about Lucas Rawlings won over her trepidation of Mr. Rawlings.

"Mr. Rawlings, it's nice to see you again." Cinda wrapped her shawl about her shoulders. Although she managed to speak pleasantly, her stomach tightened. She turned to her aunt and said, "I'm going to look in on Allison. She was feeling poorly

37

last night when I left her. I want to make sure she's doing better today."

Lucas replaced his hat and opened the gate for Cinda. "Good day, Mrs. Crawford." When the gate closed, Lucas offered his arm to Cinda. She took it and the two left the annoyed Aunt Ginny behind.

"You spend a lot of time at your friend's house, don't you?" Lucas said.

"Yes. We've been best friends since we were twelve. I don't know what I would do without her." Lucas's arm tensed.

Cinda felt as though the eyes of the whole town were on her as she walked along with this tall handsome stranger. She had wanted to talk to Allison before she saw him again. Last night in her sleeplessness, Cinda decided to tell Mr. Rawlings she couldn't possibly leave her best friend in her time of need. She would tell him she would come along later, then write a letter saying she had had a change of heart. She would tell him she was terribly sorry for his inconvenience and wish him well. But she needed to talk to Allison first to gain her courage. Allison could even tell him how much she needed Cinda to be around, this being her first baby.

Lucas drew in a deep breath. "Cindy."

She cringed slightly at the mispronunciation of her name. Her whole life she had corrected people on her name.

"I feel like I know you fairly well from your letters."

She knew him a little, too, through his letters that she had read three more times last night. It was evident he worked hard, loved God, family, and his land.

"I think we should talk about the arrangements. . .for the wedding, I mean."

Cinda bit her bottom lip. He had done it now. She couldn't avoid it any longer. He sounded as uncomfortable as she felt. What should she say? "Yes, I suppose we should" fell out of her mouth. Her knees went soft and she hoped they didn't give out on her before she reached Allison's.

"I'll find a minister for this afternoon. . .if that's all right with you?"

"No!" This afternoon definitely was not all right. "I mean," she took a moment and a deep breath to calm herself, "the ministers are usually very busy on weekends."

"I suppose we can wait until Monday if we have to," Lucas said. "I was hoping to be on our way home by Monday."

Home? "You may not be able to get anyone until Tuesday." The longer she put it off, the more time she had to think.

He stopped her on Allison's lawn and said, "You haven't changed your mind, have you?"

Since she never agreed to marry him in the first place, she could honestly say no. "No, I haven't *changed* my mind."

He walked her up to the door. Cinda hoped he wouldn't stay; she couldn't very well talk about him to Allison with him there. He knocked on the door.

Allison answered the door and her usual friendly smile broadened. "Good morning."

"Good morning, Mrs. Swan. I hope you're feeling better this morning," Lucas said, removing his hat.

"Much better, thank you. A good night's sleep was all I needed." Her eyes flitted back and forth between Lucas and Cinda.

"I'm glad to hear that." He turned to Cinda and said, "I'll see you here later then."

Cinda nodded with a forced smile, and he was gone.

The two women sat in the parlor. "You seem to be getting along fine with Mr. Rawlings." Allison still smiled, quite pleased. "Last night, now early this morning, and he'll see you later. I take it things are going well with you two."

"It's awful. He's going to make arrangements with a

minister." Cinda's voice cracked as she spoke.

"Then I take it you didn't tell him the truth?"

"I sort of told the truth," Cinda confessed. "I told him I hadn't changed my mind."

"Giving him the impression you are going to marry him."

"Allison, I know when I was younger I thought I could only be happy if I married and had children, but I have realized since then I can be happy by myself as well."

"I know you can, but isn't this an answer to your prayers?" Allison asked.

"I never prayed for this." Cinda's anguish painted every syllable. "I can't. I don't know how to be a wife. I can't even cook. What did Vivian and Eve tell him about me? Do you think he knows I can't cook?"

"You can learn."

"Who will teach me? Mr. Rawlings? I can't very well ask him to teach me to cook. He's expecting me to be the one who can cook."

"You're smart. You'll learn."

"No, I can't."

"Remember when Mrs. Pennywell had her baby? You went over and helped her with the housekeeping and her other three children while she was gaining her strength back. And what about Miss Stern? She was sick for nearly three weeks, and you took over her schoolroom. I believe her comment was 'If I'm not careful, Cinda Harrison, you'll steal my job right out from under me.' She was glad she had someone dependable and competent to call on. You didn't know what you were doing those times either. There are a number of other times you have helped out in a pinch. I don't believe there is anything you couldn't do. You always seem to rise to the occasion."

"That was different. I already knew those people. This is permanent."

Allison shook her head. "I thought I knew David well before we married. We grew up together, but I find out more and more about him all the time. The more I find out, the more I realize I don't know."

Allison's words did nothing to settle Cinda's anxiety.

Later, Vivian and Eve showed up to find out what had happened the previous night. The four women were chatting out on the porch when David returned home.

"I can't go through with it," Cinda said.

"Go through with what?" David asked.

"Marrying Lucas." Eve answered for her and giggled.

Eve sounded so chipper about this whole thing. After all, she wasn't the one expected to uproot herself and move hundreds of miles away and perform tasks she had never done before. He would find out and be angry with her. "I can't. I just can't."

"If you don't want to marry him, don't. I would be happy to break the news to Mr. Lucas Rawlings." David normally didn't like to speak on someone else's behalf, but since his wife was partly responsible, even in a small way, he would step in if Cinda wanted him to.

"Oh, David," Allison said.

Cinda wrung her hands in her lap. "I don't know what to do."

"You had better decide quickly because here comes Prince Charming," Vivian said.

David looked across the lawn at Lucas then back at Cinda. "Do you want to marry him?" His tone was urgent.

She pressed her teeth into her bottom lip. She wasn't sure what she wanted anymore. "No," she said, "I don't think so."

David bounded off the porch and stopped Lucas from coming any farther. "You are not welcome here."

Lucas took a controlled breath. "I'm here to see Miss Harrison. She's expecting me."

"She doesn't want to see you—ever again." The emphasis

David put on "ever again" carried an unmistakable message.

The two men glared at each other for several minutes, then Lucas looked up at Cinda on the porch. She diverted her gaze, unable to look him in the eye. Lucas turned and walked away.

On her way home, Cinda couldn't stop worrying about whether or not she had done the right thing. She wrapped and rewrapped the end of her shawl around her hand. Mr. Rawlings was never ill-mannered and his intentions were honorable. She feared he might insist upon seeing her when David sent him away, but he left without making a scene. A scene David probably wanted. Why was David so itchy to get in a fight with a man so much bigger than himself?

Near her home, she saw Lucas Rawlings leaning casually against a tree, watching her approach. Her heart lurched up in her throat, and she came to a sudden halt. Had he really waited all this time for her? She continued walking slowly, not looking at him. When she was almost to him, he said, "Mr. Swan said you don't want to see me. I assume that means the wedding is called off?" His voice was level and calm, controlled.

Cinda stopped and sunk her head lower. "I–I'm sorry. I–I can't marry you." She nearly choked on each word. He said nothing. *What must he be thinking? Is he mad at me?* She inched her gaze up until she met him eye to eye. He didn't look mad, only disappointed and maybe hurt. She regretted her tactlessness.

"I thought you were the right woman. Obviously, I was mistaken."

A sudden pang inside her made her want to be that right woman. He turned and walked away without saying another word.

How could she have hurt the poor man? He had been kind and gentlemanly. She in turn cut his heart out. Tears burned Cinda's eyes as she ran into the house.

six

"I saw you out there with him again." Her aunt's curt words stung. "Don't tell me there is nothing. Twice yesterday and then twice again today. He's got designs on you. You shouldn't encourage the likes of him."

Cinda wanted to ignore her aunt and go to her room, but her aunt was insulting an innocent man. It wasn't his fault. She turned to face her aunt. "What do you mean the likes of him? There is nothing wrong with. . .Lucas." She felt funny using his first name when she hardly knew the man, but she did it to irritate her aunt. "And I'm not encouraging him."

"Lucas is it now," Aunt Ginny said with shock in her voice. "If that isn't encouraging a man, being so familiar with him, I don't know what is."

"Yes, Lucas." Cinda swallowed hard, then blurted out, "He's my—fiancé."

"Fiancé!" Her aunt glared at her. "Then there has been something going on and for sometime, I would say."

"We've been corresponding for months, and he has now come to marry me. You have no say about it." Cinda had no idea why she was saying such things. She wanted her aunt to see she couldn't run her life entirely.

"I have plenty to say about it." Aunt Ginny perched her balled fists on her hips. "Your father would be very disappointed in you, sneaking around like this."

"I'm not sneaking around, and you leave my father out of this. You have no idea what he would think." She hated it when her aunt mentioned her father. She did it to get Cinda to

43

do what she wanted her to do. Not this time.

"You don't think he would actually approve of that. . .that giant?"

Cinda walked across the room and said tersely, "He's just the kind of man my father would have chosen for me. He's a hardworking farmer, conscientious, and a perfect gentleman, too." In fact, Cinda thought him a lot like her father.

"Gentleman!" Her aunt shook her finger in the air as she spoke. "A true gentleman would never wear such an ill-fitting suit. He may have a few manners but no real sophistication. Your father was a true gentleman, and I know he would never—"

Cinda turned on her aunt, leveling her gaze. "My father was a caring, forgiving man who saw the good in people, who could see the good in anybody—even you." Her sharp tone surprised even herself.

"Your father spoke kindly of me?" Aunt Ginny's voice suddenly became soft.

Cinda noticed the change in her aunt but ignored it because of her own anger. "Of course. He never had a bad word to say about anyone."

After a moment, her aunt took a quick breath. "I still don't think he would approve of this Mr. Rawlings."

"You know nothing about Lucas, but you can easily judge him." Cinda shook her head and turned to leave the room.

"Well, you can't think much of him or you would have mentioned him before now. You must be embarrassed by him. Why else wouldn't you have introduced him to your uncle and me? I don't believe one word of this, not one word," her aunt called to Cinda's back.

"Believe what you like, you will anyway," Cinda shot back over her shoulder as she ascended the stairs.

Cinda closed herself in her room and ignored her aunt's

knock at suppertime. Her stomach churned with misgivings, and she didn't have the vigor for another round with her aunt. She wanted to be alone.

She flitted from the dresser, to the window, and over to her writing desk, finally landing on the edge of the bed. As quickly as she sat down, she was up again making the rounds.

This was all Vivian's and Eve's doing. They were the ones who got Lucas and her mixed up in this. She felt sorry for Lucas Rawlings. He hadn't asked for their cruel joke. They hadn't meant for it to be cruel, but it had turned out that way. He believed every word they wrote and got caught in the snare with Cinda. Eve might have done it for the sheer thrill, but Cinda believed Vivian actually wanted to help. But Lucas Rawlings was innocent in all this. He had been led along and ended up with nothing. Cinda could give him one thing—the truth. It was the least he deserved.

If he really was in such a hurry, he would probably be on the first train he could catch. There was no reason for him to stick around now. She would have to go tonight before he left town, if he wasn't gone already. She whisked down the stairs.

"It's about time you came down," her aunt called out to her before she could reach the door. "I want you to tell your uncle what you told me this afternoon. He won't like it any better than I, and don't expect him to believe you either. Go on, tell him."

"Ginny," her uncle said, "if you want Cinda to tell me something, hush up so she can speak."

"You won't believe it, I tell you." Her aunt paused briefly. "Well, go on and tell him, or are you too ashamed?"

"Virginia! Not one more word from you until Cinda has spoken."

Ginny pinched her lips together.

Cinda looked from her aunt's accusing face to her uncle's

kind, gentle face. He waited patiently until she had her thoughts collected and was ready to speak. "What Aunt Ginny is talking about is. . ." She hesitated. Where should she start—with Mr. Rawlings himself or with Vivian and Eve?

"The gentleman caller you had yesterday?" he asked when Cinda had trouble continuing.

"And today. He called again—" Her aunt stopped short when Uncle Barney shot her a look of reproof.

Cinda, too, had looked at her aunt but now she turned back to her uncle. "Yes, the gentleman caller. His name is Lucas Rawlings. He has a farm in Montana." Cinda tried to keep her tone even, unsure of how to say everything. She knew her aunt wouldn't let her get away before she had told him the whole story.

"Montana? He's a long way from home. What's he doing way out here?" her uncle asked. "Does he have business in town?"

Cinda looked over at her aunt. She had a smug look on her face. Cinda took a deep breath and turned back to her uncle. "He came to see me." Cinda dropped her gaze to the floor. "To marry me."

"Cinda? Why would Mr. Rawlings come all this way to marry you?" Her uncle's words were filled with shock and concern.

"We've been corresponding, sort of."

"You've been writing back and forth, and now he has come to ask you to marry him without consulting with me?" Her uncle's tone wasn't one of anger but rather concern.

"Not exactly." Cinda nervously told her uncle about the letters and Vivian's and Eve's part in the whole thing.

"I knew there was more to this than you were letting on," Aunt Ginny said, then shut her mouth and folded her hands primly in her lap.

"So you've decided to marry him?" her uncle asked.

"I don't know what to do, Uncle Barney." Cinda looked at her uncle, almost pleading for the answer. "I don't think I want to marry him, but I feel awful he came all this way for nothing. It's not right what they did to him."

"What are you going to do?"

"I think I should tell him the whole truth before he leaves. He at least deserves that." She didn't sound convinced.

Maybe she just wanted to see him one last time. She felt a little sad at the thought of never seeing him again. She felt a tugging, a longing where he was concerned. Now that she had had a chance to catch her breath, this was kind of exciting, like something she might read in a book. He was a nice, Christian man and deserved a good wife, whoever she was.

"Honesty is always best. Do you want me to walk you over?" her uncle said, offering to give Cinda a little courage.

"No. It's not far. I can manage by myself. I need to think about what I'm going to say."

"She can't go by herself," Ginny scolded.

Cinda was exasperated with her aunt and spoke curtly, "Of course I can. I'm a grown woman, not a child."

"Ginny, leave her be," Barney said.

Cinda swung her cape around her shoulders and caught a glimpse of her aunt's critical glare.

Cinda marched down the street. The gall of her aunt telling her what to do. Cinda was twenty-three years old. By most, she was considered an adult, but her aunt insisted on treating her like a child, telling her what she could and couldn't do, what to wear, and how to stand. As the thought crossed her mind, Cinda purposefully slouched. She had had it with her aunt; she would like to do something to prove to her aunt she was in control of her own life. She should run off and marry Mr. Rawlings, a stranger, just to show her aunt.

The more she thought about it, the more it appealed to her. She would have her own life then and do what she wanted. She could get out from under her aunt's thumb. It would be just her and Lucas. She would be far from her meddling aunt, though Cinda would miss her uncle. Cinda liked the idea, getting away from her aunt and caring for a man who maybe loved her, someone with whom she could possibly fall in love one day and build a life.

Was she crazy? Marry a stranger?

Other women had done it. Why not her?

No, the idea was absurd.

She prayed for him as she walked, that he would not be too angry with her and for the Lord to send him the right woman to be his wife.

Maybe she could think of someone suitable for him, so his trip wouldn't be a waste. Eve certainly was interested, but she didn't think Eve was his type. What was his type? The images of her unmarried friends and acquaintances skipped through her mind. None seemed right.

Not only did she feel a pang of jealousy when she unsuccessfully tried to picture him with someone else, but when she prayed she got the distinct impression she should be the one to go with him. If he left without her, she would be thwarting God's plan.

What a ridiculous notion. God might work in mysterious ways, but there was no mystery about this. It was Vivian's and Eve's doing. And it was downright odd. That's how she felt. . .odd.

She turned and headed for Allison's. A talk with her would straighten out her turbulent emotions.

&

"I mean, it is a good thing that he was willing to come and all," Cinda said, fidgeting with her skirt folds. "He has that big farm to run and all those animals to look after. It must be a lot of trouble to find someone to look after things."

Allison raised her eyebrows. "It sounds to me like you are trying to talk yourself into this."

"I am not! I just feel bad for him coming all this way for nothing."

"It doesn't hurt that he is the proverbial tall, dark, and handsome gentleman. May I emphasize the *tall* part. You'd not find another man like him if you searched the rest of your life. He has a lot to offer a woman. He has a lot to offer you."

"I'm not interested in—"

"You are too," she interrupted with a dismissive wave of her hand. "But that is neither here nor there. He's probably left town by now."

Cinda didn't tell her friend she was sure he hadn't. If he had left straight from Allison's when David turned him down for her, he could have. But he waited to hear the bad news from her. She was sure the next train wouldn't be until tomorrow, probably not until the afternoon. She also didn't tell her friend she was on her way over to see him.

She left Allison's more confused than when she arrived. Was she the right woman for Lucas Rawlings? When she again tried to imagine him with someone else, like Eve or Vivian, the pang of jealousy startled her. Why did she keep thinking of herself being with Lucas? Was it a leading from her heavenly Father. No! This couldn't be from God—just her confused imagination playing tricks on her. She might have a few wayward emotions, but one thing was for sure, she was not marrying Mr. Rawlings.

seven

Tomorrow's train was not soon enough for Lucas. He had just come from the station to find out when the next train would leave. He entered his hotel room, shed his coat, and flung it to the floor. Next he shucked off the tight suit pants and slipped into a comfortable pair of Levi's.

He bathed and washed the grease from his hair. He hated having his hair slicked down, but it was necessary to keep his wavy hair out of his eyes and under control. He normally liked to run his hand through his hair, but he wouldn't touch it with that junk in it. He had been an idiot running around for two days in a suit with that stuff in his hair after a woman who probably never had any intention of marrying him.

The whole trip was a waste of time. He should have known he couldn't pull it off. At least one good thing had come from today—he wouldn't have to wear those tight suits or put grease in his hair again. He ran his hands through his hair just because he could. His room was warm, so he took off his shirt and stood by his open window to breath in the fresh air. He couldn't wait to get back to the wide-open space of Montana.

Where had he gone wrong? He had worn his best clothes so the lady wouldn't think him uncivilized. He slicked back his hair so she wouldn't think he was unkempt. He was a gentleman and acted politely, and he was sure he hadn't said anything offensive, not even to the intolerable David Swan.

From the start, jealousy churned in Lucas where Swan was concerned. The man obviously had a close relationship with the woman he had come to marry. Lucas had hoped she would trust him that much someday. Now there wasn't a chance of that. He had come all this way just to make sure she didn't change her mind. The farm and everything else was suffering because of his fool-hearted notion of getting married. He should have been more certain, waited a little longer. Why was he so impatient? Maybe he had been isolated on the farm far too long. He obviously didn't know how to properly act around a pretty woman. He had made a muck of the situation and would go home empty-handed, though he wasn't quite sure what he had done wrong. Now who could he marry—Eve? He shuddered at the thought.

He looked into the night sky. *What do I do now, Lord? My way failed. I want to do Your will. I thought that's what I was doing. I guess I answered my own prayers and claimed it was You. I'm staying out of it from now on. I'll do the best I can with what You've given me. If You have a woman out there for me, You will have to bring her to me. I'm not chasin' after another one.*

A knock at the door interrupted his prayer. He didn't want to see anybody. Should he even bother to open it? It was probably one of the hotel staff. He raked his hands through his clean hair as he strode over to the door. Just as he reached it, he heard a second, lighter knock. He grabbed the doorknob and yanked the door open. "What?" he barked.

Miss Harrison stood in the hallway; long dark lashes framed her wide green eyes. Her mouth dropped open. "Oh my!" She covered her gaping mouth with her hand.

Lucas's mouth hung open as well. He couldn't help but stare. "M–Miss Harrison, Cindy. . .I–I mean Miss. . ." He took a slow breath to calm his rattled nerves. She was the last person he expected to see at his door and looking so pretty. "Won't you come in?" he offered politely, motioning with his hand into the room.

"Oh," she squeaked and looked away blushing.

"No. I didn't mean that." Inviting an unchaperoned woman

into his hotel room, especially at this late hour, would be scandalous and certainly tarnish her reputation. Flustered, he continued, "What I meant was—I don't know what I meant. Wait there while I get my shirt." He retrieved his shirt, but when he turned back around, she was gone.

He fumbled with the buttons and crammed the tails into the waist of his jeans. He would have to hurry to catch her. He raced down the stairs and headed straight for the doors, but stopped when he saw her sitting in a lobby chair hunched over with her face in her hands, shaking.

Why do women always cry when they are in stressful or awkward situations? Lucas walked over to her and took a deep breath. "Miss Harrison? Are you all right?" he asked softly. "I didn't mean to scare you."

She drew in a quick breath and held it, trying to control herself. She looked up slowly.

Her smile surprised him. In fact, she looked as though she was struggling not to laugh. He smiled instinctively. "Did I miss something here?"

"It's this whole situation." She almost laughed again.

"You find this funny?" Lucas pulled his brows together.

"I was just looking at this whole situation from your point of view." She looked down at her reticule, fussing with it to avoid looking at him. "You wrote those letters and came out expecting to find a willing bride. Instead you find me shying away and putting you off. Then I show up now, at night, and you half dressed."

"I assure you I find nothing humorous in all this." A hard edge crept into his voice. "I paid good money to travel all the way out here. I have a farm to run. I have obligations. There are things to be done. This isn't a joke."

Cinda took a deep breath. "I know. Mr. Rawlings, I truly am sorry about all your troubles. You must think me capricious. You have to understand, I received your letter yesterday only hours before you showed up. It was quite unexpected, I assure you." For some reason the nervousness she had felt the past two days melted away.

Lucas Rawlings had every right to be very cross with her for all the trouble he thought *she* had put him through, but he was gentle and was clearly trying to be understanding. She knew she wasn't making that easy for him. He had always spoken politely and with respect, even to her aunt and David, and never once had he tried talking her into anything.

There was no pretense in him now. He looked comfortable and no longer out of place in his clothes. He was much more suited to Levi's than a suit. His wavy hair around his face was less stiff. He looked more. . .natural. It was time to confess the truth and let him be on his way in peace. She couldn't make more a fool of herself than she already had.

Cinda looked him straight in the face to tell him the whole mixed-up story, Vivian and Eve included. When she gazed deep into his blue eyes, she saw her future. Lucas Rawlings was in that future. She imagined being on the porch of a small farmhouse arm in arm with Lucas looking out at their spread. Lucas's deep voice pulled her back from her reverie.

"Miss Harrison, you were going to say something?" He combed a hand through his thick dark hair. She wondered if it felt as nice as it looked.

For a brief moment her dream was within reach. Could she find the courage to reach out and grab it? "Yes," she whispered. She couldn't push aside the feeling this was from the Lord.

"You certainly had a purpose in coming all the way down here," he paused and looked around the empty lobby, "alone."

Cinda snapped out of her daydream. "I've changed my mind." She forced the words out in one big gasp before she could change her mind again.

"I know. You made that clear this afternoon."

"No. I mean, I've changed it back." Cinda could feel her

cheeks flush and her heart race.

"Are you sure?" Lucas furrowed his brow. "You said this before. Don't feel you have to. I don't want you to do this unless you are sure."

"I'm sure this time," she said, barely able to keep the quiver from her voice. She wondered if Lucas suspected how nervous she was at this moment.

Lucas looked at her for a moment, not sure if he should believe her this time. "It's getting late. Maybe we should talk about this in the morning. Here." He pointed to the lobby. "Just you and me. No Mr. Swan and no aunt."

"I can't in the morning."

Lucas rolled his eyes. She was putting him off again. "I'll walk you home, Miss Harrison."

She stood up to walk with him out of the hotel. "Tomorrow's Sunday. I have church."

"My train leaves in the afternoon. I'm not changing it again." The sooner he got out of town the better.

"I understand."

Lucas stopped and turned to her, studying her face. "You understand what?" He narrowed his eyes.

"You no longer want to marry me. . .after everything I've put you through." She shifted uncomfortably.

He wondered if she was playing some sort of game with him or if she had genuinely had a change of heart. "It's not that. I'm not sure you really want to get married. I don't have the privilege of idle time to dillydally in town to be turned down again." He raked a hand over the back of his neck. "I have a farm to run."

"I won't change my mind; I give you my word."

"We'll talk tomorrow." He would leave it at that and if by God's grace anything came of it, there might be a wedding after all.

eight

"You are going to what?" Aunt Ginny had an irritating shrill in her voice.

"I'm going to marry Lucas Rawlings." She had made up her mind.

"Are you sure about this?" Her uncle's loving concern had always been a comfort.

"Yes, I'm very sure," she said to him. "I feel this is somehow in God's divine plan. I know this sounds all a bit. . .well, strange, but I believe in my heart this is God's will for my life."

"Just when do you plan on marrying this stranger? I remind you, he is a stranger." Her aunt tilted her nose in the air, her lips pinched.

Cinda turned slowly to her aunt. "Tomorrow." She swung her gaze back to her uncle and said with a touch of urgency in her voice, "It has to be tomorrow, Uncle Barney. He's leaving on the afternoon train."

He studied his niece's face for a moment, trying to read her heart. He always could. "If this is truly what you want," he said slowly and paused. Cinda nodded. "Then we had better get busy. There is a lot of work to be done." Her uncle took her by the hand and led her upstairs. Dumbfounded, her aunt remained behind in the parlor.

Her uncle opened the door to the third room that they used for storage. Cinda had seldom been in this room. He pointed to two trunks and told her she could pack her belongings in them. Then he took her over to the corner where a dusty old trunk sat.

He knelt down beside the trunk and patted it lovingly. "These were your mother's things." He opened the lid and turned to look up at Cinda, still standing. "Now they're yours." Cinda's mother was Uncle Barney's younger sister.

Cinda caught her breath. She touched the cameo at her throat as she slowly sank down beside her uncle at the treasure chest. She skimmed her hand over the beautiful quilt that topped the trunk.

"These have always been yours. I was never sure when to give them to you. Now seems like the right time." His voice was heavy with emotion.

Cinda turned to her uncle and hugged him. "Thank you. Thank you so very much." Pulling away she asked, "But how did you do this? I thought everything was sold at auction to pay my father's debts?"

"I managed to save a few things. I couldn't let my baby sister's whole life be sold off to strangers." Tears welled in his eyes, threatening to spill over, but he kept them in check.

However, Cinda's tears ran free as she hugged him again. Cinda wanted to sift through her mother's things, but she knew she didn't have the time to dwell on the past. Her future was at hand.

Closing the trunk, her uncle said, "Let's get those empty trunks. You have a lot of packing to do."

❧

Lucas arranged to meet his fickle bride immediately after church. He came in a little late to the service and stood in the back. He chose to wear olive green pants with a matching green and tan plaid shirt. He debated whether or not to wear one of his ridiculous suits. He decided if these clothes were good enough for church back home, they were good enough here. He was tired of pretending to be someone he was not.

He leaned against the back wall, resting one foot on it. He

looked around until he spotted the back of Cinda's head. She was seated near the front with her aunt and a middle-aged man Lucas assumed was her uncle. If the aunt was any indication of what the uncle was like, he wasn't so sure he wanted to meet him.

He supposed the sermon was good. His thoughts bounced back and forth between his bride-to-be and praying for guidance. Was marriage to this woman the right answer? He thought it was, but maybe in his eagerness to solve his own problem, he was stepping on God's toes. When he left Montana, he was sure of God's will. Now he wasn't as confident.

When the service ended and people filed out, he watched Cinda as she made her way down the narrow aisle, greeting friends along the way. She wore a white linen dress with a touch of ruffles and lace at the neck, elbow cuffs, and the skirt hem—a lovely vision. Was it possible that she was really going to marry him?

He remained against the wall, gazing at her. When she finally caught sight of him, he smiled and tipped his head to her. She blushed and bit her bottom lip. She turned away and headed back up the aisle.

He had his answer. She had changed her mind once again and didn't even have the courage to tell him. He shoved away from the wall and exited at the tail end of the masses, though several people remained inside.

Halfway across the church lawn he heard a female voice call his name. "Mr. Rawlings!"

He turned to see Cinda coming toward him with her aunt and uncle and Mr. and Mrs. Swan. He surveyed the small mob descending on him and braced himself, for what, he wasn't sure.

The group stopped in front of him. Cinda looked from him to Allison and David. "You've already met my very best friend and her husband, Mr. and Mrs. Swan." Lucas nodded at Allison and shook David's outstretched hand. Distrust still lingered in David's eyes, but he said nothing. Cinda drew Lucas's attention. "You've met my aunt, Virginia Crawford."

The aunt's condescending expression told him she probably had a thing or two to tell him, but she held her tongue.

He nodded to her. "Ma'am."

Then Cinda's smile broadened. "This is my uncle, Barney Crawford."

Lucas shook the man's hand. "Good to meet you, Mr. Crawford." At least he hoped it was a good thing.

"It's good to finally meet you, too, and it's Barney." Barney's casual nature and warm smile put Lucas at ease.

Lucas scanned the group and settled his bewildered gaze on Cinda. He wasn't sure what this little get-together was about.

"We should be getting along. Pastor Cooke doesn't have much time," Allison said.

"We'll meet you two inside." Uncle Barney guided the group toward the church.

With raised eyebrows, Lucas looked down at Cinda. She understood his unspoken question of *What is going on?*

"Pastor Cooke can perform the ceremony, now, before he goes off visiting." Cinda diverted her eyes to the buttons of his shirt. "If you want, Mr. Rawlings."

"Get married right now?"

Cinda nodded, looking up only as far as his chin.

"How did you manage that?" Lucas folded his arms across his chest. "I thought your pastor was too busy on the weekends."

"Pastor Cooke and my uncle have been best friends since they were babies." Cinda looked him in the eye with a boldness he had not seen in her yet.

Lucas gazed into those rich green eyes and lost himself. She was going to marry him. Somehow he knew he didn't deserve her. After a few moments of silence, he said, "If indeed we are getting married, Cindy, I think you should start calling me Lucas."

Her cheeks tinged pink and her gaze dropped back to his chin. "Then. . .Lucas. . .you should start calling me Cinda."

"What?" He had gotten caught on the melodious way his name sounded on her lips, so he didn't quite catch what she said.

"My name is Cinda, not Cindy."

"Cinda," he said to himself, to establish the sound of it. "Why didn't you tell me I was saying your name wrong?"

"It didn't seem important."

"Because you weren't planning on marrying me, and I would soon be gone."

Cinda nodded.

They walked side by side back to the church. Lucas wasn't sure if he should really believe she was going to go through with it this time.

Uncle Barney was waiting for them at the door. Another man ushered Lucas to the altar, across from where Allison stood as matron of honor. Lucas looked out over the curious crowd.

In the front sat Cinda's aunt, Mr. Swan, Miss Van Dornick, and Miss Weston. A half dozen others Lucas didn't know were huddled in the first few pews. Was this really going to happen? Or was this the grand finale to the whole big joke? He should cut and run while he had the chance.

The first note of the wedding march startled him. The door at the back of the church opened. Barney Crawford proudly escorted his niece down the aisle. Lucas realized she had a specific reason for wearing that white linen dress today. A piece of lace covering her head and face served as a veil. Since there were no flowers in bloom yet, her bouquet was a nicely done bundle of white ribbons and lace.

The woman coming down the aisle would be his wife now and forever. Should he really do this? She was sweet, and he could see she had gone to a lot of trouble since her change of heart last night. But then, he, too, had gone through a lot of trouble to come all this way for her. He hoped he was doing the right thing.

Lord, right or wrong, please bless this marriage.

❧

Cinda tried to calm the butterflies swarming in her stomach. This was it. She couldn't—wouldn't—back out now. She was really getting married. To think, three days ago she had never even heard of Lucas Rawlings, and now their lives would be forever entwined.

The ceremony rushed by in a blur. Lucas placed an aged silver wedding band on her finger. Her stomach danced at the thought it could be a family heirloom.

When Pastor Cooke said, "You may kiss the bride," she drew in a quick breath. She knew this was coming. She had been to weddings before. The groom usually grabbed his bride and kissed her passionately. Once she even saw one groom who kissed his young bride for a whole minute while his friends whooped it up. The poor girl was red-faced before he let her go.

Lucas lifted the veil, put his finger under her chin to lift her face, and softly pressed his lips to hers. The tingling started at her lips where they touched and spread like wildfire throughout her body. She hadn't expected such gentleness from this large man. Much to her surprise, she found she liked his tender kiss.

❧

Cinda stood on the train platform with her friends and family.

Eve waved a gloved hand in the air. "I can't believe you got to the altar before I did. I had better hurry up or I'll be the only one not married. Can you imagine me an old maid?" Eve giggled.

Vivian shook her head and rolled her eyes. She gave Cinda a quick hug and whispered in her ear, "You take good care of *our* Lucas."

Cinda wanted to laugh but settled for a smile.

Allison handed Cinda her copy of the *American Frugal Housewife*. "All my favorite recipes are marked."

"I can't take your cookbook."

Allison leaned into her so only she could hear. "You need it more than I do."

Cinda took a deep breath. "What am I going to do?"

"You'll do great. Just don't worry about it."

"Thank you, Allison. Good-bye, David, Eve, Vivian. I'm going to miss you all." Cinda turned to her aunt and uncle who were waiting a few feet away.

Aunt Ginny handed her several envelopes bundled together, each containing a different type of vegetable seed. "Here. You should plant a garden right away."

"Thank you." Cinda gave her aunt a quick peck on the cheek.

Her aunt had a shrewd look on her face and gave her head a little shake. "I hope you don't regret your hasty decision."

Cinda noticed a sad expression skim across her uncle's face as he looked at his wife.

"All aboard!" the conductor yelled.

Lucas put his hand on the small of her back. "We need to get going."

Cinda kissed her uncle on the cheek and hugged him. "Good-bye, Uncle Barney. I'll miss you most."

"I'll miss you, too, Sweetheart. You're like my very own daughter." He couldn't keep a tear from falling to his cheek and quickly brushed it away.

Cinda's tears cascaded down her cheeks as Lucas assisted her onto the train. She kept turning her head away trying to hide the tears. Her lacy handkerchief wasn't sufficient enough to capture all the moisture.

Lucas pulled out his and handed it to her. "If you're going to have a proper cry, you need a proper handkerchief."

"I'm sorry. I don't mean to cry all over the place." She sniffled. "I'm just going to miss everyone."

"My mother used to say, 'If you don't let the tears free, they will singe your heart until you have no feelings left.' " He pointed his finger and shook it in the air at an invisible person and said in a false voice, " 'You can't rightly be human without feelings now, can you?' "

She took the handkerchief with a smile, but somehow she didn't feel like crying any more.

nine

After the train was underway, the conductor came by to check for tickets. While Lucas showed their tickets, Cinda rested her head and closed her eyes for a second. The events of the past three days had caught up to her.

"Are you all right? Is anything wrong?"

Lucas's concerned voice woke her. The conductor was just passing. She hadn't realized it possible for a person to fall asleep that fast. "I'm fine. I'm just tired. I was up all night packing and getting ready."

Lucas's concerned look softened. "Rest your head on my shoulder." He wrapped his arm around her slender shoulders and drew her close.

Cinda knew she should protest. A lady never slept in public. But she was exhausted. She would rest her tired eyes for a few minutes; there would be no harm in that.

&

As his new bride drifted off to sleep, her hand slipped from her lap to his. Startled by the sudden touch, he realized she was already asleep. He wrapped his big calloused hand around her slender, feminine one. He wasn't sure how he would feel about the added responsibility of a wife. It surprised him that he kind of liked it. Had he made the right decision? Was this really the only solution? It was the only one he could think of at the time. He still couldn't think of a better one. It was now done, and he would do what he could to make her happy. He gently squeezed her hand.

❧

Cinda descended from the train, relieved to be off of it. Two days of rattling around on a train had made her joints sore. "How many more days will it take to get to your farm?"

"Our farm," Lucas corrected. "We should be at *our* farm the day after tomorrow if all goes well."

"If all goes well?"

"Sometimes travel out west can be. . .unpredictable."

Unpredictable? Just what did that mean?

She was glad to hear they wouldn't catch the stagecoach until the morning. The worst of the trip was over, she hoped. They stood at the front desk of a local hotel.

"One room, Sir." The desk clerk confirmed Lucas's request while pointing at the register book.

Lucas, poised to sign, suddenly turned to Cinda. "Unless you would prefer two? I have money enough for separate rooms."

She looked up into his caring face and saw understanding in his blue eyes. It was still difficult to get used to having to look *up* to him.

"This isn't that kind of hotel," the desk clerk said sharply. "We don't rent rooms to unmarried couples."

Lucas ignored the clerk's curt remark, patiently waiting her reply.

She was his wife; he was her husband. There was no point in wasting money or putting off the inevitable. "One room will be fine," she replied softly.

Lucas studied her a moment before turning back to the registry, signing their names, Mr. and Mrs. Lucas Rawlings. He plucked the key from the speechless clerk, and they headed up the stairs with their bags.

He knew he should have automatically suggested they get two rooms until they knew each other better, but he wanted to make her completely his before. . .things. . .got difficult. The more he had to tie her to himself, the more she would feel as though she belonged with him. He wouldn't have pressed if she wanted separate rooms, but she had agreed to one. As it was, they lay in bed next to each other and did nothing more than sleep.

୨ଈ

Lucas and Cinda took the last two seats on the crowded stagecoach. After an hour of bouncing and rocking along, Cinda concluded this was definitely worse than the constant rumblings of the train. Lucas seemed unaffected by the jouncing and kept his arm securely around her to keep her from bouncing off the seat.

As the morning wore on, the road got bumpier. She would rattle to pieces if this kept up. The jarring made it impossible to have any kind of conversation. Everyone sat in silence, if you could call the knocking and banging silence.

"You can trade seats with me, Ma'am," offered a heavyset man with dark hair and a full face of whiskers. He wore a business suit and sat in the front seat that faced the rear of the coach. "It's a little less bumpy up here."

Cinda's eyes widened with hope. Less bumpy sounded wonderful.

"No thank you, Sir," Lucas answered before Cinda could accept. "We'll stay put."

How dare he speak for her! She wasn't a child. Didn't he realize how uncomfortable she was? Besides she was offered the seat, not him. "But Lucas—" she started to argue, then decided a full stagecoach wasn't the proper place to question her new husband. She would suffer for now and discuss it with him later. She hadn't thought she might be going from Aunt Ginny telling her what to do to another.

Lucas pointed to the slender blond man also seated in the

front. "Most people get sick riding backward."

Cinda stared at the peaked man just as he lunged for the window and heaved his breakfast. She looked up at Lucas. "Oh."

Lucas shrugged his shoulders. "Change if you think your stomach can handle it."

Cinda raised her eyebrows. "I–I think I'll stay put." She realized Lucas wasn't trying to treat her like a child but was protecting her from further discomfort.

Just then the coach tipped down on one of the front corners and came to an abrupt halt. Everyone piled out. A wheel had broken. After the driver and the rest of the men helped in the repairs, they were on their way.

It was only a quarter of an hour before they stopped at a station for lunch and to change the team. The driver would only allow a fifteen-minute stop. They had lost much time with the broken wheel.

At the station they were served a barely palatable meal. Cinda could only choke down half a biscuit at Lucas's insistence. Getting back on the stage held little appeal, but she was glad they weren't staying at the station longer than necessary. She just wanted the trip to be over. She would have to endure this the remainder of today and again tomorrow.

The stage went faster than it had in the morning, while the ride got rougher and bumpier. She feared the coach would shake apart. Cinda noticed Lucas's grip grow tighter around her. She wondered if the jolting trip was finally getting to this strong, seemingly calm man next to her.

Since they had stopped for food and fresh horses, the old lady in the back had repeated in agony, "We be over. We be over." The woman's words grated on Cinda's nerves. She also wished for the ride to be over. When Cinda thought she couldn't take any more of the jarring, the coach teetered.

Lucas wrapped both arms around her, cradling her protectively against himself and whispered, "Here we go."

Cinda held on tightly and heard herself scream as the coach toppled over onto its side. They quickly came to a stop. The horses couldn't drag the overturned coach far.

Lucas quickly pushed people off Cinda. "Are you all right? Are you hurt?" People were moaning and groaning all around them.

"I–I'm f–fine." At least she thought so. She was not quite sure what had happened, but at least the bouncing had stopped.

"Is anyone hurt?" Lucas asked the whole group. The responses were all negative.

Someone flung open the side door that was now on top, and the driver helped pull out the passengers. Lucas helped Cinda and the others before he climbed out.

Once outside, Lucas rushed over to Cinda. "Are you sure you're not hurt?"

"I'm fine." Cinda looked at him, amazed. "You knew the stagecoach was going to overturn." She was both astonished and accusing. "Why didn't you warn me?"

"It doesn't always happen. I didn't want to worry you unnecessarily. The trip is hard enough without worrying about that, too."

He reached out to touch her, but she pulled away. Anger rose in her. How could he not warn her?

"If you've ever ridden a coach before, you would already know it could happen." He lifted his shoulders slightly.

She glared at him.

"And if not," he held his hands out palms up, "there is no sense worrying about it needlessly."

Consoling her would do no good. She was too shaken and angry, as much at him as herself for letting it scare her so.

He looked uncomfortable and pointed back to the stage. "I

should help the others right the coach so we can be on our way again."

After the bone-jarring box was set on its wheels, Lucas came to escort Cinda.

"It's time to get back on that thing, isn't it?" Cinda sneered at the stage.

Lucas nodded with a sympathetic smile. "I'm sorry."

"That was the most terrifying experience in my entire life. I will not soon forget it." Cinda took a shuttered breath to keep the tears at bay and shook her finger at him. "And I'm mad at you for not warning me. I don't like surprises." She strode off in a huff, not really so much mad as scared.

They bumped and bounced along mile after mile. Three more people got sick, one inside the coach. But at least they stayed upright the remainder of the day. Cinda's stomach had knotted from worry. Lucas had been right not to forewarn her. At least she had half a day with peace of mind. When they finally stopped in a town slightly larger than the one the night before, Cinda was so overwrought she could hardly stand, let alone think about food.

She clutched Lucas's arm as she got off. "I can't do that again."

"You don't have to."

She looked up at him. "Really?" Didn't they have another day of travel before they reached their destination? Relieved, she hung onto his arm, still unable to stand on her own.

"Really." He smiled down at her. "We'll take my wagon."

Cinda snapped up straight and let go of him. "You had a wagon and made me ride on that awful stagecoach?" Why would he do that to her?

"I didn't have a choice." He held his hands out in front of him. "The axle broke on the way. If I had waited for it to be fixed, I would have been late in arriving at your place. I didn't want you to think I wasn't coming. I wanted to have the wagon waiting in town when we got off the train, but traveling out west is unpredictable."

Cinda nodded. She was beginning to understand these unpredictabilities. "Lucas, are there any other surprises I should know about? I would like to prepare myself. There isn't anything else you're keeping from me, is there?"

Lucas raised his eyebrows but remained silent.

Cinda put her hands on her hips. "Is there anything else I should know about on this trip? Any more traveling unpredictabilities?"

"No. The wagon should be a better ride, and I promise not to turn the wagon over." His smile asked for forgiveness.

They checked into the hotel for the night, but Cinda refused to eat. Her stomach was still in knots from the trip.

≈

Though they got only one room again, he let her go to sleep undisturbed. She was frazzled after her harrowing day. She needed sleep and looked so peaceful in her slumber. He hated to wake her for another day of travel.

She seemed better in the morning, and he was glad to see her eat a healthy breakfast.

The wagon was loaded with Cinda's trunks, some food and water, blankets, and a few tools. Cinda hesitated, staring at the wagon, when Lucas reached out his hand to help her aboard. "You promise this will be better?"

Lucas smiled. "I promise. We can stop whenever you want."

With a heavy sigh, Cinda climbed up and sat on the thin cushion on the seat. At least by tonight the grueling trip would be over.

True to his word, the trip was calm and smooth. Lucas even made a place for her to lie down in the back if she wanted. After the noon meal, they walked in silence alongside the horses for awhile.

She wondered if her new husband felt he had made a mistake in marrying her. He hadn't tried to touch her at night as was his husbandly right or even kiss her since the wedding. Was he disappointed in her?

❧

Lucas rolled his eyes as he thought about how different today's travel was from yesterday's. If the lady was mad about not being warned about an upset coach, she would be livid before long, because the end of this journey was full of little surprises.

She wasn't very much like her letters. She was better, so much better in every way. She wasn't nearly as uppity and high-strung but every bit a lady. It was like getting to know her all over again. She was so quiet. He had expected to be plied with questions like in her letters. He was glad he wasn't. There were some questions he wasn't ready to answer just yet. There was nothing stopping him from asking the questions, though.

"How did you come to live with your uncle and aunt?" He wanted to know as much about her as he could.

Cinda snapped up straight. She looked up at him, staring for a moment before answering. "My mother died when I was nine and my father three years later. Uncle Barney and Aunt Ginny are my only relatives, so I came to live with them."

Her answer came out smooth, without a drop of emotion. Then she turned the question back on him. "What about you? Do your parents live near you? Will I be meeting them?"

"They passed away nine years ago," *and left me with the farm and everything that goes with it*. He noticed his answer also came out sounding rehearsed and emotionless. He wondered what thoughts tailed her answer.

"I'm sorry to hear that," she said, her voice full of emotion now. After a pause and a breath, she asked, "How much farther to your farm?"

Lucas looked down at her. "Our." He had to get her thinking of the place as hers, that she belonged there with him.

Cinda smiled shyly. "All right. How much farther to *our* farm?"

Lucas smiled. "I suspect just after lunch tomorrow."

"Tomorrow?" She halted. "But I thought we were going to get there today. No more traveling unpredictabilities. You said there was nothing more about the trip I needed to know."

"We aren't traveling at the same reckless speed as the stage coach. I thought you would appreciate the slower pace." Also he could use the extra day to get her used to the idea of belonging on the farm with him. He didn't want this peaceful time with her to be over so soon.

"I do." Cinda's gaze dropped to the dry prairie grass. "I just thought the trip would finally be over."

"Well hop in, little lady," he said in an old-timer drawl, thumbing his hand back to the wagon, "and I'll see if we can make it home before the moon is high in the sky. You'll have to hold on tight. I can't promise we'll stay upright, but I'll do my best."

Cinda laughed at his antics. "No, thank you. I think I'll walk."

❧

Cinda knew Lucas was a man with whom she could and would fall in love and they could build a life together. She found she was comfortable around him. He made her laugh and feel at ease, never pushy, always letting her make her own decisions, like where to sit in the stage. It was a small thing, but it was the type of thing her aunt wouldn't have let her do—end of discussion.

She couldn't remember the last time she walked with

someone who could match her own natural stride. It was her father, she supposed, but then he had generally altered his gait to match hers as she normally did for others. Her new husband was probably doing the same for her. His long legs glided along smoothly. He didn't seem to mind slowing down for her. In fact, he stopped for breaks before she needed them. For a man who was in an all fire hurry to leave town, he wasn't in much of a hurry now.

Lucas gave her the option of going a little out of their way to a town to stay the night in another hotel or cutting across the countryside and sleeping in the wagon. She opted for the shortcut. Lucas wouldn't have suggested it if it weren't safe, and he had a feather mattress in the wagon that would be as comfortable as any hotel. She felt rather adventuresome and seemed to surprise her husband.

They stopped by a babbling creek among the trees and ate beans, potatoes, and biscuits Lucas amazingly cooked over the open fire. She caught him staring at her again. While he was doing every little chore, whether building the fire or tending the horses, he stole glances at her. What was on his mind? She felt her cheeks warm as he came closer.

"If you're tired, you can go to bed." He pointed to the back of the wagon. "I know the traveling has been hard on you."

"I'm not tired. I slept well last night, and today's travel was pleasant as you promised."

His mouth curved up slightly, seemingly pleased at the fact she noticed he had tried to make today more enjoyable. "Montana is a might prettier place now that you're here."

She smiled at his compliment.

His gaze softened. "You're very beautiful."

"Me?"

"Yes, Ma'am. You are the only one here. Hasn't anyone told you that before?"

Her uncle and friends had, but she didn't think that counted. "I didn't think you thought so. I mean you never—I mean, you don't exactly get to choose a mail-order bride on looks. It's a sight unseen deal."

"Oh, I noticed," he said with a grin. "Don't get me wrong, I've wanted to make this marriage real. It's just that you have been so overwrought and tired from the journey. I thought it best to wait; but I don't want you to think I don't want you, because I do."

She diverted her gaze to her husband's chin, his shirt front, the trees in the distance behind him. "I'm not tired tonight."

He stepped closer and caressed her upper arms. "Are you sure?"

She looked up at his tender face and nodded.

He kissed her tenderly before taking her in his arms.

ten

Lucas pointed to the horizon. "There it is. Our farm." He wrapped his arm lovingly around her shoulder and drew her close. "We're home."

Home. That sounded nice. Her very own home. A place for the two of them to build their lives together. She looked up at her new husband and straightened herself. For the first time in years she didn't feel tall. In fact, next to Lucas she felt short. . . almost.

As they got closer, Cinda could see the house was quite large. The other homes they had passed on their journey were considerably smaller. "It's so much larger than I expected."

"My father built it for my mother. Most of what my father did was for my mother." He gave her shoulder a little squeeze. "She said when they were first married, she was afraid my father would go broke. He would get her everything she said she liked. She quickly learned to keep quiet except for her deepest heart's desires. This was her deepest of all desires—a home in which to raise a family."

He looked down at her, warmth in his bright blue eyes. "Now it's our turn." He paused then said, "How many children do you want?"

"A whole house full," she said shyly and looked away. "I was an only child. I always wanted brothers and sisters. I was very lonely when my parents died. I would dream about belonging to a big family. That probably sounds silly to you."

"No, it doesn't."

He sounded so sincere she was drawn to look back up at

him. His smile consumed his entire face, even his eyes were smiling. She couldn't help but smile back.

"A big family sounds real nice." His soft tone caressed her.

As they pulled into the quiet farmyard, Cinda took in the full view at once. She could see the weathered two-story house was missing curtains in the windows and probably a woman's touch on the inside as well. Across the yard stood a great barn with a chicken coop nestled next to it. There were several chickens wandering free around the yard pecking at the ground. On the other side of the barn was a corral with two horses at the water trough. When the wagon rolled in the yard, the two corralled horses raised their heads and nickered a greeting. The team hitched to the wagon snorted in response and bobbed their heads.

They recognize each other. How cute.

Lucas pulled the wagon to a halt with a "whoa." He seemed anxious, looking around for something. He jumped down and turned, lifting Cinda to the ground. She noticed he had a strange look on his face, like he was nervous, expectant.

He probably wondered what she thought of the place. She wouldn't keep him waiting any longer. "It's wonderful, Lucas."

He gave her half a smile before the barn doors burst open. Two identical, carrot-topped, ragamuffin girls ran across the yard squealing, scattering squawking chickens. Their worn dresses were too small for them and so dirty you could hardly tell the dresses were once yellow. At least Cinda thought they were yellow.

Lucas took a few steps forward and knelt down on one knee with open arms. They plowed into him, but he remained solid and scooped them up.

"We missed you soooo much," they said in unison, then smothered his cheeks with kisses.

"I missed you both soooo much." His voice thick with adoration.

A young man exited the barn and came toward them. He was built a little more slender than Lucas. In his Levi's and tan shirt he could pass for Lucas's twin at a distance. As he reached Lucas, Cinda could tell he was a couple of inches shorter and didn't have quite the same pronounced features as Lucas. He was a younger version.

"We expected you back two days ago," the young man said. She realized he must be Lucas's brother.

"It looks like you were expecting us," Lucas said, letting his gaze run up and down his dirt-covered brother. "We ran into a few snags."

The brother looked past Lucas and eyed Cinda. "She's a pretty one. Didn't expect that. Tall too. Have you sampled her cooking? I can almost taste a good home-cooked meal."

He was in for a surprise the first time he came visiting for supper and found out she couldn't cook. What Cinda really wanted to know about was the two dirty five-year-old girls in Lucas's arms. He said he had no children, but these two greeted him with a great deal of fondness, and he returned the feelings. Were they the brother's girls?

Cinda was rooted in place next to the wagon. She wanted to know who these people were, but she couldn't get herself to move forward. Lucas turned around with his arms still brimming with the two wiggly little girls and led his brother over to her. She took a deep breath.

"Trev, this is Cinda."

"Howdy," he said, touching his thumb and finger to his hat.

"Cinda, this is my brother, Trevor." Lucas looked at Cinda, waiting.

"It's nice to meet you, Trevor." Why hadn't she thought to ask if he had any siblings? "Are these your girls?" she asked

Trevor. It would set her mind at ease when he said yes.

"Nope," was his simple reply.

No! Then who did they belong to? She wasn't sure what to say to the unexpected brother, but she wanted to be polite. "Do you live near here?"

Trevor looked to Lucas, then back to Cinda. "Not near. Here." He said it so matter-of-factly, like Cinda should have known already.

Cinda looked up at Lucas. He had a look that Cinda could only interpret as surprise.

Lucas seemed uncomfortable and couldn't hold her stare. He jiggled the two girls in his arms and asked, "Who is who?" He looked from one redheaded little girl to the other and back again.

The girls giggled and said together, "You know."

Lucas moved each girl up and down as if weighing them and said to the one in his left arm, "You feel like you weigh just enough to be Davey."

The little girl giggled a yes.

Lucas turned to the girl in his right arm and said, "That must make you Dani."

"Yes," the girl chuckled.

He looked hesitantly back at Cinda and said, "These are my nieces."

Cinda was relieved. They weren't his.

Lucas raised the girl on the right a little higher and introduced her. "This is Daniella." Then he raised the other girl a little. "And this is Daphne."

"Hello, Daniella. Hello, Daphne. It's a pleasure to make your acquaintance." She curtsied slightly to the girls. "And where are your mommy and daddy?"

"They died," Daniella said.

"Bofe of them," Daphne said sadly.

She noticed Lucas eyeing her cautiously.

Cinda's insides tightened. "The girls live here, too?" It was more a statement of recognition than a question.

Lucas nodded.

Surprise!

Two bachelors trying to raise a pair of little girls must be hard. She could understand why they wanted a woman around. She just wished her husband had forewarned her.

At that moment a horse and rider came racing across the pasture. Everyone turned to watch the rapid approach. The pair entered the farmyard at full speed. When they were almost upon the group, the rider pulled up the horse. Cinda let out a little yelp as the horse skidded to a halt, spraying her dress with dirt. The boy jumped down off his mount before it came to a complete stop. Horse and rider panted. He slapped the dirt from his denim pants.

"Marty, this is Cinda," Trevor offered with an eager grin.

"Howdy," Marty greeted gruffly.

Another brother. Surprise.

"Marty, take off your hat," Lucas reprimanded. The boy did as he was told. "Cinda, this is my sister, Martha."

Sister! There was absolutely nothing about her that would give anyone reason to believe she was a girl. She was dressed like her brothers, including the hat. Her curly, dark hair was cropped just below her ears and tucked behind them. She walked like a boy. She behaved like a boy. And she looked like a boy.

"Hello, M–Martha," Cinda stammered out.

"Marty," the girl spat back.

"Aunt Marty, can we ride Flash?" Daniella asked.

Marty looked to Lucas for approval.

"Please?" Daphne begged, lacing her hands together.

Lucas nodded and raised each of the girls up onto Flash.

"You go slow with them. No trotting."

Lucas gave Cinda a quick, shy glance as he went to the back of the wagon and carried her trunks and the other supplies to the porch. Trevor offered to take care of the horses and led them off to the barn.

Lucas took Cinda inside the house to show her around. There was a sitting room with a couple straight-backed chairs, a worn settee, and a wooden rocker. The dining area had a large wooden plank table with a bench along each side and a chair at each end.

Next to the dining area was the kitchen. It was obvious this was not a room they cared much for. The small worktable was dirty like the rest of the room and piled with semi-clean dishes. The sink had the really dirty dishes. The few shelves were either broken or looked unstable. The whole house looked like all traces of a woman's care had been erased over time.

Lucas looked ashamed at the house, like he was seeing it for the dump it had become. He probably had been so busy in the fields, with other farm chores and his nieces, that the inside of the house never mattered as long as the roof didn't leak.

As Cinda looked around the kitchen dumbfounded, Lucas's brother came in through the kitchen door. He certainly made short work of caring for the horses. He came skidding to a halt and hollered, "Yahoo, home cookin'."

He surely had a one-track mind.

"Did you leave your manners in the barn?" Lucas glared at his brother.

He removed his hat and held it to his chest. "Howdy, Ma'am. It's nice to meet you."

Cinda looked at him, confused. Had he forgotten they had already met in the yard?

"Cinda." The tentativeness in his voice caught her attention.

"This is my brother Travis."

Cinda looked up at Lucas. "I thought his name was Trevor?"

"No. I'm Trevor," came a voice from behind them in the dining area.

Cinda whirled around to face Trevor smiling back at her. Then she looked to the smiling face of Travis. Twins!

Surprise!

"Most people cain't tell us apart, so we'll answer to either name," Travis offered.

Cinda looked one more time at the smiling brothers and didn't know how she would ever tell them apart. She looked up at Lucas, who gave her a half-hearted smile, as if to say, *please don't be mad.*

Mad? How could she be mad? She was too overwhelmed.

eleven

Lucas showed Cinda the upstairs. There were four bedrooms;
the largest one was theirs. He left her with her trunks so she
could rest awhile before getting supper ready.

Rest!

She plopped down on the bed. She would never rest again.
She put her hands to her cheeks. Oh, what had she done?
What had she gotten herself into? Too much was expected of
her. Mother to a pair of dirty little girls she couldn't tell one
from the other. She was sure they would have fun fooling her.
A tomboy for a sister-in-law. Her hands dropped into her lap.
She assumed she was supposed to make a lady of her. A pair
of indistinguishable brothers with a single mind—home
cooking. Cooking! She couldn't cook. She had hoped to start
out slowly cooking for just one man and hope she didn't
make a mess of it. Instead, she had a whole family that
expected her to cook edible meals. Besides the washing and
mending, there was the cleaning. This house needed a good
scrubbing from top to bottom. She noticed Lucas seemed to
realize how bad it was.

It was too much. How could he do this to her? She balled
up her hands. Hate and anger vied for dominance which was
unlike her, but she couldn't help herself. She wanted to go
home and leave this place far behind. But that was out of the
question; she was married now, and this was her home, like it
or not. Her aunt's words came back at her and slapped her in
the face. "I hope you don't regret your hasty decision." She
did regret it. Had her aunt known something she didn't?

So much was expected of her. It would be hard enough to learn to care for and keep house for one man, but now, there was suddenly a house full. She ran a hand over the threadbare quilt. No doubt they all needed new quilts and clothes, and she was expected to make them. She had no experience. She couldn't do it. Anger rose in her as she contemplated all there was to do. She wouldn't do it. She would go down right this minute and inform her new husband that they must live in their own house. His family could stay here, but she would not. She would demand it.

She got up, straightening her dress, and smoothed her hair. Drawing in a deep breath of courage, she glanced in the mirror on the dresser to give herself a quick nod of encouragement. Horrified by what she saw, she stumbled back to the bed and sat down. Her face now had the same scornful look her aunt had worn for years. The pinched lips. The knitted brow. The cold squinty, disapproving eyes.

She was turning into her aunt!

Still able to see herself from where she sat, she stared for several minutes at her reflection in the mirror. She opened her eyes wide, raised her eyebrows, and rubbed at the corners of her mouth. She refused to turn into her aunt.

Her aunt's words came crashing back to her. "Put hard work in front of you and you will crumble. Mark my words." Was her aunt right? Was she crumbling at the work put before her?

And whatever ye do, do it heartily, as to the Lord, and not unto man, the calm voice of the Lord whispered to her soul.

That was in Colossians. She had memorized it years ago. But could she really do all this family expected and needed her to do? *Lord, what have I gotten myself into? What am I to do?*

She got up and walked over to the mirror and said to her reflection, "You got yourself into quite a pickle, Cinda

Harrison. What are you going to do about it?" She stared at herself for a minute mulling over the question. "I guess I go downstairs and get that kitchen cleaned up, then pretend to cook supper."

She put on an old calico dress she rarely wore but thought it would be good for the job ahead. She dug through her travel bag and clutched the cookbook Allison gave her. "Thank you, Allison," she whispered and trudged down the stairs.

Cinda surveyed the kitchen, trying to decide where to begin. The counter and the dishes in the sink—that needed to be done first. She marched over and removed a stack of dirty metal plates from the sink. When she turned to put them on the worktable with the other dishes, an old man stood between her and the table. Instinctively, she screamed. Plates clattered to the floor as she braced herself against the counter.

"A rose, a rose," he began but stopped when she screamed.

Lucas was the first to race into the kitchen. He scanned the room and came over to her. "It's okay. It's only—"

The others quickly piled into the kitchen. "What's the matter?" Trevor asked.

"Dewight scared Cinda," Lucas explained.

"Why's she afraid of Dewight? He wouldn't hurt no one," Martha mocked.

Cinda stepped away from Lucas. "If someone," she shot Lucas a wicked glare, "had bothered to tell me about your grandfather, I wouldn't have been so terrified when he appeared out of nowhere."

"He's not our grandpa," Travis said. "Lucas found him two winters ago caring for a hog of ours that got out and wandered away. We don't even know if Dewight's his real name."

"He's really harmless. He'll do pretty much anything you ask him," Lucas explained.

Cinda settled her hands firmly on her hips and turned her

glare on Lucas. He shrank back from her slightly. "Is there anyone else? Any more brothers or sisters lurking around the corner? Any other relatives or non-relatives," she gave a quick glance at Dewight, "that are going to pop up out of nowhere? Anyone at all that I haven't met yet? Anyone?"

"No, this is all of us," Lucas said sheepishly.

"Then unless you want to be put to work," she said to the whole group, "get out of the kitchen." She pointed to the open door.

Martha, Trevor, and Travis practically fell over each other to get out. Lucas scooped up Dani and Davey and exited without another word.

Dewight stood rooted in the place he had been standing. He stared at her, cocking his head to one side. She supposed he was waiting for something, so she dropped her hands from her hips and said, "It's nice to meet you, Dewight."

He said nothing. He just stood silent, staring at her.

What was he waiting for? His constant gaze made her nervous. She replaced her hands on her hips. If he really wanted to stay, she would put him to work. "Fine, Dewight. I need some wood to start a fire in that stove," Cinda pointed to the stove without looking at it. "Could you get some for me?"

He didn't move or speak.

Cinda threw up her hands in resignation. She would just clean around him. She knelt down to collect the plates that had crashed to the floor. When she stood again, Dewight was gone. Cinda shrugged her shoulders. She piled the plates and other dishes from the sink on the table. Dewight came back in with an armful of wood and built a fire in the stove while Cinda cleaned the kitchen. He prattled on about a rose dying in the desert or some such nonsense.

It took Cinda two hours to get the kitchen clean enough to attempt cooking. She found the root cellar and took stock of its contents. With supplies in the kitchen and root cellar in mind, Cinda sat at the kitchen table and began to read her recipe book.

ɞ

Daniella and Daphne came skipping in the kitchen and took a big whiff.

"Mmm. Smells good," one of them said.

"Mmm. Smells good, too," the other echoed.

Cinda eyed the pair suspiciously. The brothers had probably sent these two in to find out when supper would be ready. *Cowards.* She bent down and said, "Supper's just about ready. Can you two tell everyone to wash up and get to the table?" She heard immediate scrambling outside the kitchen door, and the girls scampered out to wash up at the outside pump.

One by one they clambered to the table and sat, waiting. Lucas came in last and sat down at the head of the table with Trevor and Travis on either side. Cinda placed a pot of slightly burned succotash on the table with the not-quite-done boiled potatoes and a mound of overdone biscuits. She sat at the other end of the table with Daniella and Daphne on either side. Martha and Dewight sat on the middle of the benches across from each other. Although their faces and hands were clean, there was a perimeter of dirt around each of their faces where the water hadn't quite reached. Lucas was the only one without any dirt showing. They all bowed their heads while Lucas said grace.

Cinda watched while the food made its way around the table. She took very little. Her appetite had left her long ago. She held her breath as Trevor and Travis shoveled in their first mouthful. They looked across at each other, then glanced at Lucas who ate heartily, ignoring them. Cinda could tell it wasn't quite what they expected. She almost felt sorry for them as they ate in silence. The only ones she could have pity on were the innocent five year olds. They so desperately needed a woman's care.

ია

When the meal was over, his beautiful bride stood to clear the table. *Oh, no. That won't do.* Lucas took the dishes from her hands and put them back on the table. He reminded his brothers and sister how they used to do the supper dishes while their parents had taken a walk around the farm after supper. He was reinstituting that tradition. He guided Cinda outside where they walked in silence.

What could he say to her after all the surprises? She had taken it well, considering she hadn't left. . .yet.

They stopped by the corral. Lucas leaned against the fence. "Supper was good."

Her mouth dropped open and she swung her gaze to him. "It was awful. I can't cook, if you didn't notice."

"That's okay. You'll learn." He kicked at the ground. It hadn't been that bad. He had eaten a lot worse.

"In the meantime, everyone will starve." She shook her head. "Isn't that why I'm here, to cook and clean for the masses?" She swept her hand about to encompass the whole farm.

He shook his downcast head. He could see how she could think that.

"If you don't care that I take perfectly good food and turn it into slop not fit for the pigs, then why am I here?" Frustration and impatience coated her words.

"It wasn't that bad." He took a deep breath. "I was just nineteen when my folks passed on." At times like these, the ache in his heart was fresh and painful. "I had to look after a farm and four younger brothers and sisters. Lynnette was barely fifteen. The twins were eleven, and Marty was only four."

Cinda couldn't help but feel sorry for Lucas saddled with the enormous responsibility at a young age.

He took another deep breath and continued, "The next year Lynnette married a man on a wagon train heading for Seattle. Trevor and Travis had to quit school to help out here. I didn't know how to raise a little girl, so I raised Marty like a boy, as you can see." All he could do was shrug in excuse for his actions.

He had been so caught up in running the farm, he hadn't noticed when Marty had grown up. He turned around one day and found his baby sister was a boy. He couldn't tell her from his brothers. The irreparable damage was done.

Lucas stared out over the corral. "About nine months ago, Lynnette came home to die. I looked at her girls and saw Marty all over again. Lynnette was feminine and ladylike, like you. I couldn't do to Lynnette's girls what I did to Marty. I had a choice this time. I could make it different, better."

"Why didn't you just tell me about everyone and everything?"

"Would you have come if I had?"

Cinda looked to the ground, giving his question serious consideration. He waited.

"No."

He appreciated her not giving a quick, easy lie to placate him. "They need a mother. I know you'll be a great mother." He wanted to convince her it was going to be all right.

He was uncomfortable with her silence. Should he say more? Had he said too much? "You can go ahead on in. I'm going to put the animals to bed."

Cinda nodded but remained silent as she turned toward the house.

He wanted to make everything right for her, make it all perfect. But what in life was? "Should I be sleepin' in the barn with Dewight tonight?" Lucas called after her tentatively.

Cinda stopped but didn't turn around. After a moment she

shook her head and continued to the house.

❧

Though Cinda felt sorry for the nineteen-year-old boy who had a great burden placed on his young shoulders, she couldn't help but be angry with the man who had thrown his burdens upon her. At least she wouldn't have to worry about the supper dishes.

When she entered the sitting room, the conversation ceased. Travis, Trevor, and Martha were busy playing with the little girls. And who knew where Dewight was? He seemed to appear and disappear in a snap.

Cinda looked at the cluttered table. They hadn't even moved one dish. She could tell they were waiting to see what she would do. Cinda gathered up the dishes and took them to the kitchen. She would let Lucas deal with them when he came in and found her doing what they had been told to do. They were *his* family.

Lucas came in just after she had finished and was taking the little twins up to bed. He gave an approving nod at the clean kitchen. He never knew. Cinda dressed the still dirty girls in their too-small night shirts and tucked them in bed. Tomorrow they would get baths and something different to wear.

Although Lucas slept soundly, sleep eluded Cinda. She lay awake, nervous about having to fix a proper breakfast for everyone when they rose. She prayed but couldn't seem to give up her anxiety. She didn't even know what to make, so she got up and took turns reading her cookbook and the Psalms by candlelight until dawn. The struggles and praises of King David always comforted her.

twelve

Lucas leaned on the doorjamb and watched Cinda rush about the kitchen. He admired her diligence. She was trying so hard to please everyone, and it was important to her that she did. As the sun peeked over the horizon, it streamed in the kitchen. Her straight auburn hair blanketed her back down to her waist. Whenever her hair fell forward, she pushed it back over her shoulder. When she crossed the stream of sunlight, it set her hair ablaze. Lucas couldn't help but stare.

"Oh." Cinda startled when she saw Lucas grinning in the doorway. "Is everyone getting up already? I'm not ready yet. I don't have anything cooked."

He felt like a schoolboy caught gawking at the saloon gals. His mother had given him a month of extra chores the one time that had happened. She said if he didn't have enough to keep busy, she would see to it he didn't have time to think about those strumpets.

"Don't worry about it. There are morning chores that need to be done before breakfast." He wanted to soothe her worries. "The cow needs to be milked, the chickens fed, and the eggs gathered—" He was going continue, but Cinda jumped in.

"I already collected the eggs." She nervously pointed to a bowl of eggs. "I didn't know I was supposed to feed them. I'll do that later and remember it tomorrow. I don't know how to milk a cow, but if you show me I—"

Lucas shook his head, stopping her in mid-sentence as he stepped up close to her. He placed his hands on her shoulders to stop her flitting about. "You don't have to do everything.

89

Marty takes care of the chickens and eggs, and I'll continue to milk the cow. Don't worry so much."

"But I don't know anything about farms. There is so much to learn." She rubbed her scratched and pecked hands.

Lucas took her hands in his and caressed the red marks. "My brothers, Marty, and I will run the farm. You just have to take care of Dani and Davey. Everything else will work itself out."

Cinda wasn't as confident as her husband. There was so much she didn't know. He said she didn't have to do much, but what did he really expect?

She noticed him staring at her disorderly hair. She pulled her hands from his and scooped up her wayward mane. Pulling it over one shoulder, she began twisting it. Her hair was straight as a board and difficult to do anything with—a constant burden to her. "I'm sorry it's a mess. I haven't done a thing with it today. I didn't want to disturb you."

He took the bundle from her grasp and rubbed it between his fingers. "It shines like fire in the morning sun." He studied each feature of her face and settled his gaze on her mouth. As he leaned closer, Daniella and Daphne came bounding into the kitchen. Lucas took a deep breath. "I had better go milk that cow."

❧

Cinda spent that first morning after breakfast trying to figure out how to tell the little redheads apart. She sat down with them and studied their giggling faces. She discovered that Daniella had a distinct freckle, larger than the others, slightly off center on the bridge of her nose. Daphne had a similar freckle high on her left cheek under her eye. Now, as long as they were facing her, she could tell them apart.

Later in the afternoon, Cinda made Daniella and Daphne lie down to rest, and she ignored the filthy house while she explored her mother's treasures. She pulled out a worn wedding-ring quilt that had graced her parents' bed. She spread it across her own bed. Beneath it in the trunk was a new wedding-ring quilt top her mother had been piecing together before she died. Cinda caressed the new quilt as memories of helping her mother flooded back. She pushed away tears and vowed to finish it.

Among the items below the two quilts were her mother's Bible, a handful of other special books, a rag doll, and wrapped in a blue cloth were the pieces to her mother's once beautiful ceramic jewel box. It was smashed into a million teeny, tiny pieces, no doubt broken when the stage overturned. Cinda's heart was crushed as well. The box had been a wedding present from her father. He promised her mother on their wedding day that he would fill it with jewels for her, and he had, but they had all been sold at auction to pay the debts. Cinda saw a glimmer of gold and carefully flicked through the shards and rescued her mother's wedding ring.

"Don't cry."

Cinda looked toward the doorway as Daphne and Daniella rushed in the room.

"She hurted herself," Daphne said on the verge of tears.

"No, no. I'm not hurt," Cinda said, trying to console the pair. "I'm just sad. This box belonged to my mother. She died when I was young, and I miss her." Remembering the girls' loss as well, she added, "Do you have anything of your mother's?"

Both girls scrunched up their face as if thinking. "I got her eyes and Dani got her nose."

"Don't worry 'bout your box," Daniella said, patting Cinda on the shoulder. "Uncle Lucas can fix it. He can fix anything."

"He fixed the pitchfork Aunt Marty busted, and he made a cradle for our dolls," Daphne said.

"And he fixed the corral so the horses couldn't get loose no more," Daniella added.

Cinda smiled. Neither one wanted to be left out when there was a story to tell. "I think this is beyond repair, even for your uncle Lucas."

Daniella looked at her real serious. "What does 'yond pair' mean?"

"Be–yond re–pair," Cinda said slowly so they could hear each syllable, "means it can't be fixed."

"Uncle Trevor and Uncle Travis say that we are quite a pair," Daphne said with big eyes.

Cinda smiled.

Yes, she had to agree. They were quite a pair and had a way of jumping straight into your heart.

She held her arms open and they plunged into her arms, enjoying a group hug.

Cinda threw out the pieces of the destroyed box so the girls wouldn't get hurt when curiosity got the better of them.

The rest of the week, she spent her mornings cleaning up the twins and making them dresses from one of her old calico dresses. She spent the evenings, after her quiet walks with Lucas, doing the dishes.

She would heat bath water during breakfast and bathe Daniella and Daphne right after they ate. Within two hours they were filthy again, even when they remained in the house. The inside of the house was as dirty as the outside.

Lucas, Trevor, Travis, and Martha spent long hours preparing and planting the fields. Dewight mulled around the house and farmyard doing odd little chores and talking to himself. When Cinda was within earshot of him none of his words made sense. He would go on about a rose wilting, an apple tree blooming, and fighting some war. Those were only the ones she understood.

One morning she took the bathtub out behind the house and filled it with warm water. Dewight happily helped her until she informed him it was for him to bathe in. Cinda didn't know when he had bathed last, if ever. Dewight made himself suddenly scarce. Cinda hoped she hadn't scared him. But when it was time for supper, Dewight was seated at the table as usual, bathed and wearing clean clothes, though they were wrinkled.

Everyone looked at him oddly. Cinda just smiled.

≈

One evening on their nightly walk, Cinda looked out at the budding fields. "Lucas?"

"Yes."

"What's out there?"

"What?"

"What do you grow? Everyone else has cattle around here. Why don't you?"

"We grow alfalfa." He looked at her. "And we grow alfalfa because everyone else around here has cattle. Cattle eat alfalfa."

Cinda smiled to herself. She noticed the way he stressed *we*. He wanted her to know what was his was hers, that she belonged here. She just didn't feel like the farm was hers. She felt like she was visiting on some terrible vacation. She didn't feel like she belonged, on the farm or with *his* family.

≈

On Sunday morning Martha's howls could be heard all the way to the barn. "I ain't wearin' no dress." She turned defiant eyes on Lucas. "You cain't make me. My clothes was always good enough fer church before she come. They are just as clean as theirs." She motioned toward her twin brothers. She rammed her hat down on her head and stormed out, planting herself in the back of the wagon.

Cinda had taken one of her dresses that was a little small for her and altered it to fit the begrudging Martha. She figured

Martha never wore a dress because she didn't have one. Evidently not.

A sad expression settled in Lucas's eyes. "Let's get going or we'll be late." He walked outside with a look that showed his heartache over what he thought he had done to his baby sister.

Cinda decided she would spend more time with Martha and transform her into a lady for Lucas. He shouldn't have to feel badly. He did the best he could under the circumstances he had faced. All Martha needed was a little feminine intervention. Once Martha saw how pretty she looked in a dress, she would feel differently about wearing one.

&

The sparsely populated small church building stood at one end of town. The circuit preacher came around every four weeks, weather permitting. The other weeks they gathered for a prayer meeting and sing-along. A select group of men took turns leading the prayer and singing.

Cinda's cheeks warmed at all the people staring at her and whispering among themselves.

Lucas stood to lead this week's meeting. He raised his hands to hush the group. "It seems that before we begin praising the Lord in song, I should make an introduction or none of us will have our minds where they should be. You all are wondering who this beautiful young woman is." Lucas cupped Cinda's elbow and brought her to her feet. The whispers of speculation started up again. "I'm proud to introduce you to my wife, Mrs. Lucas Rawlings."

Cinda smiled politely as the group became louder in their discussion.

"The Lord's been answering your prayers," called a man from the back. Hoots and hollers came from around the room.

Lucas quieted the group again. "Let's get back to the reason we are here—worship. There will be plenty of time afterwards to meet my beautiful bride. Jed, will you open in prayer? Then we'll sing 'Amazing Grace.'"

After church, the congregation crowded around her, many people speaking at once.

"Cinda, this is my good friend Lem Dekker," Lucas said, introducing a tall, handsome blond man.

A scuffle off to the side cut the introductions short and shifted the group's attention off Cinda. Three boys were rolling around in the churchyard, fighting. No, there were only two boys. . .and Martha! Apparently they had teased her, telling her she would turn into a sissy now that Cinda was around, and she was getting the better of them.

Lucas, Trevor, and Travis pulled apart the group. The two boys gave up more easily than Martha—after all, it was her pride on the line. She kept swinging, trying to get away from Lucas as he held her by the scruff of her shirt collar, depositing her in the wagon. Cinda doubted it would be as easy as she thought to transform Martha.

Because of Martha's fighting, they left town before the noon meal, instead of eating in town as they normally did. Would every Sunday be this challenging?

❧

That night on their after-supper stroll, Cinda brought up the painful subject of Martha. "I don't think Martha should be out in the fields with you and your brothers."

"But she's a big help. She really pulls her weight out there. We need her."

Cinda realized that before Martha could see herself as a girl, her brothers needed to see her as a girl. "She's your sister, not another brother. She'll never become a lady if you don't start treating her like one." Lucas was silent. "I think for starters she should be called by Martha. Marty sounds too boyish."

Lucas shook his head. "That will go over about as well as the dress."

"But it is something we can control. Do you want her rolling around on the ground fighting with boys?" she asked in earnest.

He shook his head. "No, of course not."

"We can't force her into a dress; I realized that this morning, but we can get her used to the feminine sound of her name. When we get her to start thinking of herself as a girl, it will be easier to get her to look and act like a girl." Cinda wanted to soothe his guilt.

Lucas hesitantly nodded in agreement but didn't look convinced. He seemed willing to give it a try, probably to undo the damage he had done.

"I'm glad you're here," he said and caressed her cheek.

"Thank you." Strangely, part of her was happy to be here with him and the other part wanted to wake up from this nightmare.

Lucas went to take care of the livestock while Cinda went inside to do the dishes.

Trevor and Travis looked up at Cinda expectantly as she entered the house. Martha had a smug, contemptuous look on her face. Cinda looked over at the cluttered table. If she thought for one minute that they would have already done the dishes, she was fooling herself. She took a deep breath and started clearing the table.

They thought they were so smart getting out of the chore of washing the dishes. She felt like leaving the dishes but figured they would probably leave them for her to do in the morning when they would be twice as hard to clean. She couldn't face a dirty kitchen in the morning. Cinda didn't so much mind the task, it was the air of power they felt they had over her. Cinda continued to stew and fume. By the time she finished, she was downright mad. She grabbed the dishpan and marched to the open kitchen door. She would heave the water as far as she could. Maybe that would make her feel better.

The dishpan was already in motion when she saw Lucas in her line of fire. Lucas was passing by the door. It was too late. She couldn't stop the dirty water from heading straight for her husband. Lucas looked up in time and jumped back. The water sloshed on the ground in front of him, splashing his boots but sparing the rest of him.

At first he looked merely startled. When his shock faded away, it was replaced with what she could only determine as anger.

Cinda was too shocked to move as Lucas strode toward her and into the kitchen. He glanced around, then yanked the dishpan from her and examined her shriveled hands. He pulled her along after him out by the fruit trees.

"I–I'm sorry, L–Lucas. I–I didn't know y–you were there," she stammered as she trailed in his wake.

He stopped and faced her. "You washed the dishes?" It was more an accusation than a question.

Cinda nodded. "They can't be left 'til morning."

"Have you been doing the supper dishes all along?" His voice was harsh and demanding.

Cinda nodded again. She didn't understand why he was so upset with her. She certainly hadn't meant to douse him with the dirty water. "I–I didn't know you were there. I wasn't trying to throw dirty water at you."

"You are not to clean up the supper dishes," he commanded gruffly.

"But they have to be cleaned before I can prepare breakfast."

"Then don't fix breakfast," he snapped.

"But Lucas—"

He turned to her and put his hands gently on her shoulders. "I told my brothers and sister that it was their responsibility. I won't have them defying me," his voice softened, "or taking advantage of you. Now promise me you won't do the supper dishes, no matter what."

Cinda searched her husband's face. "But—"

"Promise me."

Cinda reluctantly nodded. She knew a pile of dirty dishes would await her in the morning if Lucas enforced this.

He pulled her into his warm embrace and held her close. "I'm sorry for being cross. I'm not angry with you. I'm angry with Marty and the boys."

The next night Lucas took Cinda with him to the barn to see to the livestock. When Cinda entered the house, she looked at the table of dishes. What was Lucas going to do? She looked at the triumphant trio. How would he confront them? The usual expectant expressions faded quickly when they saw Lucas enter behind her. They stole glances at each other. Lucas didn't acknowledge the table. He walked over and scooped up Daphne and handed her to Cinda. He scooped up Daniella in his arms and said, "It's time for you two to be getting to bed." Then he marched upstairs with a casual good night to the stunned trio.

֍

As Cinda suspected, the following morning the dirty dishes were waiting for her, still scattered across the table. She rolled up her blouse sleeves preparing to dive into the chore, when Lucas came in with a pail of fresh milk. He set the pail on the kitchen table and hooked an arm around her waist. "No you don't," he said and guided her into the sitting room. He sat her in the rocking chair and handed her a book from the nearby shelf.

"But Lucas, everyone will be hungry."

"It says in the Bible, in Second Thessalonians, chapter three, 'if any would not work, neither should he eat.' I believe that's verse ten. Hunger spurs one to work harder when the reward is food." They heard footsteps on the stairs. From where they sat, she could see Trevor and Travis stop before they reached the bottom.

Another set of footsteps trotted down the stairs. "What's for breakfast?" It was Martha's voice. "I can't smell—"

Cinda heard an umph. Martha had evidently bumped into Trevor and Travis who stood frozen on the third step from the bottom.

"Do you think she's sick or something?" Travis asked.

"They'll never get done with the three of you gawking at them," Lucas called from the sitting room. They spun around to see Lucas, Cinda, Daniella, and Daphne cozied up together sharing a book. Lucas continued, "Call us when breakfast is ready." They were speechless as was Cinda. "Could you hurry it along? We're hungry, and there's a heap of work to be done around here today."

The trio went groaning into the kitchen. They knew better than to argue and understood that the sooner they got to it, the sooner they would all eat.

Daniella and Daphne started whining about their hunger pains. Cinda's heart went out to them. "Lucas, this isn't fair to them."

"You're right, this isn't fair." He turned to Daniella and Daphne. "You two go in the kitchen and let them know just how hungry you are until they have fed you." The two girls skipped off to the kitchen, and soon the moans and groans increased.

"Lucas, how could you?"

Lucas smiled. "They'll not leave the dishes for you again. I promise you that."

Cinda hoped that was true. Caught off guard by Lucas's intense gaze, she smoothed back a lock of hair from his forehead.

He leaned over and kissed her gently. "I dare not continue or I'll never want to stop."

She smiled back at him and felt as if it had suddenly gotten warm in the house.

The next night and every night thereafter, the supper dishes were clean when she and Lucas returned from their evening walk.

thirteen

Martha sulked in a kitchen chair with her arms folded across herself. Lucas had left her to help Cinda, but she would have nothing to do with it. Cinda could feel Martha's piercing glare on her back as she finished up the breakfast dishes. She wouldn't push Martha into doing much this first day. At least she was in a more ladylike atmosphere. One step at a time. Cinda had to take it slow.

Cinda turned with a smile on her face. "Who would like to help me?"

"No one," Martha snarled.

"I wanna help," Daphne offered with excitement in her small voice at the same time Martha had spoken.

"No, you don't," Martha snapped at the girl and glared at Cinda.

Daphne stuck out her bottom lip and looked away.

"Dani, Davey, and me are going outside to ride Flash." Martha shot Cinda a gloating smile as the three left the room. Daphne looked back forlorn.

Two could play at this game. "Since no one will help me bake the cake, I guess I will be forced to lick the bowl all by myself," Cinda called lazily to their backs as they reached the front door. She had never made a cake before but thought since her cooking was improving, they could have fun trying. Following a recipe wasn't as hard as she had feared.

Daphne and Daniella came racing back. "I wanna help," they both called out.

"Great. But I think we need one more helper. Don't you?"

Cinda looked up at Martha, hoping she would relent and join in the fun.

Martha narrowed her eyes and tightened her mouth into a narrow line. She flung open the door and stormed out to the barn. Cinda was sure this wasn't the last battle with Martha. She might have resigned the twins for now, but she wasn't through yet.

They made a mess of the kitchen and themselves trying to make the cake, but Cinda couldn't remember having more fun.

She realized that with Martha around it would be a constant battle of wills for the twins' allegiance. A battle. What was it that Dewight said about battles? "A war is won, one battle at a time." Yes, this was definitely war, and with God she could win this war one battle at a time. Now, which battle should she approach first? It needed to be an easy one—one she knew she could win. She needed success early on to have the courage to endure.

The most difficult battle would be Martha. She would save that one for last. If she put off doing anything with Martha, then she really would have no trouble with the girls. The most important battle she had to win was for Daphne and Daniella. They desperately needed a mother's guidance and they already looked to Cinda quite naturally.

Cinda marched out to the barn to free Martha from her sentence of housework. She found her lounging in the ceiling rafters. She was so far up, Cinda shuddered with fear for the girl's life.

"Martha, would you come down here? I would like to talk to you," Cinda tried to be calm, but she couldn't keep a slight quiver from her voice.

"My name ain't Martha, Cindy," she called from her lofty perch.

"Your given name *is* Martha, mine however, is *not* Cindy," she retorted.

"If you say so—Cinderella."

Cinda took a deep breath. *One, two, three, four, five, six, seven, eight, nine, ten,* she rattled off in her head. She wasn't going to get into this just now, but she knew Martha thought of her as a work maid. "Would you please come down here so I may speak with you without shouting?"

"If you want me, come and get me."

Cinda really wasn't up to playing these games with her. But Martha wasn't coming down until she was good and ready. "I came to tell you that you may help your brothers in the fields, if you like."

"What?" Martha shifted positions.

"You heard me."

"If this is some sort of trick to get me down, it won't work. Lucas would just send me back, and you know it. Then I would be in trouble with him. You would love that, wouldn't you?"

"I assure you this is no trick. Tell Lucas that I told you to go, and tell him I will explain my actions this evening. If he still doesn't believe you, remind him his wife has been known to change her mind. . .often." On that note, Cinda turned and left the barn. She wasn't sure if Martha would go or stay up in the barn. It really didn't matter as long as she didn't try to come between Cinda and the twins. This was the one battle she had to win for Lucas's sake. She couldn't fail him. They were the reason Lucas brought her here in the first place.

A few minutes later, Cinda saw Martha race out of the barn on Flash full speed ahead. At least she didn't kill herself climbing down out of the rafters, but she might on that horse.

❧

At supper that night the haggard work crew filed in. Cinda wondered if they even stopped at the pump before coming in.

Maybe tonight wasn't the best night to start this. No. They shouldn't eat with all that filth on them. Cinda wondered how long it would take them. They looked around the table and at each other.

"We ain't got any plates," Trevor moaned.

"We don't have any plates," Cinda corrected. "And you won't get one as long as I can see dirt on your face, neck, and arms." She looked over each of them and shook her head. "Nope. None of you will get a plate until you're cleaned up properly." Lucas had shone her how motivational food was with his family, and her cooking was actually edible now.

"What about Lucas? Aren't you gonna check his face and hands?" Martha asked with a smug smile. She and her brothers glanced past Cinda.

Lucas had come in just after his brothers and sister. She could feel his presence behind her. He had heard the whole conversation.

Oh, no! Lucas. Cinda swallowed hard. She had forgotten about him. She couldn't very well humiliate him in front of his siblings by treating him like a child, but if she allowed him at the table unwashed, they might not take her seriously.

Cinda took a plate from the stack she held in her hands and handed it over her shoulder to Lucas. "Your brother always washes thoroughly." She hoped and prayed tonight he hadn't been careless and was still grimy.

The three filed out grudgingly. Lucas took his place at the table. Relief swept through her when she saw he was washed and clean.

"What would you have done if I hadn't been washed up?"

Died of humiliation, she thought but said, "You, my husband, have always washed up properly."

Lucas gave her a broad smile, flashing his dimple, as she strode down the table giving a plate to Daphne and one to

Daniella. The others filed back in like whipped puppies—
clean whipped puppies.

After supper Cinda explained to Lucas that too many
changes would be hard on a fourteen-year-old girl. She
remembered what it had been like at twelve, being uprooted
and having her entire world turned upside down. She would
need to go slow with Martha, very slow. She had to accept
Cinda first, so for now only her name would change.

fourteen

After three days of chasing Daniella and Daphne, Cinda was at her wit's end.

Just this morning she had read in the twenty-seventh Psalm, "Hear, O LORD, when I cry with my voice: have mercy also upon me, and answer me." She had cried out for mercy and answers and felt as if God weren't listening. In her loneliness and desolation, the Lord brought to mind a promise in Matthew, "Ask, and it shall be given you; seek, and ye shall find; knock, and it shall be opened unto you." She had asked for guidance and was fervently seeking a solution. Where was the answer?

She studied the girls, trying to figure out why they had a change in demeanor. They had been compliant before and enjoyed helping her around the house. Now they were defiant and downright disobedient. Occasionally Daphne would look at her like she wanted to be with Cinda, but she remained glued to Daniella's disobedient side. They refused to answer to Daniella and Daphne, only to Dani and Davey. They had been fine and enjoyable until—until Martha had been forced to stay behind. She was reaching back from the fields and interfering. Cinda turned thankful eyes to the Lord.

Cinda knew she had to break Martha's hold on the girls. First she had to find out what Martha was holding over them, and Daphne was just the one to tell her.

The girls were still at the breakfast table. Everyone else had left for their day's work. The twins were the last ones to finish, picking at their food. Cinda took hold of Daphne's hand, helping her off the bench.

"Where are you taking my sister?" Daniella asked, alarmed.

"I just want to talk to her. You stay here," Cinda said.

"No!" Daniella screamed, jumping off the other bench. "You can't have her." She came around and grabbed Daphne's other arm. Daphne became the object of a tug of war and started crying.

Stunned by Daniella's reaction, Cinda released the sobbing girl's hand. Daniella draped herself around Daphne. Cinda put her arms around the stiff, crying pair.

"Oh, please don't eat us," Daphne wailed.

"Eat you? Why would you think I wanted to eat you?" Cinda asked, horrified that they would think such a thing.

"Because trolls eat little girls," Daniella cried.

Trolls? "You think I'm a troll?"

The two bleary-eyed girls nodded.

"What makes you think that?"

"Aunt Marty said so," Daniella said bravely.

Martha. She should have guessed. *These two probably believe everything she says.* "How could I be a troll? I'm much too tall for a troll, you know. They are no taller than this." Cinda stood up and held her hand at shoulder height. For once she was glad she was so tall. "And they are this wide." She held her arms out well beyond her sides. "Their hair is really short and curly." Cinda took the pins from her hair and let it fall over her shoulder. "Any curl here?" She knelt down and held out her glossy hair to the girls to touch. They each caressed it gingerly, shaking their heads. "And trolls have long, pointy noses and drool all the time. Have you ever seen me drool?" They both shook their heads again. "Then how could I be a troll?" she concluded, holding her arms open. She wasn't sure if they believed her.

Daphne rushed into Cinda's embrace. Daniella held back with a pout.

"What's wrong, Daniella? Do you still think I'm a troll?"

She shook her head. "I don't want Mama to cry in heaven."

"Your mama won't cry."

"Yes she will," Daphne said emphatically, pushing away from Cinda. "She will think we don't love her anymore."

The poor girls had been so scared that they were denied love from the one person they were around all day. In Martha's attempt to get at Cinda, she clearly hadn't realized what she was doing to Daphne and Daniella. She couldn't know the effects it was having on them. Martha loved those little girls, Cinda was sure of that. It was Cinda who Martha disliked—just why, Cinda wasn't sure.

Cinda didn't want to frighten them any more than they already were. She let them play in their room with their dolls the rest of the day.

Martha and her brothers returned early from the fields. They came in through the kitchen door.

"Martha, I would like to talk with you," Cinda said, trying not to reveal her anger.

Martha completely ignored her and strode on by.

Cinda knitted her brows together. "Travis, would you stir this for me?" she asked, without even looking at him.

"I'm Trevor," he said awkwardly. Cinda had asked them to correct her when she called them by the wrong name. She wanted to learn their right names and couldn't do that if they allowed her to use the wrong name.

"I'm sorry," she said, looking at him. If she had bothered to look at him before she spoke, she would have noticed his bangs down as Trevor always wore them. If they ever changed and wore their hair the same, she would be at a loss to tell them apart. "Trevor, could you stir this for me and not let it burn?" She absently plopped the wooden spoon in his hand and took off after Martha.

"Martha, let's talk in your room where we won't be bothered," Cinda said.

Martha continued to pretend she didn't exist, thumbing through a book.

"You can talk to the *troll* now or Lucas later."

Martha's head popped up, her eyes wide.

"Now," Cinda commanded.

Martha silently stalked up to her room with Cinda on her heels. Martha crossed through her room and stared out the window.

Cinda closed the door firmly and stared at Martha's defiant back. She was waiting for Cinda to say something. Cinda wasn't sure where to begin. "How could you do it? How could you tell those sweet little girls I was trying to fatten them up to eat them?"

Martha shrugged her shoulders.

"Do you know that they have hardly eaten a thing in three days?"

Martha snapped around in surprise to look at Cinda. She was genuinely concerned.

"Yes, that's right. They are the ones suffering, not me. They are scared to death all day with no one to comfort them because you have taken that away from them. I know you don't like me, but please leave them out of it."

Martha could no longer hold Cinda's stare. Obviously, she had never meant to hurt the girls.

Cinda let her words sink in awhile before continuing. "I don't want to bring Lucas into this if I don't have to, and I don't think you want that either." Martha shook her head. "Then you better convince those two I'm not a troll and won't eat them. You better be so convincing they eat a hearty supper. Do you understand me?"

Martha nodded and made a move for the door.

"I'm not through with you yet. If they don't eat well, I will talk to Lucas after supper."

"I'll tell them," Martha said softly with downcast eyes.

"One more thing. Daniella and Daphne need all the tender loving care we can *all* give them. To make them think their mother is crying up in heaven because they hug me is hurting them as well. You let them know that no matter what they do, their mother and father will always love them. Always. Have I made myself clear?" Cinda's words were stern and not to be questioned.

Martha nodded. "Yes," she said barely above a whisper then jumped at the rap on the door.

"Marty, is Cinda in there?" came Lucas's voice through the door.

Martha looked at the door in a panic, then she looked back at Cinda.

"Yes, Lucas, I'm in here," Cinda called back and then opened the door. She smiled up sweetly at her husband, trying to douse the flames of anger she had felt moments before.

"I don't want to interrupt," Lucas said with uncertainty, looking from her to his sister and back again.

"You're not interrupting a thing. Martha was just on her way to play with the girls before supper," she said.

Martha took the hint and slipped past Lucas and Cinda without a word.

Lucas watched her go into the little girls' bedroom. "What was that about?" Lucas asked, swinging his gaze back to Cinda.

"Girl talk."

Lucas raised his eyebrows and smiled at the promising prospect. She swept past him and went down to check on supper.

Daniella and Daphne ate, but Martha spent the meal nervously watching them and Cinda. The days that followed, however, were filled with happiness and hugs for the two little girls. Martha seemed as relieved as Cinda.

Cinda focused a lot of her attention on the girls. She made new dresses for their dolls, replaced the yarn hair, and drew new faces with almond-shaped eyes, long lashes, and smiling mouths. She opened a jar of cherries they would have at supper and painted the lips red.

Next it was time to get back to the chore of scrubbing the house and making curtains. Cinda took the girls and Dewight into town to buy some scrub brushes and window fabric. Cinda also bought fabric for two more dresses for each of the girls. Dewight disappeared when they got into town and magically reappeared when Cinda was ready to leave. Cinda was grateful for the break from his annoying, nonsensical rambling.

No one was really sure of Dewight's real name, but someone in town thought he might be a man who once had a place in the hills. They thought the man's name was Dewight and his homestead burned to the ground some thirty years ago, killing his family. He'd been wandering ever since.

❧

"Ooooo," Daphne sighed.

"It's soooo prettiful," Daniella crooned.

The girls were eyeing a white handkerchief with a delicate lace border it that Cinda had put up as a prize for the best wall scrubber. Armed with scrub brushes and a pail of soapy water, the girls went to work. They each had a wall to scrub and Cinda cleaned the other two walls in their little room. Cinda helped them reach the high areas but they worked diligently for an hour. Each would check out how the other was doing, then go back to her wall and work harder. Cinda had finished two walls and half the floor when both girls were finally satisfied.

Cinda studied both walls carefully. They had both done

such a good job she couldn't reward one and not the other. "It seems as though we have a tie."

"A tie?" Daphne asked, raising her eyebrows up and down, and up and down again.

"I don't want a tie. I want the handkerchief," Daniella whined.

"A tie means you both win. Let me find another prize."

"But I don't want another prize. I want the prettiful handkerchief," Cinda heard one of them say on her way out. She was certain it was Daniella.

Cinda returned a minute later with her hands in her pockets. She pulled out the white handkerchief with the lace from one pocket and handed it to Daniella. She snatched the handkerchief from Cinda's hand and said to Daphne in an encouraging tone, "You get the other prize."

From her other pocket Cinda removed a lavender handkerchief with a purple iris embroidered in one corner.

Daphne's eyes got as round as her mouth. "Ooooh. It's beautiful." She cuddled it to her face. "I love it."

They raced each other to the barn, trying to be the first one to show Lucas. When Cinda caught up with them, Lucas was praising their work and complimenting their dainty prizes. He looked up at Cinda adoringly. His eyes sparkled with a hint of moisture. She could tell he was pleased, and it warmed her heart that he cared so much. This big, strong fortress of a man seemed as soft as a baby chick on the inside.

❧

Two nights later Daniella and Daphne came to the table after everyone was seated. Lucas had had them doing something for him. After supper they made Cinda close her eyes. When she opened them, before her sat a cake with a single lit candle and a wrapped present.

"What's this for?" Cinda asked, confused.

"It's your birthday, May seventeenth," Lucas said.

Cinda was astonished. Had time really passed so swiftly that it was her twenty-fourth birthday already? She had been there for a month and a half. "How did you know?"

"I asked Allison on the train platform before we left." Lucas held her gaze for a long moment.

"Open your present," Daphne begged.

"No, blow out the candle," Daniella countered.

"We have to sing first," Daphne corrected.

After a round of "Happy Birthday," the candle was extinguished and Cinda untied the green ribbon from the gift.

"The ribbon is for your hair. It matches your eyes. That's what Uncle Lucas said." Daniella rubbed the ribbon.

Cinda glanced up at Lucas and gave him a smile of approval. He could be so thoughtful. She looked at the gift and peeled back the paper. It was a small ceramic jewel box like her mother's, the one that had broken in transit. Cinda bit her bottom lip, trying to hold back the tears.

"See, we told you Uncle Lucas could fix anything," Daphne said.

"He certainly can," she said and looked at him not only with her eyes but with her heart as well. She felt something there. Could it be love?

"Open it," Daniella called out.

Cinda raised the lid slowly. Inside was a single strand of pearls, just longer than choker length.

"They belonged to my mother," Lucas said apprehensively.

That was it. The dam burst and the tears flowed freely. "They're beautiful," Cinda murmured through quivering lips.

Martha got up swiftly and stormed out of the house.

"What's her problem?" Travis asked, clueless.

Cinda had seen that loathsome look on Martha many times, but just now she finally understood it. The girl was jealous and hurt of the time and attention Lucas showed Cinda. Lucas was more like a father than a brother to Martha, and now Papa had a new bride. She was no longer the only woman in his life. Cinda unknowingly was taking everything that was hers—her brother, her nieces. . .her pearls. She had expected to get her mother's pearls; she had never thought they would be given to a stranger. One day Cinda would relinquish them to her. Martha's caring about something as feminine as a string of pearls was a glimpse of the woman hidden deep within.

Lucas came around the table and put the pearls around Cinda's neck. "Thank you," was all Cinda could manage.

fifteen

That night Cinda and Lucas took their usual walk. Cinda couldn't keep her hand from fingering the pearls. He had been so thoughtful from the beginning to think to inquire about her birthday, then to surprise her with a cake and such thoughtful gifts. This was just like the kind of romantic love she read about in so many books. Could this big, strong man really love her? Or was he just grateful she was raising his nieces to be ladies? She liked to think that maybe he could love her. . .someday.

They stopped at their usual spot next to the corral. After a moment of silence Lucas said, "Do you know what's the most beautiful sight to a man?"

His wife? she hoped. "What?"

"The land he owns stretched out before him," he said, making a sweeping gesture with his arm, "growing green and lush. It's your land, too, now. Isn't it a wondrous sight?"

Cinda, disappointed, looked out at the swaying green land. To her it was just a green field like so many others she had seen. Nothing special about it. She supposed she had read too many romance stories where the man falls in love with a woman and can't live without her. Real life wasn't like that. She should be happy to have a good man with whom to grow old.

She had seen love. David and Allison certainly loved one another. Alvin was in love with Vivian. Eve loved men—period. And Cinda's father had loved her mother with his whole heart. He loved her so much that life without her was impossible. Yes, a deep lasting love did happen in real life, but it was reserved for a precious few. She felt fortunate to have seen such a devoted love in her parents, but for her it was unlikely. How could it be with everything happening around here? Except for their short nightly walks, Cinda and Lucas were rarely alone or spoke to each other. His days were filled with caring for the fields, the livestock, and providing for everyone. Her days were filled with two active little girls and enough household chores to keep her busy for a lifetime. No, there would be no time for love here.

That night Cinda took off the pearls and put them in her new jewel box with her mother's cameo, her mother's wedding band, and a small emerald ring her uncle had given her on her eighteenth birthday. She knew there would be very little opportunity to wear any of them. She had worn her mother's cameo only once since the day she arrived. If she were back home, she would have had many occasions to wear each of them.

ã

Cinda had heard Trevor, Travis, and Martha talking about Dewight's odd behavior. Travis said they had never seen so much of Dewight. Normally, he would disappear for days at a time except in the dead of winter. That was the only time he generally stayed close to the farm. Trevor said he was acting different because Cinda always set a place for him at the table. He knew he was welcome with her.

Cinda thought Dewight was odd indeed but not for the same reasons the others thought so. They seemed not to notice his talking to himself and not making sense, or maybe they just ignored it. Cinda couldn't ignore it when she was around it so much.

"The apple tree always blooms in spring. Always in the spring," Dewight mumbled as he came in through the kitchen door, walked through the dining area and out the front door.

Cinda could only stare after him. He seemed to have a purpose in coming in with his message and back out again, but even the little twins ignored him. He had carved each of them a beautiful wooden pony, and that said to Cinda that he didn't have the mind of a crazy man. What he did, he did with purpose. It only made sense that what he said, he said with purpose.

Cinda looked at the apple tree already losing blooms, sprinkling petals in Martha's short, dark curls as she sat below its limbs. Sure enough, it bloomed in the spring. She wondered if in the summer he would mention the fruit, and in the fall the leaves turning, and in the winter the bare branches. Maybe he was just a senile old man ranting.

Cinda watched as Martha stood and pulled down a branch, drinking in the sweet fragrance of the blossoms. Cinda hadn't expected her to do that. Dwight's words rolled around this vision of Martha. She, like the apple tree, would bloom. She was on the verge of her own spring, and bloom she would in her own time and her own way. Next, Cinda saw Martha racing off on Flash. She was afraid of nothing. Cinda decided not to worry any more over Martha's impending womanhood. She might not have traditional feminine qualities, but she would have special qualities all her own.

Cinda's reverie was interrupted by a sudden squawking of the chickens in the yard. She ran out to see what had them fussing so. She hoped it wasn't a fox or something dangerous—the girls were out there playing. Daniella and Daphne were there indeed, watching their uncles, Trevor and Travis, duke it out. Why were they fighting? Determined to find out, Cinda marched over to them. She tried to get their attention by calling out their names. It was no use. What on earth would make them fight each other like this? Brother should not be fighting against brother. Not having any brothers or sisters, she knew siblings were something to be treasured.

Cinda stepped closer to them, ready to shout and command their attention. Before she could, one of them drew back a fist, catching her mouth with his elbow. At the same time the other one swung, grazing his brother's face and popping Cinda in the cheekbone. Cinda's hands flew to her face. Daniella and Daphne started screaming. Trevor and Travis froze in horror. When Cinda got over the initial shock, she went over to the little twins to calm their fears.

"I'm okay," Cinda said to the weeping pair.

"You have a bleed," Daphne screeched.

Cinda touched her mouth where the frightened girls were pointing. Sure enough, there was a little blood at the corner of her mouth. After she calmed the girls, she turned back to the stunned pair of fighters.

"Why'd you step into a fight like that?" Travis ventured to ask.

"Because I wanted to find out why the two of you were fighting."

"He took my biscuit and ate it," Trevor explained.

"If you would eat faster, then I wouldn't have taken it," Travis replied.

Cinda balled up her fists. "You mean to tell me that you two were fighting over a biscuit?" Two nearly grown men fighting like wild animals over a silly biscuit. "Get in the house, both of you, now."

They immediately obeyed.

"Lucas is going to kill you," one said to the other.

"Me? You hit her, too," the other shot back, backhanding his brother in the chest. Unless facing them, she couldn't tell them apart, but she could tell from the tone of their voices that they were genuinely scared about what Lucas would do to them when he found out.

"I didn't know she was there. I couldn't see her. You should have told me she was there."

"It's not my fault. I didn't see her until it was too late."

"We're both going to get it." They hung their heads.

Oh my. What would Lucas do? Travis and Trevor certainly hadn't meant to hit her. She was the one at fault. Well, maybe they could be blamed a little for fighting in the first place. She would tell Lucas it wasn't their fault, or she could just say she fell or something.

"Do you still want a biscuit?" Cinda asked Trevor once inside the house. Trevor gave a little nod. These two were like a pair of two year olds. She could deal with two year olds. Cinda set a full bowl of biscuits and another cookie sheet full of biscuits on the table. "Good. You and your brother get to eat biscuits. Every last one. Do I make myself clear?"

They both nodded and sat down. "Are you gonna tell Lucas what we done?" Trevor asked.

"Just what is it you two don't want me to know you have done?" Lucas asked. He was just returning from town, no doubt hungry for his own lunch. He looked closely at his brothers and gave a half smile. "You two fighting again? Well, I guess it was only a matter of time. The peace couldn't last forever."

They stared wide-eyed at him. Cinda almost felt sorry for them.

"They fighted because Uncle Travis took Uncle Trevor's food," Daphne explained.

"And he ate it, too." Daniella didn't want to be left out of this exciting story. "Then they hit Cinda."

"They did what?"

Cinda tried to escape into the kitchen, but Lucas caught hold of her arm and turned her to face him. He lifted her face to examine the damage. He studied the split in the left corner of her mouth and the shine on her cheek. Fire flashed in his eyes.

"Which one? Which one did this?" Lucas demanded. He turned to his brothers and brought his fist down on the table. "Which one of you?"

Oh, dear. What was Lucas going to do? There had been enough hitting for one day. "I did it," Cinda said. "I was foolish enough to walk into the middle of a fight. I am the one to blame."

"A man never hits a woman for any reason, ever!" Lucas was yelling. "I want you two outside. Now!"

"Sit down," Cinda barked when they started to stand like sheep going to the slaughter.

"Stay out of this," Lucas growled.

Though startled by Lucas's gruffness, she couldn't let him harm them. "I'll not have brother fighting brother. That's why this whole thing started. Unless you want to be the next one hitting me—"

Lucas spun around to face her. She flinched slightly. His face contorted. "I would never hit you."

"If you raise a hand to either one of them, I will step in between you and them. You'll have to knock me out of the way." Cinda could feel the anger heat her face, and her voice trembled.

Lucas's face was red as well and his nostrils flared. He stormed out of the house.

Cinda turned around to see two wide-eyed young men staring at her. "Eat," she barked. They shoveled in the biscuits.

Shaken, Cinda went into the kitchen. She had never heard Lucas speak with such harshness to anyone. He hadn't seemed upset that his brothers were beating on each other, so why had he gotten so angry?

A sudden realization hit her. He got mad when he learned they hit her.

❧

Lucas stormed out and grabbed the reins of his horse from where it was tethered to the hitching rail. He marched to the barn and threw open the door as hard as he could. It slammed against the wall. The horse nickered and pulled back.

"Come on, Boy." Lucas pulled on the reins.

He led the hesitant horse into his stall and yanked at the strap to loosen the saddle. How could his foolish brothers get themselves in a position to hit Cinda? The thought of her hurt tore at him.

"What's got you spittin' nails?" Marty said behind him.

He spun around to see her leaning over the side of the stall. He glowered at her. She was no better.

She held up her hands in mock surrender. "Whatever it is, I didn't do it. I swear."

He pointed at her. "Your brothers did." He turned back to the horse. He had never before not claimed any of his siblings. He had spent his whole adult life looking after them and keeping them together. But right now he felt like there were a few too many Rawlings around. "Why can't they solve their problems without using their fists?"

"They was fightin'?" Marty said astonished. "You're riled up because they was fightin'? Since when?"

"They weren't just fighting." He yanked the saddle from the horse's back, then flung it over the stall rail and brought his fist down on it. "They hit Cinda, both of them. She's going to have a black eye and a fat lip."

"Is that all?"

"Is that all!" he bellowed.

"A lot worse has happened to me in fights, and you never got this mad."

Lucas ignored the hurt tone in her voice. "This is different." He stomped over and grabbed a brush.

"Why? Because it's sissy Cinderella. She'll live."

"Because she didn't deserve it." He shook the brush at her with each word. "You, on the other hand, pick your fights." He turned to the horse and made a long, quick stroke down his back with the brush, then shoved the brush in Marty's hand. "Take care of my horse." He strode out of the barn.

There was one too many Rawlings in the barn for his liking. He needed to be alone. Marty was right, of course. Cinda would be fine, but just the thought of her being hurt twisted his insides something fierce—not just because she was a woman to be protected and taken care of but because she was Cinda, his wife, whom he cherished and cared for. His insides twisted more when he recalled her flinching when he hollered. How could he have yelled at her? She wasn't at fault. It was his pig-headed brothers he was angry with.

As he took off up the hill as fast as he could, he tried unsuccessfully to pray. He needed to run off some of his fury.

❧

Lucas was gone the rest of the day and didn't show up for supper, and Trevor and Travis weren't hungry after all those biscuits so they skipped supper. The meal seemed quiet with so many missing even though Daniella and Daphne couldn't tell Martha enough times about Trevor and Travis hitting Cinda. Cinda just wanted to forget the whole horrible situation.

After supper, Trevor and Travis showed up to do the dishes. Lucas came in as well.

Cinda grabbed his plate. "I'll fix you up some food."

"I'm not hungry." He motioned her toward the door and took her outside for their walk. They walked in silence around the yard and ended up at their usual spot by the corral.

"I'm sorry for yelling at you. It was my brothers I was mad

at, not you." Lucas didn't look at her.

"It really was an accident. They didn't know I was so close to them."

"I know, they told me."

"Oh, Lucas, you didn't. . .hit them?"

He faced her. "No, I didn't. And I wouldn't have this afternoon either."

"But you were so mad, I thought. . ."

"My brothers may talk with their fists from time to time, but I prefer not to. I was just going to talk to them. I wanted to know how they could get in such a fool position."

"Just talk?" she questioned.

He smiled slightly. "All right. I would have yelled the roof off the barn, but I wouldn't have hit them—not that they knew that for sure."

"I don't think they will be fighting again."

"At least not anywhere near you," Lucas said, and they both laughed.

Lucas became serious again. "Please know that I would never strike you." His eyes were pleading with her. He held out his hand for her to take.

She took his hand and smiled. "I know."

With his other hand he tilted her head up to look at her injuries. "Does it hurt much?"

"No, not really. A little when I smile. Your brothers knew just what to do. It seems they have had some experience tending these kinds of wounds."

"They've had a lot of experience." He gently touched the bruise on her cheek. His touch was so light it left her skin tingling. His eyes lowered to her split lip. He softly kissed the unharmed corner of her mouth.

She was once again surprised by the gentleness in this big, strong, proud man. Wrapping her in his arms, he held her in silence for a long while. She felt safe in his tight embrace.

Before falling asleep that night, she prayed.

Father God in heaven, I praise Thee for the grace you have bestowed on me and Thy loving mercy. Keep Daphne, Daniella, Lucas, Trevor, Travis, and Martha safe. . .and, oh yes, Dewight, too. I worry about him wandering off and getting hurt. Teach Travis and Trevor to settle their disagreements in a different way.

She paused and took a deep breath. *I know I should be thankful for this family, but I can't quite find the gratitude in my heart yet. Please continue to work in me. I always prayed for a large family. I never imagined this is how You would answer that prayer.*

Lucas rolled over in his sleep and draped a muscular arm across her waist. *Lucas is a good, kind man. I thank You for that.* She yawned. *I better end or I'll fall asleep before I finish. One more thing, could You please do something about Martha? Amen.*

sixteen

The rooster crowed, announcing the beginning of a new day. Cinda pulled the covers over her head. No, it couldn't be morning already. Hadn't she only just dropped into bed? Why were the noisy, chaotic days so long and the peaceful nights so short? She wanted to ignore the wake-up call. To sleep in just once would be so delightful, but she knew she couldn't do that. Lucas was already up milking the cow and would expect to greet her as he always did when he came in the kitchen with the pail of milk and a kiss. Then everyone else would slowly get up and the day would be underway, not stopping until after dark when it was time to fall back into bed.

Today she wanted to finish the church dresses for Daniella and Daphne, shirts for Lucas and Travis needed mending, and Trevor had a pair of pants that required a patch. Keeping the house clean was a constant battle. The kitchen floor definitely needed a good scrubbing. Then there were the daily chores of cooking and keeping up with a pair of active five year olds.

Cinda readied herself and went down to the dreary kitchen. Although she had cleaned it several times, it still looked dull. She had made some yellow gingham curtains to cheer up the window, but the rest of the kitchen was still drab. The broken and uneven shelves still wobbled. She had attempted to fix them but only ended up with a battered thumb and frazzled nerves. As soon as Lucas was not so busy, she would ask him to fix them. He'd already had so many burdens placed on him from such a young age, but never once did she hear him complain nor would she.

She wanted to do a little decorating to make the house seem more homey, but there was never time. Today would be no different.

Martha was the first one down. "What's for breakfast, Cinderella?"

Cinda took a deep breath. "I'll make a deal with you. You call me by my name, Cinda and I will call you Marty instead of Martha."

Marty looked at her for a moment, then shrugged her shoulders on her way out of the kitchen.

After a noisy breakfast, Cinda sat down and completed the mending and sewing while Daniella and Daphne played quietly at her feet. It was a nice change from their usual squabbling. Lunch was noisy as well but uneventful. Afterward, Cinda worked on the kitchen floor. With Daniella and Daphne outside with their aunt and uncles, she finished the task in no time.

Suddenly Cinda found herself with what looked like an hour to herself before she should start supper. She spent about ten minutes walking around the house making a list of the things needed to spruce up the place—curtains, doilies, maybe a rug for the sitting room. Then she settled herself in the rocking chair in the sitting room. She sighed. It was good to get off her feet and rest. She picked up a book she had been wanting to read, one she had started several weeks ago when she had a spare minute but hadn't been able to get back to until now. This was her chance to escape to another world for a little while. Even Dewight's annoying ramblings wouldn't spoil her solitude.

She reread the beginning to refresh her memory. Just as she became engrossed in the story, however, chaos sounded in the kitchen. Cinda ran in and found a muddy piglet and two muddy five year olds scrambling across her clean floor.

Daphne and Daniella squealed as much as the pig. Their mud-drenched clothes sprayed everything as the girls spun around, chasing the pig.

Cinda's first thought was to stop the flying mud. The only way to do that was to stop that grubby swine. As the squealing hunk of ham came toward her in the doorway, threatening to muddy the rest of the house, she reached for it. She fell half on it, capturing it in her grasp. "Somebody take this thing," she said, stunned by what she had done.

Marty waltzed in and took the piglet from Cinda. "Sorry, Cinderella. It just got loose," she said with a shrug.

Cinda clenched her fists. She was *not* Cinderella and obviously the chat she had with *Martha* this morning fell on deaf ears or a cold heart. Then there was her floor. Her beautifully clean floor now was smeared with mud. The cupboards were splattered as well. She gritted her teeth. *One, two, three, four, five, six, seven, eight, nine, ten,* she rattled off as fast as she could under her breath.

Lucas blocked Martha's escape. He surveyed the muddy scene and took the piglet and pointed to the twins. "See to it that those two get cleaned up."

"But Travis was the one who let them play with Chuckie."

"Now! Take them down to the creek and get as much mud off as you can." Lucas left no room for argument.

Martha huffed and held out both her hands. Daniella and Daphne each claimed one.

Lucas left with the pig, leaving Cinda sitting on the dirty floor in a muddy dress. If she got started right away, she would be done in time to fix supper.

She got a scrub brush and filled a pail with water. Her arms and shoulders were still sore from cleaning it the first time. Well at least she would be off her feet. Tears stung her eyes.

Just when she thought she had a moment to herself, it had

been viciously ripped away. Cinda clenched her fists and growled. "I can't take it any longer. There's always one more thing to do, no one to talk to, no one to confide in, no one to lean on." She rubbed her hand on the muddy floor. Frustration boiled under the surface. "Does the dirt never end?" She slapped the floor and blinked as a mist of mud sprayed her face.

Cinda angrily scanned her dismal surroundings. She marched over to the shelves. Afraid to put anything on them for fear they would fall down completely, she lifted the edge of one rotting board and let it drop on its support. The support pulled out of the side board. Cinda jumped slightly as the shelf crashed to the bottom. "Kindling, that's all they're good for."

Still fuming, she surveyed the entire kitchen. "A kitchen without a pantry is like a house without a roof. This is pathetic. There isn't a mixing bowl left that isn't chipped and cracked." She looked at the dented and bent metal plates; pushing them aside, she shook her head. They had obviously been pounded out a time or two. She held up two wooden spoons, the only cooking utensils. One had a piece missing and the other's handle was broken. "What use are these?" How was she supposed to cook decent meals under these conditions? She glanced at the room as a whole. "This whole kitchen is a joke. One big joke," she yelled, half laughing and half crying.

The anger built inside her as she scanned the room, looking for something, anything about the kitchen that was good. Even the pump creaked and was difficult to use. She turned and heaved the pair of broken spoons at the wall. She should count to ten, but this felt so much better.

Then she caught her breath. Out of the corner of her eye she saw a stunned Lucas standing in the doorway. She faced him and stared in horror. How long had he been there? She hoped it wasn't long, but from the pained expression on his face, he had heard enough. He went back outside without a word, looking dejected and downtrodden.

. How could she have said all those things? She had criticized his mother's kitchen. She hadn't meant to hurt him. Could she take it all back? No. Once spoken, words can never be retrieved. The damage was done.

"But the tongue can no man tame; it is an unruly evil, full of deadly poison," the Bible said. Her tongue had certainly spewed poison, and Lucas was its victim. She fell to her knees next to the pail of water, defeated, and started scrubbing.

seventeen

Lucas rose earlier than normal and milked the cow before leaving for town in the wagon.

He never spent much time in the kitchen, and he hadn't realized how pathetic it really was. It used to be a nice kitchen, one his mother had been proud to show off to occasional visitors.

Cinda hadn't complained once about it. She had asked him to repair the shelves when he had time, but the job didn't seem urgent, and he forgot. He couldn't blame her if she wanted to up and leave. He certainly hadn't provided a very appealing home for her. But that would change. Starting today, he would make it her home too—change whatever she wanted to make her feel like it was hers. He wondered if this was how his father felt when his mother wanted something. He had always gone to the ends of the earth to please her.

Lucas pulled into town and headed straight for the mercantile. He bought all the lumber Jed Overman had on hand, which wasn't much, and ordered more. It would be enough to get started. He bought paint, nails, and more of that yellow yard goods Cinda had at the window. At least he had noticed that much. While he was there he picked up the food supplies, so he wouldn't have to make an extra trip into town.

"You're cleaning me out, Lucas," Jed said with a whistle. "What you doin', building a whole new house or something?"

"Or something," Lucas said smiling. "You got any cooking spoons?"

"Over there." Jed pointed to an area to the back. Jed was near fifty, with one arm stumped just below the elbow. He had lost it during the War Between the States. Now he ran the store with his wife and daughter.

Lucas sifted through the kitchen stuff and came up with a metal spoon. "Is this all the kitchenware you have?"

"What are you looking for?" Jed said as Lucas moved back to the counter.

"I don't know. What do you need in a kitchen?"

"That's not my domain." He turned toward the back. "Maggie, got a customer who needs your help."

Maggie appeared from the back room and went through the catalog with Lucas. Lucas ordered everything she suggested.

"That's one lucky lady you got yourself, Lucas. Hang on to her," Maggie Overman said and returned to the back.

"I intend to, but I'm the lucky one."

"Tell me how a no-good scoundrel like you got a beautiful, refined, citified wife," Lem Dekker said, slapping him on the back. Lem had arrived a few minutes before and had leaned over watching what Lucas chose from the catalog.

Lucas had gone to school with Lem, and he took his good-natured harassing for the fun it was. "All I can say is I don't deserve her," he began but was cut off.

"We already know you aren't worthy of such a delicate flower. Whatcha do, hog-tie her?" Jed teased.

"I know, it was a shotgun weddin'," Lem jumped in with a chuckle. "That's the only way a pretty thing like her would have anything to do with a ugly mug like him." He chucked his thumb toward Lucas.

Lucas stood there with a smile and took their ribbing.

Maggie appeared from the back room again with two old dresses their daughter Becky had outgrown years ago. The fabric was still good and could be made into dresses for the twins. "I think it was Lucas's good looks and charm that won her over." She handed the dresses to him.

Lem and Jed looked at Lucas, then at each other and said, "Naw."

"Thank you, Mrs. Overman," Lucas said, tipping his head to her. "I believe it was the good Lord Himself who saw fit to bless me."

Lem's smile faded. He shoved his hands into his pockets and walked out. "Hi, Lem," Becky said sweetly as he brushed past her without a word. Lem had had eyes for Lucas's sister, Lynnette, and was just as heartbroken as Lucas was when she married and ran off to Seattle. The two men had been through a lot together. Only Lucas was blessed many times over and Lem had nothing.

Lucas shed his smile as well. He knew Lem felt cursed by God at every turn and struggled to hold on to his faith. Most of the time he simply ignored God and pretended all was well. It pained Lucas to see his friend in such agony.

"I best be getting along." Lucas picked up a sack of flour and swung it over his shoulder.

"You tell that bride of yours to come by for a visit and a cup of tea. Becky and I are dying to get to know her," Maggie said. "We have too few womenfolk around these parts."

"And the ones we do have are looking after men who aren't looking back," Jed said, staring at his daughter's back as she gazed out the window at Lem.

Lucas headed for the door. "Lucas," Jed called after him, "Sam over at the post office said to tell you to stop in if I saw you."

"Thanks, Jed. I will."

❧

Cinda regretted her little explosion the day before. She told herself it was just because she was so tired. She hadn't meant to hurt Lucas. She didn't even know he was there. She wished she could take it back at least a hundred times. If she had only closed the kitchen door, the pig wouldn't have gotten in. But she had left it open so the floor would dry faster. As it turned out, it didn't get a chance to dry at all. She looked at the floor and could see several spots she had missed in her fury. She would have to get down on her hands and knees again today to get them.

Lucas came in with a box of canned goods. "There's a letter here for you." He set the box on the table and handed her the letter. The good news quickly edged out her bad feelings.

"It's from Allison." She sat in a chair excited to read the news. "I wonder if she's had her baby." She could hardly open it fast enough.

Lucas went out and returned with a sack of flour draped over his shoulder. "I hope it's good news." He put the sack down by the flour barrel. He turned to her when she didn't answer. He asked again. "Is it a girl or a boy?"

Cinda looked up at him with tears stinging her eyes. Lucas came over and knelt in front of her. "What is it? It's not her baby?"

Cinda shook her head. "I–It's my. . .m–my. . .my uncle."

Lucas wrapped his arms around her and held her close as she cried. When Cinda composed herself, she said with a quivering lip, "Allison says he's really sick. The doctor doesn't think he is going to make it." The tear dam burst again.

"I'm so sorry," Lucas said, holding her. "It's okay. Please don't cry."

He seemed worried by her tears so she did her best to collect herself. "I'm fine now." She struggled for control. "I don't want to keep you from your chores." Lucas didn't seem to know how to handle a distressed woman. It would be best if she found someplace private to cry. She didn't want him or anyone else fretting over her. He just nodded and got up to leave.

"Thank you for getting the provisions," Cinda said. He made two more trips to bring in the rest of the food he bought, then disappeared until supper.

Cinda tried to get her work done but caught herself staring blankly into space several times. She never knew how much time passed from her last conscious thought to when she jerked back to reality. She drifted through the day not completely aware of her surroundings.

Why did it have to be her uncle? He couldn't die. He had been a second father to her. She still needed him, and now he needed her. Almost as if coming out of a dark closet into the sunlight, she knew what she had to do. She had to go to him. But would Lucas let her? Would he keep her from going? She wouldn't ask, she would just tell him. . .after supper during their walk.

Supper went along as if nothing had happened. Why shouldn't it? For his family, nothing had happened. It wasn't their uncle on his deathbed. None of them had even met him, except Lucas the day they were married and hastily departed. Cinda lost what little appetite she had. She couldn't sit there any longer and pretend everything was fine. She shoved away from the table and put her plate in the sink. She slipped out the kitchen door. She was leaning against the peach tree when Lucas joined her a moment later. He stood silently next to her.

"He is like a father to me," Cinda said with a cloud of melancholy surrounding her. "He comforted me when my father died. I was always soaking his shirt with my tears. He was my strength. I can't imagine him sick. He's never sick, or at least he would never admit it. He can't be dying. He just can't." Tears streamed down her face.

Lucas encompassed her with his big arms. "Shh. It will be all right." Now her tears drenched his shirt.

Cinda appreciated his trying to comfort her, but she knew it wouldn't be all right. Her uncle was dying. The only person on earth who loved her was dying, and she was so far away.

"So when do you leave?" he finally asked, his voice heavy.

"Oh, Lucas, could I?"

"If you need to."

In the depths of his blue eyes she could see he wanted her to say no. "Yes. He needs me."

❧

Cinda refused to pack her black dress for the impending funeral. She had to think positive. Her uncle would be fine. She did pack her dark gray traveling suit, just in case.

Lucas leaned against the wall, watching Cinda pack her trunk.

Did he have to stand there watching her every move? He was always so busy around the farm. "I'm really not sure what to pack."

"When are you coming back?" Lucas asked.

Cinda ignored the forlorn tone in his voice. She couldn't think about him right now, only her uncle. "I don't know. It depends on how sick Uncle Barney is." She heard him shift positions. When she returned to the dresser for another garment, she glanced over at him. He was leaning on the window frame, staring out the window. He was usually so confident and in charge, but right now he looked like an insecure boy.

"Are you coming back?"

Cinda froze, staring unseeing at the folded nightgown she had retrieved from the drawer. Coming back? She tried to swallow the sudden lump in her throat. How could she answer him when she didn't know herself? All she had thought about was getting away from this wretched place and seeing her uncle. . .going home. She hadn't thought about coming back or the future. She should say something. But what?

His heavy footsteps crossed the room. The door creaked open, then quietly swung shut. She quickly turned to the door. She was alone, empty and alone. His slow, even footsteps faded down the stairs. Each one stabbed at her pounding heart.

Her uncle needed her. She couldn't think about anything else right now. She forced Lucas out of her thoughts and finished packing, but she wasn't sure who her tears were for—herself, her uncle, or Lucas. It didn't really matter. She was going and going with her husband's consent, that's what mattered. She *was* going.

She went to the jewel box Lucas had given her for her birthday and caressed the top of the ceramic box before opening it. She put her emerald ring on her right hand and pinned her mother's cameo at her throat. For a moment, she held the pearls in her hand, rolling their smooth, glossy texture between her fingers and thumb. She let them pour out of her hand and back into the jewel box, and then she took her mother's wedding ring and slipped it in her reticule. Like closing a coffin, she slowly closed the lid of the jewel box.

When she opened the bedroom door, Trevor was propped up against the wall, waiting for her. He took her suitcase, and she followed him downstairs. She expected Lucas to be in the wagon, but he was nowhere in sight.

"Where's Lucas?"

Trevor shrugged and helped Cinda aboard. He climbed in after her.

"Isn't Lucas driving me into town?"

"Guess not. He told me to take you and see you got on the stagecoach all right," he said, like it was perfectly normal for her husband not to take her.

Dewight appeared next to the wagon holding out a single meadow daisy for Cinda. When she took it, he bowed and left without his usual rambling.

Trevor snapped the reins and the wagon jerked into motion. Cinda took one last look at the farm. She thought she saw someone standing in the shadow of the open barn door. The shadow disappeared before she could make out who it was. Was it Lucas or just wishful imagination?

She got on the stage and waved to Trevor. Cinda was not looking forward to the bone-rattling ride. The coach managed to stay upright, barely, the only good thing about the trip.

After two days of bouncing around in the stage, Cinda was relieved to step aboard the train. As the train pulled out of town, Cinda noticed a lone rider on a hill. She hoped it wasn't a train robber—another traveling unpredictability. Then he disappeared. Cinda looked nervously for a robber and his buddies to appear. They never did. It was probably just her active imagination running wild because of the stress of traveling alone, her uncle being so ill, and too little sleep. She let go of the image and focused on the remainder of the trip.

eighteen

Stepping off the train, her eyes moistened. The familiar sights and sounds were refreshing. She had never noticed before, but there was even a distinct aroma to her home. She drank it all in.

"Cinda," a familiar voice called.

Cinda turned to see Allison sitting in a nearby buggy, waving her arm. She rushed over to her dear friend whose stomach was as big and round as a watermelon. After a quick hug, David loaded Cinda's trunk into the back of the buggy, and they were off to Cinda's old house.

As they drove through town, Cinda took in the faces of those she knew growing up. The places seemed more wondrous than she had ever realized. The simple school building she graduated from brought tears to her eyes, and when they passed her church, her heart quickened. She and Lucas were married there. Why had that thought popped into her head? It happened so quickly, she wouldn't have thought it would have made a lasting connection with her church of many years. Of all her memories of her childhood church, why did that one memory come to mind? *Probably because it was my last memory of the building,* she told herself.

Her thoughts turned to her uncle. "How is he?"

"He's failing fast. The doctor doesn't think he'll hang on much longer." Her friend patted her hand. "It's a good thing you got here when you did."

When they pulled up to her aunt and uncle's house, Cinda's first thought was. . .*home.* Funny, she had never thought of it that way before. Being away made it seem different some-how—less cold and lonesome.

She looked woefully at the doctor's buggy parked in front of the house.

"If you need anything, just let me know," Allison said as Cinda went through the gate.

Cinda nodded. "I will. Thanks."

David and Allison drove away as Cinda closed the gate. Lucas's face flashed before her. The night they first met, she had barricaded herself behind the gate. She left the memory lingering there as she continued up the front walk.

An eerie chill swept over her as she entered the deathly quiet house. Was the house always this quiet? Or had it been such a long time since she had been in absolute quiet that now the silence seemed loud?

She set down her suitcase and went up the stairs slowly, cautiously. Each step was one step closer to her uncle's pass-ing. If she stayed on that last step, maybe she could stop time itself and her uncle's imminent demise. She stood as still as a statue, staring at her uncle and aunt's bedroom door. That would be where he rested, if. . .

When the bedroom door opened, Cinda caught her breath. The doctor exited with his medical bag and a grim expres-sion. He held the door open for her. She moved slowly to the doorway, her feet dragging like lead. Her stomach twisted.

"It's only a matter of time," the doctor said as Cinda passed him at the door. "Send for me when he gets worse. I can't do anything for him but ease his pain. I'll be back in the morning to check on him." He closed the door and left.

There was no hope then. She walked in and sat at her uncle's bedside. Her aunt stared out the window.

"I don't know why you bothered to come. He's not likely to wake again," Aunt Ginny said toward the window.

Cinda ignored her and scooped her uncle's hand in hers. He would know she was there whether he woke or not. "I'm here, Uncle Barney. Your little Cinda is home." The words seemed odd to her somehow—because she was calling herself little or because of the tightness in her chest when she said home? This would never feel like home again without her uncle to warm it.

When he gets worse. The doctor's words kept echoing in her head, louder and louder.

WHEN.

It was a foregone conclusion—Uncle Barney *was* going to die. If she could only accept it, maybe it would make it easier.

She hoped and prayed for God to grant her this one miracle and spare her uncle's life. If he would wake up so she could talk to him one last time, maybe she could will him to live.

Cinda clutched her uncle's hand. Exhausted from her jarring trip, she laid her cheek on his hand and fell asleep.

Some time later, she was startled awake by her uncle's moving hand. She lifted her head and looked into her uncle's droopy eyes. His first look was one of recognition and joy, then he furrowed his brows and frowned.

"You shouldn't be here." He struggled with each word.

What! Of course she should. Did her uncle really not want to see her? Or was it delirium from the illness and medication?

"I couldn't stay away when you were sick," Cinda begged.

"I'll live or die whether you are here or not." He strained for breath. His energy sapped. "Go home, child. Go back to your hus—band." With that he slipped back asleep.

"I am home," she whispered. A tear rushed down her cheek.

&

Her aunt looked tired and weary. Cinda wondered how much sleep she had gotten since her uncle fell ill. It didn't look like much. With fretting over arriving in time and the arduous journey, Cinda hadn't slept much either.

The house was as spotless as ever and the kitchen sparkled. Cinda finally figured out the eerie feeling in the house. There were no smells except the heat of the approaching summer and the ensuing death. No baking bread, no simmering stew, no pie cooling in the window with its scent drifting in on the afternoon breeze. Nothing. The air was stripped bare. If death itself had a smell, this was it.

Cinda's tears came and left like waves. Aunt Ginny, on the other hand, hadn't dropped a single tear; her eyes remained dry. She stayed close to her husband except to prepare simple meals.

❧

Cinda tossed and turned as sleep evaded her. She kept wondering if her uncle would still be with them in the morning or if their heavenly Father had called him home during the dark hours of the night. It was doing her no good lying there, flipping back and forth. She rose with a foreboding feeling and donned her robe. She crept down the hall, cracked open the other door, and peered in.

Aunt Ginny was seated in the chair alongside the bed. Her uncle was awake and Ginny was reading to him by lamplight. Her aunt quit reading and looked up at her, and her uncle's gaze followed. He limply patted the bed next to him. He was glad to see her.

"Doesn't my Ginny have a beautiful voice?" he strained to say. Cinda nodded. Virginia Crawford had a melodious tone in her voice when she spoke kindly, and her singing was the loveliest in church.

As Cinda sat down, she exchanged glances with her aunt across the bed. Aunt Ginny stood and crossed to the window. It was still black as midnight. Cinda wondered just what time it was. It had to be close to dawn.

Barney Crawford tried to speak. Cinda stopped him. "Don't talk. Save your strength."

He smiled knowingly. "I have no strength left. My time has come."

"Don't say that."

"I have something important to say to you. You must listen." He was insistent, a sense of urgency in his frail voice.

Cinda bit her quivering bottom lip and nodded.

"Forgive her." He glanced over at his wife's back.

Just what did her uncle expect her to forgive Aunt Ginny for? For being cold and indifferent? For making an orphaned twelve year old feel unwelcome? For treating her like an unwanted stray mutt? For squelching her dreams? If her aunt did ask for forgiveness, could she give it to her? She wasn't sure.

He squeezed her hand. "If I can, so can you." Barney Crawford drew in a final, labored breath and was gone.

"No," Cinda sobbed. She looked up with tear-filled eyes at her stone-faced aunt.

Virginia Crawford never displayed excessive emotion in public. She left without a word or a tear.

Cinda looked sadly at the doorway through which her aunt had escaped. *This isn't public,* Cinda wanted to shout after her. *We can cry together. How could she not cry? Didn't she love him? How could she be married to this sweet, caring man for all these years and not love him? Everyone loved Uncle Barney.*

Maybe not everyone. Cinda shed a tear for her bitter aunt.

nineteen

Uncle Barney's friends crowded the cemetery. Cinda cried because she would miss her uncle. She also cried because of the throng of good people who were touched by her uncle's life. She never thought that so many people would attend. Allison had delivered her baby the morning Uncle Barney died and was unable to come, but David was there. Cinda told him she would come by next week to see Allison and David Junior.

After the funeral service, Cinda and her aunt accepted the condolences of friends and neighbors.

"For goodness sake, stop slouching. I would have thought you would have outgrown that by now." Aunt Ginny handed her unused handkerchief to Cinda, who had long since soaked hers.

Next her aunt would be scolding her for crying in public. Cinda straightened her shoulders and held her chin up. It had been awhile since she felt so tall. She noticed it actually hurt to slouch.

During the somber ride home, Cinda could hear the echo of her uncle's sweet voice in her ear. *"Forgive her."* She looked over at her stoic aunt sitting stiff and proper, without so much as a moist eye.

"Forbearing one another, and forgiving one another, if any man have a quarrel against any: even as Christ forgave you, so also do ye." The words filled her soul.

No, she couldn't forgive her, not this heartless woman. There had been too much hurt at her hand.

143

"Then came Peter to him, and said, LORD, how oft shall my brother sin against me and I forgive him? till seven times?

"Jesus saith unto him, I say not unto thee, Until seven times: but, Until seventy times seven.

It was too much to ask of her. She couldn't.

"And when ye stand praying, forgive, if ye have aught against any: that your Father also which is in heaven may forgive you your trespasses. But if ye do not forgive, neither will your Father which is in heaven forgive your trespasses."

She had done nothing wrong. She didn't need forgiveness. She focused on something else so she wouldn't have to listen to the little voice in her thoughts any more. Her heart hardened. The voice was silenced.

❧

That night a noise woke Cinda. She had a hard time waking herself enough to recognize the sound. *Crying?* More than crying, she realized, a heart-wrenching sob. *One of the twins probably had a bad dream.* She sat on the edge of her bed and pried open her eyes, shaking off the confusion.

Daniella and Daphne weren't there. The only one in the house was her aunt. Cinda walked groggily to her aunt's room and found her sitting in the middle of the empty bed she had shared with her husband for years. She was hunched over her bent knees, sobbing uncontrollably.

Cinda wanted to wrap her arms around her aunt to comfort her, but she wasn't sure her aunt would let her. She never had before. In fact, Cinda could not remember ever being hugged by her aunt. Cinda sat on the edge of the bed and tentatively put her arms around her aunt. Aunt Ginny didn't resist and leaned into her niece's embrace. In the lonesome darkness they mourned side by side, yet separately.

When the tears stopped, her aunt said through sniffles, "I did love him. I loved him so much."

Really? What should Cinda say? What could she say? She had never heard her aunt say she loved her uncle before. She had never seen her show love to anyone. She had never witnessed her display this much emotion. This was not the heartless aunt she knew.

"I know you don't believe me," Aunt Ginny said, getting off the bed, drying her face with her hands. She crossed to the window and looked into the empty blackness that mirrored her heart. "I didn't love him when I married him, of course. I was in love with another man. . .or at least I thought I was at the time. Only he had married someone else. I convinced myself he did it just to hurt me. Two weeks later I married Barney to prove to him and myself he couldn't hurt me."

All these years her aunt had settled for second best. The other man must have been quite exceptional to be considered better than her uncle, who Cinda thought was the best. . .next to her own father of course.

She obviously needed to get this off her chest. Her aunt stared out the window. "I was hurt and could never quite let go of it. When his wife died, I left Barney and went to him. I was so sure he wanted me." Her voice was far removed from this time and place. "It was all in my head, of course. He never said he wanted me. He never asked me to come. He never wanted me, even from the beginning. He couldn't even see me through his grief. He wasn't the man I thought he was, the man I thought I had fallen in love with. I realized Barney was the man I had thought the other was. I came back to Barney, begged for forgiveness and asked him to take me back."

It was like the dam had broken and every pent-up emotion was freed to rush forward. "We were actually doing well for awhile. Now there is no time left to make it up to him."

When did this all happen? While Cinda was in Montana?

No, she spoke as if it all happened long ago.

"I don't know why you are crying over him. You don't have to worry, you'll see him again." The confidence in her aunt's voice both comforted and confused her.

"What do you mean? You'll see him in heaven, too."

"God doesn't let the wicked in heaven."

"We are all sinners in God's eyes."

"I don't think even God could forgive my wicked heart when my own husband couldn't. Oh, he said he did. But in his heart," she thumped on her chest, "where it counted, there was no forgiveness there."

"But he did forgive you, from deep down in his heart. The last thing he said was 'Forgive her. If I can, so can you.' " Her uncle had known his wife had a deep need to be forgiven. She didn't know why her aunt needed her forgiveness, but Cinda felt she could finally forgive this hurting woman. "I forgive you too, Aunt Ginny."

Aunt Ginny let out a shrewd, knowing laugh. "You don't even know what you're forgiving, do you? If you knew, you wouldn't throw your forgiveness around so easily, you impudent child."

"Don't tell me what I can and can't forgive. I'm long past being a child, if you haven't noticed." Cinda was regretting coming in to comfort her grieving aunt.

"Easy for the ignorant to say, hard for the knowledgeable to do." Her eyes narrowed and her expression hardened.

"Then enlighten me," Cinda snapped back.

Her aunt turned fiery eyes on Cinda. "It was your fault he couldn't forgive me. You were a constant reminder—of him." Cinda looked at her curiously, shaking her head, confused. "Don't tell me you haven't figured it out? I thought you had known since you were a child. Everett, your father, he was the one. Didn't you ever wonder why Barney never visited your home? And when you visited here, you only came with your mother."

Her father! Her aunt had been in love with her father? "My father would never—"

"You're right. Everett never would, despite my efforts," her aunt said cutting her off. "I accepted Barney's proposal to have a reason to be near his brother-in-law. I tried my best to break your father and Olivia up. He was always a perfect gentleman—and an absolute sap over your mother."

Her aunt was like an erupting volcano, spilling over, destroying everything in its path. Why was she saying these hurtful things now that they didn't matter?

"I'm the reason they moved away from here." She pointed to herself. "Then when Olivia died, I took advantage of it and tried to trick Everett into marrying me for your sake. 'A girl needs a mother I told him.' "

"Stop it! Why are you doing this?"

"You're just like Olivia, too caring and forgiving. Olivia and I were best friends until I ruined it. I was a fool for so many years. She should have hated me, but she didn't. God sent you here to punish me and hate me for her."

Is that how her aunt saw her, a constant thorn in her side? The poor woman was tormented by her own guilt. She couldn't forgive herself or accept that others could. She was trying to finally make things right with her own husband. Then Cinda's father died and she was thrust upon her aunt as a reminder of her evil deed. No wonder her aunt never made her feel welcome. With Cinda in her home, Ginny could never escape her past.

Cinda felt like she should hate her aunt for everything she tried to do and did. She always wanted to hate her aunt, but there was nothing to base it on. Now she had something to hate her for, but she found compassion instead. Anything her aunt might have done, she had long since punished herself for.

Her aunt stood there waiting for Cinda's hatred. Cinda walked across the room and stood before her aunt.

Forgive, and ye shall be forgiven.

Cinda's heart softened toward her aunt and the bitterness melted away. "I don't hate you, and I do forgive you." Cinda couldn't blame her for falling in love with the most wonderful man in the world. . .Everett Harrison, Cinda's own father.

"How can you?" her aunt asked through tear-filled eyes.

"There is nothing for me to forgive." Cinda found tenderness for her aunt. "Uncle Barney forgave you years ago. So did my father and my mother. God has forgiven you. You need to forgive yourself and accept our forgiveness." She hadn't realized until now that to her uncle she was always his little sister's child, but to Aunt Ginny she was always Everett's daughter.

Ginny buried her face in her hands. "I'm sorry for everything. I'm sorry for not treating you better."

Cinda's eyes teared up and she threw her arms around her aunt. They mourned together for an uncle and husband who would be dearly missed. They mourned for years of denied love. They mourned for a friendship long overdue.

twenty

"Allison, he's beautiful. David must be so proud," Cinda cooed over the newborn baby she cradled in her arms.

"David can't stop talking about him. He's a good papa." Allison smiled broadly. She, too, was proud of her little bundle of joy. "David fusses over us something terrible. He won't let me do a thing." She leaned close to Cinda and whispered in a teasing tone, "You won't tell him I'm out of bed, will you?"

The two laughed.

Allison grew serious and patted Cinda's arm. "How are you doing?"

"I'm doing fine. It is hard to believe Uncle Barney is really gone. I keep expecting to smell his pipe smoke filtering through the house." Cinda got a mischievous look on her face. "I even lit it yesterday just to be able to smell it. I thought Aunt Ginny was going to faint when she came in and saw me. I think she actually expected to see him in his chair."

Cinda went on to explain about Aunt Ginny having been in love with her father. She told Allison about them crying and talking together and how they were getting along wonderfully now. Her aunt's guilt had been between them all those years. Now that it was confessed and forgiven, they could be friends.

Cinda fixed some tea and poured them each a cup.

"How long will you be staying?" Allison asked her.

Cinda sipped her tea, putting off the question. "I haven't

decided." She couldn't look at Allison.

After a moment of uncomfortable silence, Allison said, "You're not planning on going back, are you?"

Cinda looked up. "I don't know, Allison. What should I do?"

Her friend shook her head with a look of sympathy and understanding.

Cinda let out a heavy sigh. "I went into this thing in such a rush. I thought it was God's will, but now I wonder. I don't know that I made the right decision. Maybe God wasn't calling me to marry Lucas. Maybe I was just trying to escape Aunt Ginny. . .and. . .being an old maid. I think I made a terrible mistake."

"Was he really awful?" Allison held compassion in her eyes. "He seemed nice enough."

"Lucas? No, he's not awful at all." Cinda drew in a long, thoughtful breath. "Lucas is wonderful. He's caring, tender, giving, and loving."

"He sounds perfect," Allison said, raising her eyebrows in question. "I don't see what the problem is."

"He has one major flaw," Cinda said tight-lipped. "Travis, Trevor, Martha, Daniella, Daphne—and Dewight."

Allison looked at her hands and moved her fingers. "I count six flaws."

"I always wanted to have a big family—and I wouldn't mind them so much, if they weren't all so impossible." Cinda huffed and closed her eyes for a moment, conjuring each one up in her mind. "Martha doesn't even know she's a girl. Excuse me, Marty. She calls me Cinderella. She knows I hate it. Then there is Dewight. He rambles and appears from nowhere."

Allison shivered. "It gives me the creeps just thinking about him."

"He's not all that bad. I figured out that most of what he says actually makes sense if you have the time to figure out what it means. He really is harmless, unlike Travis and Trevor."

"Those are Lucas's twin brothers you can't tell apart?"

Cinda nodded. "They fight each other over the most ridiculous things. They were actually fighting about their food. I ended up with a black eye and a split lip."

"They hit you?"

"They didn't mean to. I really shouldn't have gotten so close."

"Was Lucas mad?"

"Furious, but he didn't lay a hand on them. Despite his size, he is really very gentle. You should see him with Daniella and Daphne. They can be quite a handful at times. He's a good father to them."

Cinda paused for a moment, then focused on her friend. "I feel really wicked for not wanting to go back. It would be so much easier if I stayed here."

"Maybe. But you'll never be at peace."

"You think it's peaceful there?"

"I'm not talking about peace on the outside. I know you won't be content here, not really. The Lord won't let you. You don't belong here anymore."

That's just what her uncle had told her. "I thought you would want me to stay."

"I do, but more than I want to satisfly my own selfish desires, I want you to be happy. You won't have the joy of the Lord going against Him."

"I told you, I'm not sure it was God's will. I think I acted hastily without the Lord's blessing."

"Mistake or not, Lucas is still your husband, and God wants you at your husband's side. It's not like Lucas has hurt you. You admitted that yourself."

"No. He has never hurt me. He's always been so. . ." Her words trailed off as she thought of Lucas. No doubt he was out in one of the fields seeing to it nothing got neglected. Or riding out on his horse, sitting tall in the saddle. Or hunting for food to put on the table. Or tending to a scraped knee. She took a deep breath and exhaled. "Selfless. That's what Lucas is. Everything he does is for someone else."

"I'll miss you." Allison had a wistful expression.

"What?" Cinda asked, coming out of her dreamy state.

"When you leave, I'll miss you."

"Am I leaving?" She had hoped for someone to make the decision for her, though she knew it was hers alone to make.

"Yes. You'll go. You're only putting it off for a little while."

"How can you be so sure, when I'm not?"

"I just know, and I know you. It's something in your eyes when you talk about them. . .about him. They are a part of you now. They're your family, and family has a way of getting under your skin."

*

Cinda didn't remember her bed being so terribly uncomfortable and cold. She pulled the covers around her neck. How could she be cold? It was almost summer. It had been colder in Montana, but she had never felt it.

Cinda had unconsciously slipped back into the routine of being "home." She thought the peace and quiet was wonderful, and she enjoyed being able to sleep in. She actually got to read a book, and she was getting along with her aunt better than she ever imagined possible. With the barrier of guilt stripped away, they had nothing to stop them from being friends, at last. Her aunt even let her in the kitchen. All the while, though, Cinda couldn't shake the uneasy feeling, like something bad was going to happen; but hadn't it already?

Cinda took her place in the doorway of the kitchen. She

watched her aunt kneading bread dough.

Aunt Ginny caught sight of her. "Come help me make these pies for the church social tomorrow." She turned the kneaded dough into the greased bowl and draped a towel over it to let it rise.

Cinda stood dumbfounded in the doorway. Had Aunt Ginny really invited her into the kitchen? Maybe she had imagined it. . . wishful thinking.

Aunt Ginny heaved a bowl into Cinda's arms. Cinda clutched the bowl and cautiously stepped into the room, afraid to disturb anything or make a mess in the spotless shrine. Her aunt gave her the ingredients and guided her through the steps of preparing the piecrusts. Cinda soon relaxed and the two spent the afternoon in the kitchen baking and talking pleasantly. Cinda cherished the time they spent together and would savor it forever.

They both conveniently avoided mentioning Lucas or Cinda's leaving.

≥

Cinda went to a schoolmate's wedding. Sally was three years younger than Cinda, and now she was marrying Emery, a boy who had been in Cinda's class. As long as Cinda could remember, Sally had been in love with Emery. Love. What was love? Cinda couldn't put a finger on it.

After the wedding ceremony, Cinda gathered with her friends—Allison and David, Vivian and Alvin, and Eve and her banker fiancé, Leon Livingston. They stood together under an oak tree in the churchyard.

Eve held out her hand so everyone could see her grand engagement ring. "Isn't it gorgeous? We're getting married next month. I couldn't let you have all the fun."

"Next month?" Vivian asked. "Isn't that a little fast? I mean, to get a proper wedding together."

"Leon says he loves me too much to wait any longer than that to make me his wife." She flashed the ring in the sunlight to show everyone just how much Leon loved her. Leon stood proud. Proud of the expensive ring and proud of being the one to catch the beautiful Eve Weston. *Love?* Cinda wondered. Was this love?

"My wedding will be the most splendid this little town has ever seen. Too bad you'll be going back soon," Eve said to Cinda.

Cinda looked away, not knowing what to say, but she knew Allison understood.

twenty-one

Cinda wandered around the empty, quiet house. There was no arguing. No talking. No conversation at all. No playful laughter. No giggling girls chasing after one another. No love crossing the table between the many occupants. Nothing— just peace and quiet. Very quiet. She should have been happy in the stillness. It was what she had longed for ever since she left, wasn't it?

She found herself thinking more and more about Lucas and his entire family. They were loud, sloppy, and sometimes even a bit rude. Chaos always reigned in that house—and love. There was no mistaking the love that enveloped the house. They were a tight-knit family. Any one of them would go out on a limb for another. She missed the love that seemed to be floating about in the air in that crowded, rundown house.

She couldn't believe she had been here for three weeks already. At times it seemed like she had never left this home. At the same time it seemed like she had long since overstayed her welcome. Her uncle was right. She didn't belong here anymore. It was time to go *home*. Home to Lucas.

I struggle against my own flesh, Father, my selfish worldly desires. I am so weak. I must confess what You already know. I don't want to go back. I know You want me to return, so I will. I will try with Your help to do so with a cheerful heart. Believe it or not, I actually miss them, and I think I have come to love the husband You gave me. Thank You for letting me not grow old alone. Amen.

She seemed happier somehow knowing she was going

155

home. It felt like a weight had been lifted from her soul.

⁂

Cinda sat at the writing desk in her room. She would write Lucas a letter, letting him know she was returning—immediately. She wasn't quite sure how to say it. She mulled it over so long, she noticed the mailman heading down her street before she had written one word.

"Oh, I don't have time to run to the post office, and it must go out today." Cinda scribbled, *Dear Lucas, I'll be home soon. Love, Cinda.*

It wasn't at all what she wanted to say, but the mailman was almost at her door. She rushed down and caught him just as he had turned to leave.

The next day a letter from Lucas arrived. Cinda tucked herself safely up in her room before opening it in private. She took a deep breath.

> *Dear Cinda,*
> *I'm sorry to hear about your uncle. I hope your aunt is doing well under the circumstances. Everyone here misses you.*

Everyone?

> *The twins are asking when their mama is coming home. The boys miss your cooking, even your biscuits. I even caught Marty looking at that dress you fixed for her. I've done some fixing up myself, around the place.*

What about you, Lucas? Do you miss me?

> *Looking around, I can see that there's something missing. It's hard for me to believe what you took.*

What?

He was accusing her of stealing? She took nothing but her own clothes. She didn't even take the pearls he gave her. She left more behind than she took. All her mother's treasured things. Now she wished she hadn't written that letter saying she was coming back. Just what did he think she had stolen? Whatever it was, she would be sure to return it. She read on with fury burning in her eyes.

When I sat down to write that very first letter to you nearly a year ago, my thoughts were not of myself. All I could think about was Lynnette's girls. They needed a mother, nothing else mattered to me. Now it seems I can only think of myself.

I know I'll never get back what you took, for how does one retrieve his heart when it has been stolen? For that is just what you've done. My heart is yours, now and forever.

> *Lovingly,*
> *Lucas*

Cinda slipped her fingers across the word "lovingly," caressing each letter. A tear dropped on the paper, smearing Lucas's signature.

"Oh, no." She pulled out her white handkerchief and dabbed at the drop. The ink came off, ruining her best handkerchief. She didn't care. The signature was almost illegible. She clutched the letter to her chest.

"I'm coming, Lucas," she whispered, hoping it wasn't too late. *He loves me!* She dashed down the stairs.

"Really, Cinda. Ladies do not run," Aunt Ginny said in disgust.

"Well, maybe they should." Cinda smiled broadly and

pecked her aunt on the cheek. "I'll be back later to pack."

Cinda raced in a most unladylike way all the way to Allison's to show her the letter and to say good-bye.

twenty-two

Cinda entered the house and smelled the familiar aroma of freshly-baked bread. She went to the kitchen door. The sight of her aunt in the kitchen warmed her, but something seemed wrong. Her aunt stood still at the sink with her back to Cinda. She wasn't washing dishes, though it looked like she was going to. She wasn't even looking out the window over the sink.

"I'm home, Aunt Ginny," Cinda said with a cheerful lilt in her voice.

Her aunt jumped slightly and brought her hands to her face. If Cinda hadn't been looking at her, she would have missed it.

"Aunt Ginny?" Cinda walked over to her and touched her shoulder.

"I didn't hear you come in," she said in a shaky voice.

"What's the matter? Did something happen? Did you get some bad news?"

Her aunt shook her head to all the questions.

"What is it?"

"I'm going to be alone." A tear ran down her face. She wiped it away. "All alone."

Cinda hadn't thought that her aunt might be lonely when she left. She couldn't leave her now. She also knew she couldn't stay. It was simple. There was only one solution. "Pack your things. You're coming with me."

"Where are you taking me?"

Cinda smiled. "Montana, of course."

"I couldn't. That's your home."

"And now it's your home, too. I can't leave you here alone, and I can't stay," she said with a shrug. In Cinda's mind it was easy and settled. She ignored her aunt's protests and started deciding what they would take with them. She remembered the list she had made a few days before she left Montana—the items she wanted to get for Lucas's house. She located all of them and more from her aunt's house.

"What we don't take with us and can't sell, we can give to the church." There were a few larger pieces Cinda knew she could sell to interested parties.

"Are you sure this will be all right with him?" Aunt Ginny asked. "Most men wouldn't take to their wife's relations being put upon them unexpectedly."

"*Him* has a name. It's Lucas." Cinda smiled to herself. "And Lucas will make no arguments. I can guarantee that." Not after his little surprises when she first arrived in Montana.

❧

Three days later they stood on the train platform. Cinda was glad her uncle and aunt had rented their house. Now she didn't have to worry about selling that, too.

The two-day train trip seemed to take forever. Cinda was anxious to get back to Lucas. She had herself so worked up her stomach flipped and turned the entire train ride.

"The first thing we are going to do when we get off this train is find the town doctor," Aunt Ginny said.

"Are you feeling ill?" Cinda hoped not. She didn't know if she could handle more trouble after her uncle's death.

"No. But you obviously are." She had a no-nonsense look on her face. "The doctor can give you something to settle your stomach."

"I'm fine." Cinda tried to assure her. "I'm just anxious."

"You haven't eaten a thing since we got on the train. It won't do any good for you to faint into your husband's arms.

Mr. Rawlings will think I have been neglectful in taking care of you."

Cinda didn't think it would do any good to argue, and it would be nice for her stomach to settle.

After seeing the doctor, they went to the livery to rent a wagon and horses. Cinda wasn't going to trust their precious cargo with the stagecoach or some other freight service she didn't know about. Fortunately Lucas's name was known throughout the region or the liveryman wouldn't have even bothered with them.

They started out early the next morning with their loaded wagon. Cinda hoped their journey wouldn't take more than three days. She also hoped they wouldn't get lost. She didn't think she could cut across the prairie like Lucas did. If she followed the road the stage took to the town south of Lucas's land, then headed north, she couldn't miss. She hoped.

Mid-morning they stopped at a stream to water the horses. When they climbed back aboard and got on their way again, Cinda noticed a horse and rider on the next rise. The silhouette looked vaguely familiar. She soon realized it was the one she had seen when she left on the train. *Please don't see us.* Visions of bandits raced through her mind.

He hadn't really threatened the train Cinda was on. Maybe he wasn't really a bandit but a regular person out for a ride. Cinda racked her brain about what to do, turn and run or continue on, hoping he stayed put. The road forked up ahead. In case he wasn't a figment of her imagination and posed a real threat, she would take the south fork. It led away from him. Then she would loop back around to the northwest.

As soon as she veered to the south, the rider prodded his horse in motion and headed straight for them. Cinda snapped the reins, urging the horses faster. The rider would overtake them in no time. He came at them so swiftly, his hat swept off his head and bounced on his back.

Cinda could see his brown hair bouncing in time with his hat and his strong, determined jawline. *Lucas!* Cinda reined the horses to a halt as he caught up to them. His horse was lathered from being ridden hard for some time, not merely the short distance he just closed between them.

"You're going the wrong way," he said, jumping down from his mount.

"Lucas!" Cinda exclaimed as he pulled her down off the wagon seat.

He was out of breath from the ride and cupped Cinda's face in his hands. He studied her and then pulled her close. She could hear his racing heart. He pushed her away. "Are you all right? You're not hurt are you?" Concern etched his face. Before Cinda could answer he was squeezing her again. He pushed her away again and looked around. "What are you doing out here alone?"

"I'm not alone." Cinda pointed up to the wagon seat. "Aunt Ginny is with me."

Lucas frowned. He obviously wasn't comforted by that fact. "Don't you know it's dangerous for women to travel alone in the West?"

"I didn't—" Cinda started, but Lucas pulled her into his chest again. The back and forth motion turned her stomach. She wished he would make up his mind, hug her or hold her at arm's length.

When his breathing slowed, he stepped back from her and cradled her face in his hands. "You're really safe?"

Cinda nodded with a weak smile.

Lucas looked deep into her eyes. "They're greener. I couldn't remember if they were greener than alfalfa or not. They are definitely greener." He leaned down, kissing her long and hard. Then he tied his horse to the back of the wagon.

Cinda thought about Lucas up on the hill on his horse before he raced down. Was he the man she thought was a train robber? Were they one and the same? "Lucas, did you follow me to the train when I left?"

His broad mischievous smile emphasized his dimple. He kissed her again. She had her answer. He had seen her safely to the train. Now he helped her up onto the wagon seat and climbed aboard.

"It's good to see you again, Mrs. Crawford." Lucas replaced his Stetson.

"Not as good as it is to see you, Mr. Rawlings," Aunt Ginny said with a formal air.

He turned the wagon north and headed across the prairie. "This is a good pair of horses you got here. I'm surprised they didn't try to push some plugs on you."

"If it weren't for Aunt Ginny, they would have."

Lucas leaned forward and eyed the older woman.

Her aunt kept her gaze forward, sitting properly. "My father was a horse breeder."

Lucas raised his eyebrows. "You made wise choices."

The corners of her aunt's mouth turned up ever so slightly at the compliment, and she sat a little taller.

twenty-three

Three days later they pulled into the quiet farmyard. The only activity was the chickens mulling around, pecking at the ground. It was just like the last time. Lucas helped Cinda down and then her aunt. All was quiet, but Cinda knew it wouldn't last. She eagerly waited, listening for that first sound.

There it was!

Cinda's smile broadened. "Here they come."

"Here who—" Aunt Ginny started to ask when the barn door burst open, and Daniella and Daphne, dirty from head to toe, raced full speed toward them, scattering the chickens.

"Mama, Mama," they yelled.

"I hope you don't mind?" Lucas removed his hat. "They asked if they could call you Mama. I said it was okay."

Cinda nodded. Tears filled her eyes as she knelt down to catch the racing pair.

"We missed you sooo much," Daphne said with Daniella chiming in on the sooo.

"I missed you both, sooo much." Cinda hugged and kissed them both.

Trevor strolled out of the barn just like last time. "We weren't sure what happened to you, Lucas. Jed said you got a letter and raced out of town." He looked at Cinda and her aunt. "I see everyone's all right."

Lucas nodded in agreement and introduced Trevor to Cinda's aunt. Cinda had already introduced the twins.

Travis and Marty came racing toward them on horseback.

They were neck and neck until Travis veered around a pyramid of three bales of hay at the edge of the yard. Marty sailed over them and into the lead. She skidded to a stop. "Yee haw." She jumped off Flash. "Better luck next time," she gloated to Travis, who was just coming to a halt. "You do my chores for a whole week."

"Mrs. Crawford, this is my other brother, Travis, and my sister, Martha," Lucas said, pointing to the pair.

Aunt Ginny had a horrified look on her face that she quickly replaced with a sterner one. "I have never seen such rowdy behavior from a young lady."

Martha stepped directly in front of the older woman and planted her balled fists on her hips. "I ain't no lady."

Aunt Ginny stood taller. "That's obvious." The battle of wills had begun. It was a toss-up as to who might win.

Cinda knew her aunt wouldn't back down as easily as she had. In fact, her aunt wouldn't give up at all. She would have Martha in a dress if it were the last thing she did. And it just might be, if Martha had anything to do with it. Life would be interesting with those two.

Aunt Ginny stepped away from Cinda when she saw Dewight approach, eyeing him suspiciously.

"A rose, a rose. To see its beauty. At last it wilts in the desert sun." Dewight looked up to the clear blue sky, smiling and shouted, "The rain comes!" He began twirling around with outstretched arms. "The rose will bloom again." He spun away.

Daniella grabbed one of Cinda's hands and pulled her toward the house. "Come on. You gotta come see the new kitchen."

Daphne quickly grabbed the other hand and pulled as well. "It's so beautiful. Hurry, hurry."

Cinda allowed herself to be dragged in and through the

house to the kitchen with everyone tagging along behind. She stopped and caught her breath at the sight.

The worn floorboards were replaced, and the whole floor and the walls had been whitewashed. Cinda ran her hand along the worktable that had been sanded and refinished. Her gaze settled on what used to be the broken-down pantry. The old shelves were gone and replaced with what appeared to be new pantry shelves draped in yellow gingham. Cinda stared at the bright, cheerful room.

Daniella and Daphne pulled back the curtains of the pantry to reveal the shiny new metal mixing bowls and new ceramic serving bowls. The tears Cinda was trying hard to hold back broke free. She tenderly touched the bowls.

"And new spoons, too." Daphne held up an array of metal and wooden spoons.

Daniella snatched a spoon from Daphne's grasp and handed it to Cinda. "Uncle Lucas carved this one hisself."

Cinda clutched the spoon with tear-stained cheeks. He had done all this for her.

"It isn't much, but I guess it will do," her aunt said, looking around.

Lucas looked down.

"No. It's perfect. Absolutely perfect." Cinda smiled lovingly at Lucas when his eyes met hers. "Thank you."

He smiled back.

twenty-four

Over the next couple of days, Lucas became more and more distant. He was scarce all day. He didn't come in for either lunch or supper. He didn't even come in after supper for their walk. Cinda's stomach twisted, wondering what was wrong. She fixed a plate of food and took it out to the barn where Lucas stood, brushing his horse.

"I brought you something to eat." She held out the plate for him.

"I'm not hungry." He kept stroking his horse.

"You haven't eaten since breakfast. You need to eat."

Lucas yanked the plate from her hand and plopped it on a nearby crate. "I said, I'm not hungry."

Cinda realized she had been wrong—it did bother him that she brought her aunt without asking him first. "I'm sorry for bringing Aunt Ginny without asking you first. I just couldn't leave her all alone."

"You're sorry. *You're* sorry." He dropped his head, shaking it. "It's not your aunt. She's welcome, if you want her here."

"Then what is it?" Cinda was confused. "What have I done to upset you?"

"You haven't done anything," he said softly. "And you have done everything."

Cinda cocked her head sideways. Her confusion was compounded with each passing moment.

"You have done everything I hoped for in a wife and more. I deceived you and dumped my whole family on you. I only heard you complain once. I don't deserve you." He paused, struggling with his emotions. "Why did you come back? There certainly isn't much for you here."

"You're here."

He stopped her before she could say more. "I know you never wanted to marry me."

"But I did. It was my choice."

Lucas pulled a stack of letters out of his back pocket. "I've been asking God what I should do about these. He keeps giving me the same answer. . . 'Ask her.' So I'm asking." He divided the letters into two piles. He held up the group of four letters. "These were written before we were married. Those two were written after we were married. Your handwriting changed." He weighed the two stacks. "Who are you? You're not the woman I asked to marry me."

Cinda reached for the four letters Lucas held. He gave them to her. The writing was Vivian's.

"Are you really Cinda Harrison? Is our marriage even legal?" he asked, sounding as though he really didn't want to know.

Cinda felt bad she hadn't told him about the letters. "Vivian," was all she could manage to whisper.

"Your name is Vivian?"

Cinda shook her head. She looked up at him. "It's Vivian's handwriting."

"Then you are Cinda Harrison?"

Cinda shook her head again and stood up tall. "I'm Cinda Rawlings." Lucas stared at her suspiciously, waiting for her to continue. "Vivian and Eve decided to find a husband for their shy friend before she became an old maid." A tear splashed on her cheek. "It was kind of a joke. I didn't know anything about it until I got your letter the day you arrived."

Lucas caressed the tear away. "Why didn't you tell me? I wouldn't have bothered you any more. You know that."

"I was terrified. I didn't know you then. I didn't know how you would react to being tricked like that. How do you tell a stranger he came a long way for nothing? When I got to know you a little in those few days, I felt God leading me to you. I thought maybe life with you would be easier than with my aunt."

"But it wasn't, was it?" Shame coated his words.

"No, it wasn't. It was hard in a different way. But something strange happened. I was needed here. I needed to be needed. I was an only child and wasn't used to all the commotion of a large family. I'm still not used to it, but I do know this is where I want to be—with you."

Lucas grabbed her and held her tight. "Whatever did I do to deserve a blessing such as you? The more I get to know you, the more convinced I am I don't deserve you." He stepped back from her. "When I married you, I wasn't thinking of you as a person with feelings. To me you were the solution to a problem. And if you were the woman of character I hoped and prayed you were, you would stay out of a sense of duty even after you met my family."

He leaned against a stall post and looked down at his boots. "I always wanted to have a loving relationship like my parents, but I had to give that up a long time ago."

"When your parents died?"

He nodded and continued. "I didn't have time for anything. My brothers and sisters needed me. The farm needed me. Then Lynnette and her girls needed me. I thought if I could find a good mother for Lynnette's girls, that was all that was important. I didn't have to have love as long as they did." He turned his focus back to Cinda. "I'm sorry for not being honest about my family. I have always felt bad for not telling you. Can you ever forgive me?"

"Of course, Lucas." Cinda stepped up to him, wrapping her

arms around his waist.

He held her close for a long while. "I thought I was going to die when you left. I never expected to love you."

"I love you, too." She could feel Lucas's arms tighten around her. "You really don't mind about my aunt? I just couldn't leave her all alone."

"If you can live with my family, I can live with yours. You only have one relative, I sprang five on you. Six if you count Dewight."

Dewight definitely counted. Cinda decided now was a good time to spring another one on him and held up two fingers. "Two relatives."

"Two? I thought your aunt and uncle were your only ones?" Lucas pulled his brows together. "You have another relative coming? When?"

Cinda shrugged her shoulders and smiled. "In about seven months. But it's not just my relation, it's yours as well." She patted her stomach.

Lucas looked from her stomach up to her face and smiled broadly, his eyes bright with hope. "You're going to have a baby?"

"*We* are going to have a baby."

Lucas picked her up and spun her around. "I'm so happy."

"Me, too."

"You know what this means?" he asked, putting her down.

Cinda shook her head.

"No more my family and your family." He gently put his hand on her stomach. "This baby ties us all together as one big family. *Our* family."

Cinda nodded. They headed to the house. She hadn't slept well since she left, but she would tonight. She didn't know if it was the hard work or the company—maybe both. She didn't care. She was home with her family and the man she loved.

A Letter To Our Readers

Dear Reader:

In order that we might better contribute to your reading enjoyment, we would appreciate your taking a few minutes to respond to the following questions. We welcome your comments and read each form and letter we receive. When completed, please return to the following:

Rebecca Germany, Fiction Editor
Heartsong Presents
PO Box 719
Uhrichsville, Ohio 44683

1. Did you enjoy reading *Cinda's Surprise?*
   ☐ Very much. I would like to see more books
   by this author!
   ☐ Moderately
   I would have enjoyed it more if _____

   _____

   _____

2. Are you a member of **Heartsong Presents**? Yes ☐ No ☐
   If no, where did you purchase this book?_____

   _____

3. How would you rate, on a scale from 1 (poor) to 5 (superior), the cover design?_____

4. On a scale from 1 (poor) to 10 (superior), please rate the following elements.

   _____ Heroine   _____ Plot

   _____ Hero   _____ Inspirational theme

   _____ Setting   _____ Secondary characters

5. These characters were special because_____

_____

_____

6. How has this book inspired your life?_____

_____

_____

7. What settings would you like to see covered in future
   Heartsong Presents books?_____

_____

_____

8. What are some inspirational themes you would like to see
   treated in future books?_____

_____

_____

9. Would you be interested in reading other **Heartsong
   Presents** titles?   Yes ☐   No ☐

10. Please check your age range:
    ☐ Under 18   ☐ 18-24   ☐ 25-34
    ☐ 35-45   ☐ 46-55   ☐ Over 55

11. How many hours per week do you read?_____

Name _____

Occupation _____

Address _____

City _____ State _____ Zip _____

British
COLUMBIA

The early twentieth century not
only births the town of Dawson
Creek, British Columbia, but
changes it from a prairie village
into the southern anchor of the Alcan Highway. Follow
the fictionalized growth of author Janelle Burnham
Schneider's hometown through the eyes of characters who
hold onto hopes, dreams. . .and love.

This captivating volume combines four complete novels
of inspiring love that you'll treasure.

paperback, 464 pages, 5 ³⁄₁₆" x 8"

♥ ♥ ♥ ♥ ♥ ♥ ♥ ♥ ❤ ♥ ♥ ♥ ♥ ♥ ♥ ♥ ♥

♥ ♥ ♥ ♥ ♥ ♥ ♥ ♥ ❤ ♥ ♥ ♥ ♥ ♥ ♥ ♥ ♥

·······Presents·······

Great Inspirational Romance at a Great Price!

Heartsong Presents books are inspirational romances in contemporary and historical settings, designed to give you an enjoyable, spirit-lifting reading experience. You can choose wonderfully written titles from some of today's best authors like Peggy Darty, Sally Laity, Tracie Peterson, Colleen L. Reece, Lauraine Snelling, and many others.

When ordering quantities less than twelve, above titles are $2.95 each.
Not all titles may be available at time of order.